TEXAS KILL
OF THE
MOUNTAIN MAN

TEXAS KILL
OF THE
MOUNTAIN MAN

WILLIAM W.
JOHNSTONE

and J. A. Johnstone

PINNACLE BOOKS
Kensington Publishing Corp.
www.kensingtonbooks.com

PINNACLE BOOKS are published by

Kensington Publishing Corp.
119 West 40th Street
New York, NY 10018

PUBLISHER'S NOTE
Following the death of William W. Johnstone, the Johnstone family is working with a carefully selected writer to organize and complete Mr. Johnstone's outlines and many unfinished manuscripts to create additional novels in all of his series like The Last Gunfighter, Mountain Man, and Eagles, among others. This novel was inspired by Mr. Johnstone's superb storytelling.

All Kensington titles, imprints, and distributed lines are available at special quantity discounts for bulk purchases for sales promotions, premiums, fund-raising, educational, or institutional use. Special book excerpts or customized printings can also be created to fit specific needs. For details, write or phone the office of the Kensington sales manager: Kensington Publishing Corp., 119 West 40th Street, New York, NY 10018, attn: Sales Department; phone 1-800-221-2647.

ISBN-13: 978-0-7860-4061-2
ISBN-10: 0-7860-4061-0

First printing: December 2020

10 9 8 7 6 5 4 3 2 1

Printed in the United States of America

Electronic edition:

ISBN-13: 978-0-7860-4062-9
ISBN-10: 0-7860-4062-9

THE JENSEN FAMILY
FIRST FAMILY OF THE AMERICAN FRONTIER

Smoke Jensen—*The Mountain Man*
The youngest of three children and orphaned as a young boy, Smoke Jensen is considered one of the fastest draws in the West. His quest to tame the lawless West has become the stuff of legend. Smoke owns the Sugarloaf Ranch in Colorado. Married to Sally Jensen, father to Denise ("Denny") and Louis.

Preacher—*The First Mountain Man*
Though not a blood relative, grizzled frontiersman Preacher became a father figure to the young Smoke Jensen, teaching him how to survive in the brutal, often deadly Rocky Mountains. Fought the battles that forged his destiny. Armed with a long gun, Preacher is as fierce as the land itself.

Matt Jensen—*The Last Mountain Man*
Orphaned but taken in by Smoke Jensen, Matt Jensen has become like a younger brother to Smoke and even took the Jensen name. And like Smoke, Matt has carved out his destiny on the American frontier. He lives by the gun and surrenders to no man.

Luke Jensen—*Bounty Hunter*
Mountain Man Smoke Jensen's long-lost brother Luke Jensen is scarred by war and a dead shot— the right qualities to be a bounty hunter. And he's cunning, and fierce enough, to bring down the deadliest outlaws of his day.

Ace Jensen and Chance Jensen—*Those Jensen Boys!*
Smoke Jensen's long-lost nephews, Ace and Chance,
are a pair of young-gun twins as reckless and wild as
the frontier itself . . . Their father is Luke Jensen,
thought killed in the Civil War. Their uncle Smoke
Jensen is one of the fiercest gunfighters the West has
ever known. It's no surprise that the inseparable Ace
and Chance Jensen have a knack for taking risks—
even if they have to blast their way out of them.

CHAPTER ONE

Laramie County, Wyoming Territory

Emma was hanging up her wash when she saw a rider approaching. At first she felt a sense of joy, thinking perhaps her husband was returning from his trip, but as that rider came closer, her joy turned to dread.

"My husband isn't here," she said, when her unwelcome visitor rode right up to her and dismounted.

"That's good, because I didn't come to see him. I came to see you."

"What do you want, Marvin?"

"You know what I want, Emma. I want you. I've always wanted you. Come with me now. We can start a new life somewhere else, just you and me."

"No, Marvin. I made my choice a long time ago."

"How can I convince you that you made the wrong choice?"

"You can't convince me. I didn't make the wrong choice."

"All right, then, at least invite me in for a cup of coffee. I've come a long way today, and you owe me that much."

"What do you mean, I owe you? Why would I owe you anything?"

"Let's just say it's for the memory of the way it once was between us."

"There was never anything *real* between us, Marvin," Emma said. "Except in your imagination."

"But I thought we were *enga*— Well, at least let me leave with some dignity. A cup of coffee together? Would that hurt?"

"All right," Emma replied with a resigned sigh. "One cup of coffee, then I want you to please leave." She nodded toward the clothes basket which was half-filled with just washed items she had not yet hung up to dry. "I need to finish hanging out my clothes."

Minutes later, Marvin followed Emma into the house. As soon as the door was closed behind them, he grabbed her, then turned her around, and even as she was fighting him, he forced a kiss on her. "You want me, you know you do."

"No, no, go away. Leave me alone!" Emma slapped him.

Marvin smiled at her, but the malevolent smile was without warmth. "All right, bitch. As you said, you have made your choice." He pulled out his pistol and brought it down on her head.

She dropped to the floor and he fell upon her, ripping off her clothes and having his way with her. She regained consciousness in the middle of his attack and tried to fight him off, but he was too strong for her.

When he was through he stood and looked down at her naked and bruised body. "If I can't have you, he can't either." Marvin pulled his pistol and shot her in the stomach, then left her moaning on the floor behind him.

The clothes on the line were flapping in the wind as he rode away.

Three months later

Smoke Jensen sat on the top rail of the corral looking at the horses that had just been brought in. These were five of the one hundred horses he had just sold. The contract not only called for the delivery of one hundred horses, it also specified that the horses be saddle broken.

Four of the horses had been broken, but so far, three riders had been unable to break the fifth. His ranch hand was about to try.

"Cal, there's no need for you to break your neck trying to ride that horse," Smoke said. "Turn him loose. We'll just keep him as a stud for breeding. We can replace him with another."

"Now, Smoke, if you order me to do that I will," Cal replied. "But I'd like to give it a try. I don't like to think that a horse can get the better of me."

"Ha!" Pearlie said. "If you ask me, that horse already has the better of you. Why, I wouldn't doubt but that he could beat you at checkers."

"We'll see," Cal said as, without any preliminaries, he swung into the saddle.

The reaction of the horse was instantaneous and violent. The horse leaped straight up with all four legs leaving the ground. Coming down on four stiff legs jarred Cal, but it didn't dislodge him from the saddle. On the next move, however, the horse kicked his back legs into the air so that his back formed about a sixty-degree angle pointing to the ground. The maneuver caused Cal to be tossed forward over the horse's head, where he wound up lying on his backside.

"Cal! Are you all right?" Smoke shouted. Jumping down from the fence, he hurried over to the young man who had become more like a son than an employee. "Are you hurt anywhere? Is anything broken?"

"Nah, I'm all right," Cal said as Smoke and Pearlie helped him to his feet. Cal put his hands, gingerly, to his backside. "I'll tell you this, though. I don't think that horse is going to let anyone ride him."

"That's because he hasn't had anybody who knows what they're doing try it yet," Pearlie said.

"Are you telling me that you can ride him?" Cal asked.

Pearlie smiled. "You just watch."

The horse was tethered by a long rope to a pylon in the middle of the paddock. The idea was to let the horse run in concentric circles, the circles decreasing as the rope wound itself up on the pylon.

Pearlie mounted the horse but he, too, was thrown from the saddle perhaps even more quickly than Cal had been.

"I'll tell you what," a sheepish Pearlie said as he regained his feet. "That horse just pure dee doesn't want anyone to ride him."

"It's not worth someone getting a broken neck," Smoke said. "Turn him loose and bring in a replacement."

"All right, Punch. It looks like you're going to get

your way," Pearlie said as he began removing the saddle. "Out you go."

"Punch?" Cal said.

Pearlie nodded. "He punched three others out of the saddle before he took us on," Pearlie said. "Can you think of a better name?"

"He's Smoke's horse," Cal said. "It's up to Smoke to name him."

"Punch it is," Smoke said.

"Are you going to try and ride him, Smoke?" Cal asked.

Smoke chuckled. "No, and I'm not likely to try and stick my hand up a bear's butt, either. I told you. We've got enough horses to meet the contract, so we don't need this one."

"Which just goes to show how smart you are and how dumb we are," Pearlie said.

"I'm going to check with Herman and see how he's doing," Smoke said, turning away from the others to complete his task.

"I hate confessing that the horse beat me."

Smoke heard Cal's remark as he headed toward the toolshed that was being remodeled by Herman Nelson.

As he approached, Smoke heard sawing and knew Herman was gainfully occupied. Behind only Pearlie and Cal, Herman was the most dependable of all his permanent hands. One thing Smoke particularly appreciated was how efficiently Herman took over the ranch and ran it during the many times Smoke, Sally, Pearlie, and Cal were away.

When Herman saw Smoke approaching, he stopped

sawing. "Hello, boss. Is there anyone left that's crazy enough to try and ride that horse?"

"Did you try?" Smoke asked.

Herman laughed. "Oh, yes, I have to admit that I was the first one dumb enough to get throwed by 'im. 'N I'm tellin' you right now, even if you ask me to, I don't plan to try again."

"I'm not going to ask anyone else to try," Smoke said. "I don't want to take a chance on anyone getting his neck broken. How are you coming in here?"

"I need some angle iron for the shelves, and I'll have this place looking like some grand mansion somewhere," Herman said proudly.

"How many do you need?"

"Three per shelf, four shelves, so I'll need twelve."

"All right. I'll make a run into town," Smoke said.

"Great, I would love to go into town," Sally said enthusiastically in response to Smoke's announcement of his plans a few minutes later. "I have so many errands to run."

"I was just going to run into town and come right back. I hadn't really planned on you—" Smoke stopped in midsentence.

"You hadn't planned on me what?" Sally challenged.

"Uh, I had no idea you would be willing to go into town with me. What a pleasant surprise this is. I'll be happy to have you go into town with me."

"Oh, Smoke, you say the sweetest things to me," she teased. "I can be ready right away."

Kansas and Pacific Railroad Depot, Big Rock, Colorado

Roy J. Clemmons and Sue Martin were two of the six passengers who stepped down from the train. They stood out from the others—four men were wearing jeans and cotton shirts. Clemmons was wearing a black suit with a red vest over a white, collared shirt with a black string tie. His dark hair was perfectly coiffured, and his moustache, which didn't extend beyond each end of his lips, was well-trimmed.

Sue stood out, not only because she was an exceptionally pretty woman with bright red hair, but also because of what she was wearing. The provocative V-neck of her dress was low enough to show the tops of her breasts.

"Our train doesn't leave for six more hours," Clemmons said. "There is plenty of time for us to earn a coin or two."

As they walked away from the depot, they paid no attention to the two riders, man and woman, just coming into town on Jensen Pike, the road that came in from the west.

"I'll go on down to Earl Cook's place," Smoke said. "You can do whatever it is that you have to do.

"It shouldn't take me too long," Sally said. "If you don't mind, I'll just go on back home when I'm done."

"I may be a little later," Smoke said.

"Tell Louis I said hello."

"What makes you think I'll be going to Longmont's?"

"I don't know. What makes me think the sun will set in the west tonight?" Sally replied with a little laugh.

CHAPTER TWO

Smoke Jensen was in Longmont's Saloon sitting at Louis Longmont's special table with Louis.

"What are you doing in town at this time of day, anyway, Smoke? Is there not enough to keep you busy out at Sugarloaf?" Although Louis Longmont was a longtime resident of Big Rock, he still spoke with the lilt of a French accent.

"We're gathering some horses to take down to Texas, but Pearlie and Cal seem to have things well in hand," Smoke answered. "Who's your new girl?"

"What are you talking about? I don't have a new girl."

"That one," Smoke said, pointing to an attractive young red-haired woman who was setting drinks before the card players. Though what she was wearing was as provocative as what was worn by any of the other bar girls, even Smoke could tell that her dress was more expensively made.

He recognized only two of the players.

"Oh, *non, monsieur.* She isn't working for me. She came in with the man in the suit. But you have changed the subject. What brought you to town in the middle of the day?"

"Sally had some things to do, so I volunteered to come with her, to help out."

Louis chuckled. "*Oui,* one can easily see that you are being a big help."

"I *am* being a big help. Sally said I would be most helpful just by staying out of her way."

"You could have stayed out of the way by staying out at the ranch."

"That's true," Smoke agreed. He held up his beer. "But then I couldn't be sitting here talking with you. Anyway, I had to take care of something down at Earl's."

"What did you need done at the blacksmith shop?"

"Nothing major. I just needed some braces made for a few shelves I want to put up in the machine shop."

Their conversation was interrupted by a woman's scream. They looked toward the source and saw that someone had grabbed the red-haired woman who had been the subject of Smoke's earlier observation. The woman's assailant had his arm around her neck. He was holding his pistol to her head, but he was yelling at the well-dressed man sitting at a card table.

"You've been cheatin', mister! You've been cheatin' from the moment I sat down here. And this woman has been helpin' you."

"What are you talking about? I haven't done anything!" the woman said, her voice breaking with fear.

"Don't give me none o' that, lady. Do you think I don't know how you've been sneakin' around behind all of us, givin' him signals 'n such on what cards we was holdin'? Now all of you, get up and leave the money on the table. We've been cheated out of a lot of money, and I plan to get back my share of what he stole."

Smoke stood up and walked toward the table while aiming his pistol at the man holding the woman hostage. Because everyone's attention was on the scene playing out before them, neither they, nor the man with the gun, saw Smoke until he was within ten feet of the table. When the man did see Smoke, he jerked around, still holding his gun to the woman's head.

"Stop right there, mister!" he called out, angrily. "What is it you think you're about to do?"

"I'm not real sure, but it could be that I'm about to kill you," Smoke said, his voice flat and completely emotionless.

"What do you mean, you're about to kill me? Are you blind? Don't you see that I have a gun pointed toward this woman's head?"

"Now that you mention it, I have noticed that. By the way, you might also have noticed that my gun is pointed at you."

"Drop the gun, mister. Drop it now, or I'll kill the girl."

"All right, go ahead," Smoke said easily.

"What?" the man asked, shocked by Smoke's response. "Look, you don't understand. If you don't drop the gun now, I'm goin' to kill her!"

"Yes, you keep saying that. The truth is, mister, you're in a bit of a quandary here, aren't you?"

"A bit of a what?"

"You're in a bit of a fix. If you move that gun toward me, I'll kill you. If you shoot the woman, I'll kill you.

So if you are going to shoot her, go ahead and do it. If you don't drop it, I may just go ahead and shoot her myself so we can get this over with."

"I . . . I don't believe you."

"Why not? I don't know her, so she doesn't mean anything to me."

The man who was holding the woman looked at Smoke and saw the black hole of the end of the pistol pointing straight at him. His eyes grew wide in fear, and small beads of perspiration popped out on his forehead and his upper lip.

"I'll give you to the count of three to make up your mind," Smoke said. "One."

"You're crazy!"

"Two."

"No, no!" The man dropped his gun and took his arm away from the woman's neck.

Quickly, and with a little cry of relief, the woman darted away from her would-be assailant to join the suited man at the table.

"Thank you, mister. You saved my life," the woman said.

"Yes, well, this would have never come up if you hadn't been helping your man cheat," Smoke replied.

"What? Why, I never!" the woman said.

Smoke didn't know the gunman, nor the card player the woman had run to, but he did recognize the other two players, though he knew the name of only one. Ivan worked at the stable, the other player he knew only as a cowhand who worked on one of the area ranches.

"Ivan, are you a winner or a loser?"

"Ha, are you kiddin'? I'm down fourteen bucks,"

Ivan said. "Dobbins is losin', too," he added, nodding to the cowhand across the table from him.

"How about it, Dobbins? How much money are you down?" Smoke asked.

"I'm down twenty-two dollars," Dobbins said. "It was damn foolish of me to lose that much money. That's a month's pay for me."

"What is your name, mister, and how much have you lost?" Smoke asked the would-be gunman.

"My name is Crabtree, Buster Crabtree, and I've lost twenty-eight dollars, all to him!" Crabtree pointed directly across the table.

"And who would you be?" Smoke asked the winner.

"My name is Clemmons. Roy J. Clemmons." The man spoke with the accent of someone from the Northeast.

"You're a little out of your territory, aren't you? What are you doing in a place like Big Rock?"

"Sue and I arrived by train this morning. We are on the way to San Francisco, where I have taken employment at the Blue Chip Club. I'm sure someone like you has never been to San Francisco, so no doubt, you've never heard of the club."

"The Blue Chip Club is a gambling establishment on Lombard Street," Smoke replied.

Clemmons's eyes opened wide in surprise. "You know the place?"

"I know the place. I also know that it has a reputation for hiring gamblers who can assure the house wins by manipulating the cards."

"I-I don't know what you are talking about," Clemmons stuttered.

"Mr. Clemmons, there is no doubt in my mind

but that you were cheating these three men, and I'm quite sure your woman was involved in some way. I don't approve of what Mister Crabtree did, but I can understand what drove him to do it. So here's what you are going to do. You are going to return the twenty-eight dollars to Mr. Crabtree, the twenty-two dollars to Mr. Dobbins, and the fourteen dollars to Ivan. Then each of you are going to take out whatever money you have put in the pot for this hand. Gentlemen, this game is over."

"Now, just why in the hell should I do such a thing?" Clemmons asked, angered by Smoke's demand.

"Because I'm holding a gun and you aren't," Smoke replied easily. "And I could kill you long before you can get to that holdout gun you are keeping just under that bright red vest."

"And here I thought you were my hero for saving me," the woman said as Clemmons began counting out the money, then reluctantly returning it to the other three players. "Why, you are nothing but a thief with a gun."

"Yes, ma'am. Well, some folks steal with a gun, and some folks steal by using a good-looking woman to signal what the other card players are holding." Smoke replied.

The three men began counting their money and putting it away.

"Mr. Crabtree, we aren't going to have any more trouble with you, are we?" Smoke asked.

"No, sir, I'm satisfied that all is well. And I apologize for makin' such a damn fool of myself. I also thank you for bein the only one of the two of us to show any sense this morning."

Louis had come over to the table. "*Monsieur* Clemmons, I believe you said that you arrived on the morning train?"

"I did."

"Then it is my suggestion, *monsieur*, that you return to the depot and await the earliest train that can take you out of town."

"You've got no right to order me to stay in the depot," Clemmons said

"*Oui*, that is true. I can only offer that as a suggestion. However, as the owner of this saloon, I am telling you to leave my establishment now and never come in here again."

"Yes, well you certainly don't have to tell me that. I've no intention of remaining in an establishment owned by somebody who would countenance robbery at gunpoint." He glared at Smoke. "Nor do I intend to stay in this town any longer than the very next train. Come, Sue, let's get out of this place."

The others in the saloon applauded as Clemmons and the woman left.

Smoke returned to his seat.

"Annie," Louis called to one of the girls who did work for him. "Bring us two more beers, would you, *mon cher*? These have grown flat."

"So, when are you going to Texas?" Louis asked when the beers were delivered.

"Just as soon as we get the horses gathered and broken, we'll be taking them to Big Jim Conyers at his ranch near Fort Worth."

"Why do they call him Big Jim?"

"Well, he's six feet seven inches tall, and he weighs nearly 300 pounds. Does that give you a hint?" Smoke asked with a chuckle.

"*Mon Dieu*, that is a big man," Louis said.

"Yes. He's also a pretty big man in Tarrant County, and I'm not just talking about his size."

Sugarloaf Ranch

Seeing a plume of dust in the long, dedicated road that approached the ranch, Sally Jensen smiled, then stepped out onto the wide porch so she could watch his arrival. The road—on the state and county maps it was called Jensen Avenue—came from Big Rock and served at least four more ranches and half a dozen remote houses before; reaching the eastern boundary and passing under the entry arch with the name of the ranch, *Sugarloaf*, fashioned from wrought-iron letters above. But she knew Smoke had no intention of riding under the arched entry.

He left the road, then, urging his horse Seven into a mighty jump, sailed over the fence almost as if on wings. After successfully negotiating the fence, he galloped into the compound before pulling the horse to a stop and leaping down from the saddle.

Sally stepped out to the railing to look down at her husband. "Well," she said with a wide and welcoming smile. "It does my heart good to know you still think of me as someone you would gallop home to."

"Sally, my love, I would soak my trousers in kerosene and ride through a forest fire to get home to you."

"What? And expose Seven to such danger?" she quipped.

"If I asked it of Seven, he would do it without hesitation. He is the greatest horse in the world!" Smoke augmented his comment by patting the hard-breathing animal on its forehead.

Sally laughed. "Smoke, you have said that about every other horse you have ever owned. And you have named every one of them Seven."

"That's true, and they were the greatest horses in the world, too."

"Don't be silly. There can only be one greatest," Sally reminded him.

Smoke held up his finger and waved it back and forth. "No, that's the schoolteacher in you talking. If you love horses, you know there can be as many greatest horses as you want."

Again, Sally laughed. "If you say so."

"How are things going here?" he asked.

"Here comes Pearlie. You can ask him yourself."

Smoke's foreman was Wes Fontane, though not one out of a hundred people who knew him knew what his real name was. He was *Pearlie* to one and all.

"Is Earl goin' to be able to get them angle irons done?" Pearlie asked as he approached.

"Pearlie!" Sally said in a chastising tone.

For just a second, Pearlie looked confused, then he smiled and nodded. "I said *them* angle irons, 'n I was supposed to say *those*, wasn't I?"

"Very good."

"So, Smoke, did—"

Smoke held up his hand. "Just say the word *those*."

"What?"

"I already heard your question. Just change *them* to *those* and I'll answer. There's no need to repeat the whole question."

"Those," Pearlie said.

"Yes," Smoke replied, and both men laughed.

"God help me, I'm surrounded by crazy people," Sally said, but she laughed as well.

"How's the gather going?" Smoke asked.

"It's going great," Pearlie said. "We found forty-seven new colts to brand, and Cal's out there with them now. I expect they are pretty close to being done."

"What about the horses we're taking down to Texas?"

"We don't have 'em all, but we've got most of 'em picked out. Then, of course, they will have to be broken," Pearlie said. "It'll be good to see the Colonel again. Are you going, Miz Sally?"

Pearlie's reference to Big Jim as *the Colonel* was because he had been a colonel in Hood's Division during the War Between the States.

"Yes, Julia has invited me. When the train leaves next Monday, I'll be on it."

"Hey, Smoke, is Live Oak as big as Sugarloaf?"

"I think the two ranches are within a few hundred acres of each other. I'm not sure which is"— he paused and looked at Sally before finishing the sentence— "the *bigger* of the two."

"Very good," Sally said with an approving smile.

Pearlie stretched. "Woowee, I'll be glad when we're done here. I'm just about all tuckered out."

"You aren't too tired for peach cobbler, are you?" Sally asked.

"Are you kidding? Even if I couldn't walk, I'd be able to pull myself in on my belly to get some of your cobbler."

"You don't have to go to that extreme. Just be cleaned up when you come to the table."

"The only thing is, I feel bad about all the others. All the hands have worked as hard as Cal and I have, and I feel a little guilty about being the only ones to enjoy the cobbler."

Sally smiled. "You don't have to feel guilty. When I was in town, I acquired sufficient ingredients for Mr. Peabody to make enough peach cobbler for all the hands."

"Great!" Pearlie said with a wide smile. "Now, I not only won't feel guilty, I can eat here, then go out to the cookhouse and have seconds."

CHAPTER THREE

Live Oak Ranch, Tarrant County, Texas

Live Oak Ranch was just north of Fort Worth and consisted of 120,000 acres of gently rolling grassland nurtured by scores of year-round creeks and streams that made it ideal for cattle. But the cattle that enjoyed the grass and water were different from most of the cows in Texas. They weren't longhorns, and they weren't even Herefords. These were Angus cattle introduced to the range some time earlier when Duff MacCallister, Smoke Jensen, Sally, Pearlie, and Cal, as well as Matt Jensen, made a long drive to bring the very first Angus cattle into Tarrant County. Converting his herd to Angus cattle had been a particularly good investment for Big Jim Conyers. At the current market price one Angus cow brought half again as much as a Hereford and almost twice as much as a longhorn.

A dozen full-time employees of the ranch and another eight seasonal employees lived in a couple of long, single-story bunkhouses—white, with red roofs. A cookhouse big enough to feed all of the single men, a barn, a machine shed, a granary, and a large stable were also working parts of the ranch.

Big Jim's son, Dalton, and his wife, Marjane, lived in their own house, as did the foreman, Clay Ramsey, his wife Maria, and their young son Manny. The most dominant feature of the ranch was what the cowboys called the "Big House." Its architecture was an example of Spanish Colonial Revival, with an arcaded portico, stained glass windows, and an arched entryway.

Big Jim was in his office working on his books when his wife, Julia, stepped in, holding an envelope. "We just got a letter from Sally and Smoke Jensen. Sally has accepted my invitation, so she's coming, too. She says she is looking forward to the visit."

"Well, I'm sure you and Tamara and Marjane will be able to come up with some way to make her feel welcome."

"I was thinking we might have a big party and invite folks out from town. That is, if it's all right with you."

"Of course it's all right with me." Big Jim closed the tablet he was writing in and went over to give Julia a kiss. "Anything you do is all right with me, Julia, simply because you're the one doing it."

"Horses? What are you talking about?" The question was asked by Boone Caulder, one of the young cowboys in the bunkhouse.

"Clay said we was gettin' in a hunnert new horses from Smoke Jensen," Willie Blake said.

"Who's Smoke Jensen?" Calder asked.

"He's a feller that raises quarter horses up in Colorado," Gene Finley said.

In addition to Boone Caulder, Roy Baker, and Gene Finley, at least six others who called this bunkhouse home were present for the conversation.

"Folks say that his horses is the best mounts there is, 'n they're worth a hunnert, to a hunnert 'n ten dollars a head," Bert Rowe said.

"A hundred dollars a head? You can't be serious." Boone said in disbelief.

"I'm just tellin' you what folks is sayin' they're worth."

"That's a lot of money for a horse when you can get a pretty good one for forty-five, maybe fifty dollars," Boone said.

"Smoke Jensen has been real careful 'bout growin' horses, 'n he knows the best kind to breed 'n all," Roy said.

"You know this Smoke Jensen, do you?" Boone asked.

"Oh yeah, me 'n Gene 'n Clay 'n Dalton all met 'im a few years ago."

"He's a gunman," Gene Finley said.

"He's not a gunman. What are you talking about?" Roy replied.

"You ever know anybody that could draw a gun faster?" Gene asked.

"Well, no, but that don't make him a gunman. I generally think of a gunman as someone who ain't always on the right side of the law, 'n Smoke always is."

"I wonder if Smoke Jensen is faster than the Professor," Dewey Gimlin, one of the other cowboys, asked.

"I doubt it," Donnie Webb said.

"Why do you say that?" Roy asked. "You ain't never seen neither one of 'em draw, have you?"

"No. But I've heard of both of 'em, 'n from what I've heard, Smoke Jensen is more 'n likely twenty years older 'n the Professor. That bein' the case, it stands to reason that the Professor, bein' a lot younger 'n all, would have to be faster."

"Well, I've never seen the Professor draw, but I don't need to," Roy said. "I've seen Smoke Jensen draw, 'n I'm tellin' you, he is faster than the Professor or anyone else you might want to name."

"Nine thousand dollars," Boone said.

"What?"

"One hundred horses at ninety dollars apiece is nine thousand dollars. That sure is a lot of money."

Fort Worth, Texas

Drew Burgess wasn't yet fifty years old, but he looked older, his hair and deep sideburns laced with gray. He had a rather prominent nose and a face that was always red. At the moment he was standing at the bar in the Red Light Saloon. He had just bought a beer for Boone Caulder.

"Is it true that Conyers is buying a hundred head of blooded quarter horses?" Burgess asked.

"Yes, sir, that's true, all right." Boone said. "Mr. Burgess, you deal with livestock 'n all. Do you have an idea how much them horses cost?"

"I own the Fort Worth Livestock Exchange, Mr. Caulder. I make it my business to know such things. Yes, I'm quite aware of the value of such horses. How did Conyers acquire them? Was the purchase arranged by Preston Miller?"

"I don't know," Boone replied. "You'd have to ask

Clay that. He's the cow boss and he probably knows such things. I'm just one of the cowboys."

"I'm sure Miller has made the contract for him. Conyers uses Miller for all his stock deals."

"Him 'n Mr. Miller has been friends for a real long time," Boone said. "I do know that."

"Yes, they have been. And I fear that friendship has blinded Conyers to anyone else who would try and do business with him."

"That's right. You and Mr. Miller are enemies, aren't you?"

"I would not say that we are enemies. *Enemy* is much too harsh a word," Burgess said. "We are business competitors, though, and I have to admit that we are a long way from being friends."

"Miller does a lot of business, though, doesn't he?"

"He does more business than the Fort Worth Livestock Exchange and the Trinity River Cattle Brokerage combined. Conyers uses him exclusively, and Conyers does as much business as all the other ranchers in the county, combined, so it stands to reason that with Trinity and me having to divide the remaining business, Miller is going to be the biggest."

Small one-room house, Grove Street, Fort Worth

When Eb Lattimore slapped his wife, she called out in pain. "Ouch!" Maggie put her hand to her cheek, which was already turning red from the blow.

"Are you telling me you worked all night 'n five dollars is all you got?"

"Business was real slow. I didn't have anyone who stayed all night. I only had two for just a short time, 'n of the five dollars apiece they give me, I had to give half of it to Miz Watkins. For crying out loud, Eb, you know how that works."

Eb Lattimore, who was a tall gangly person with dark hair and eyes, and about a week's growth of whiskers, stroked his chin as he stared at his wife. "If you'd get yourself a crib like I told you, you wouldn't have to share nothin' with that Watkins woman. Me 'n you could keep it all."

"No, I'm not goin' to get a crib. There don't nobody but the dirtiest and the meanest kind of men that go to the cribs, 'n I'm afraid of men like that. Miz Watkins keeps a clean house, 'n the men that come there are more likely to be clean 'n act like a gentleman."

"What the hell do you care whether they're clean or a gentleman or not?" Lattimore demanded. "You ain't lookin' to marry any of 'em. You done married one of 'em already."

"Yeah, I . . . married one of them," Maggie said, rubbing her cheek.

"Get breakfast fixed. I've got to go to work," Lattimore demanded.

After Lattimore left, Maggie cleaned up the breakfast dishes and considered her situation. She had been on the line for three years, and though she was still an attractive woman, the dissipation of her profession was beginning to take its toll. It had been her ambition, as it was of many of her sister soiled doves, to find some man who either didn't know of her past, or knew of it, but didn't care, who would marry her and allow her to quit the "profession."

When she met Lattimore, she had thought he might be just the man. Lattimore obviously knew what she was because that was how they had met. When he'd asked her to marry him, she'd jumped at the chance. After they were married, she was shocked to learn he intended for her to continue working as she had.

"This way I can have you anytime I want without havin' to pay you anythin'. 'N whatever you get from the other men will be mine."

"Eb, how long do you intend for me to keep working?" Maggie had asked.

"Until I tell you to stop," Lattimore replied.

"Yes, well, here is the problem with that. I've noticed that women like me, well, it seems they get to lookin' just real old a lot faster 'n other women. Another year, or two at the most, there wouldn't be nobody but the most needin' man would want 'nything to do with me. 'N more 'n likely they wouldn't be willin' to pay no more 'n a dollar for it."

"Yeah, well, just keep on a-doin' it for as long as you can get anyone to pay."

After Maggie finished washing the breakfast dishes she went into the bedroom, pulled open the third drawer in the chifforobe, lifted the false bottom, and looked at the money she had hidden there. One hundred and ten dollars. It was money she had accumulated by holding out on every third man she "entertained."

* * *

Working as a hostler for the North Texas Stagecoach Company, Lattimore was in the barn assembling an eight-horse team when someone called out to him.

"Lattimore?"

"Wait," Lattimore replied, looking around to make certain that he was alone, except for the person who had hailed him. "Yeah, it's all clear."

Delbert Catron, the man who hailed Lattimore, was just under six feet tall, and weighed 180 pounds. He stood out among his contemporaries. While most had beards, or moustaches, or even just an unkempt growth by going days at a time not shaving, Catron was always fastidious in his personal grooming.

"I saw the signal and presumed it meant you had some information you wished to convey," Catron said. Called *the Professor* by most, the signal he mentioned was the red bandana Lattimore had hung from a nail on the outside of the barn.

"There's a stagecoach a-goin' to Fort Worth that's goin' to be carryin' near a thousand dollars today," Lattimore said

"Meet me at the Red Light Saloon tomorrow," Catron said.

Lattimore watched him walk away and thought of the one hundred dollars he had just made by giving him the information about money the coach would be carrying. Maggie need never know.

CHAPTER FOUR

Big Rock

For the first few seconds after he woke up, Buster Crabtree had no idea where he was. He knew only that he was outside, lying on the ground somewhere. When he sat up his head began to spin, and he had to put one hand on the ground to keep from falling back again. The last thing he remembered was standing at the bar in the Brown Dirt Cowboy. He didn't know exactly how much he had drunk, but he seemed to remember having asked for a whole bottle of whiskey.

Why did he do it? It didn't make the pain any less.

With some effort Buster stood up, then looked around to get his bearings. He was just outside the edge of town, and he could see the backs of the houses on Moore Street, which meant he was just east of town. But what was he doing out here? Why had he spent the night on the ground? He had a hotel room, and it was paid for until the end of the week.

For just an instant, a partial memory popped up. Someone, not anyone he knew or could remember having ever seen before, had "helped" him leave the saloon. He remembered that they were going the wrong way; he told his benefactor that the Big Rock Hotel was at the west end of Center Street. That was the last thing he remembered.

Buster checked his pockets, and his worst fear was realized. All his money was gone. He started back toward the hotel room, realizing that he didn't even have enough money to buy breakfast.

For the moment, that wasn't a problem. He didn't feel like eating anything anyway, but he was sure to be hungry before nightfall. Without money and without a job, how would he eat?

Buster had tried at the livery stable, the freight office, and the stagecoach depot to get a job, but was told nothing was available. None of the other businesses in town—the Cattlemen's Association, a couple of law offices, and a bakery—seemed to offer any opportunity. He knew he had nothing to offer any of them.

Frustrated and anxious as to what lay ahead of him, Buster went back to the hotel, then up to his room, where he lay on the bed. He saw his holster and pistol hanging from the head of the bed, and he got an idea.

Strapping the pistol on, he walked up Ranney Street to Front Street, then down to the bank.

"This is foolish," he said aloud.

Suppose he did go in there and rob the bank? How would he get away? His horse was in the stable. He couldn't get the horse out because he had no money. It would be foolish to rob the bank, then, carrying the bags of money, walk down to the livery and pay to get his horse out.

Mo's Meats was just across the corner. It was a business establishment certain to have some cash on hand, otherwise how would they do any business? Because it was a business, it was unlikely the proprietor would be armed. Twenty dollars. He would just steal twenty dollars then leave.

Buster stepped across the street and stood in front of the meat market for a moment, then realized that the same problem existed. His horse was in the livery and he had no money to get his horse out. Besides, the sheriff's office was right next door to Mo's Meats.

Buster smiled, and that's when he got another idea.

Sugarloaf Ranch

Smoke Jensen was on top of the U.S. Wind Engine windmill, tightening the vane that kept it pointed into the wind, when he saw a rider approaching by Jensen Avenue. Since it ended at his ranch, whoever it was had to be coming to the Sugarloaf. As the rider came closer, Smoke smiled. He recognized Sheriff Monte Carson.

Climbing back down the windmill, Smoke wiped his hands off with a damp cloth and waited as Sheriff Carson came through the gate then rode up to the see him. "Hello, Monte. What brings you out here?"

Monte dismounted and led his horse to the watering trough, where it began drinking thirstily.

"Didn't you have a run-in with a man by the name of Buster Crabtree a few days ago?"

"Yes, I did, but nothing really came of it. Why do you ask?"

"He wants to see you."

"You didn't have to come out here for that, Monte, not that you aren't always welcome. But you could have just sent Crabtree out here."

Monte shook his head. "Nope, I couldn't have done that. He's in jail."

"Why is he in jail?"

Monte chuckled. "It's a little confusing. I think you might want to talk to him about that."

"All right. Let me change into a clean shirt and I'll come into town. By the way, Sally has made some lemonade if you would like to wait and ride into town with me."

"Yes, a glass of lemonade would taste very good right now."

"Thanks for comin' to see me, Mr. Jensen," Crabtree said when Smoke went into the jailhouse with Monte.

"Monte, why don't you open the door and let me go into the cell with him," Smoke said. "I don't like talking through the bars."

"Oh, I'll do better than that. I'll open the cell and let Mr. Crabtree out. The three of us can sit around my desk and have a cup of coffee while we talk."

"Thanks, Sheriff," Crabtree said, as Monte opened the door to the cell.

"Now, Mr. Crabtree, Monte says that the reason for

you being in jail is confusing. Can you tell me what it's all about?"

"I turned myself in to the sheriff and asked him to put me in jail."

"Well, like Monte said, that is confusing. Why did you ask Monte to put you in jail? Are you a wanted man?"

"I hope to be wanted."

"I beg your pardon?"

"I'm hoping you'll want me. I'm in jail because I want to get a job with you."

Smoke laughed and shook his head. "I've hired a lot of hands in my day, Crabtree, and I'll admit that I've even hired a few from jail. But as far as I know, none of them have ever had themselves put in jail just to get a job with me. I'm sure you will agree that that is a most unusual approach."

"Yes, sir, I suppose it is. But let me begin by talking a little bit about our run in the other day. When I pulled a gun on that woman for helpin' that card sharp, well, that wasn't me. I ain't never done nothin' like that before in my whole life. The way you handled it, I mean, the way you stopped to find out what was going on before doin' anything, told me more about you than anyone ever could tell me about you. That's why I told the sheriff I wanted to see you."

"I appreciate your confidence in me, Mr. Crabtree, but that doesn't explain why you asked Sheriff Carson to put you in jail."

"I know I'm goin' a long way around to get to the point," Crabtree said. "But hear me out. It may be that I need to explain this to you in order to figure it out myself. I woke up this morning, not in my hotel bed, but lyin' out in the gully that's just east of town. I had a hangover, a lump on my head, no idea of how I got there, and no money in my pocket. Someone had hit me over the head and took twenty-one dollars from my pocket, which is all I had left.

"I tried to get a job at a few places, but nobody was interested in hirin' me. Then, I actually started thinkin' about robbing a bank, or some other such thing. I've not only never done nothin' like that before, I ain't never even *thought* about nothin' like that. But there I was this morning, makin' plans that, if I had gone through with them, would have set me on the wrong side of the law for the rest of my life. The fact that I actually was thinkin' about it scared me to the point that, well, I thought the best thing for me to do would be to turn myself in to the sheriff's office before I really did something. So that's what I done."

"And here I thought it was just the lunch I fed you," Monte teased.

Buster chuckled. "Yeah, well, I have to confess that did figure into my consideration."

"Buster . . . that's your first name, isn't it? Buster?" Smoke started.

"Yes, sir. Well, that's what I'm called, and that's what I prefer, but my actual first name is Gabe."

"Buster, you keep saying that this isn't you. But you did hold a gun on that woman, and by your own admission, you did think about committing a robbery. I'm willing to accept that this isn't the real you. What I don't understand is why you did these things that aren't you."

Buster was quiet for a long moment, and Smoke

was surprised and a little embarrassed to see that Buster's eyes had filmed over with tears.

"I'm sorry," Smoke said. "I didn't mean to—"

Buster waved his hand to interrupt. "No, I've asked you for a job. You have a right to know as much of my background as there is. For the last several years I have been up in Wyoming, making a living by breaking horses for ranchers. That's how I came by the name Buster. Often I would go off for weeks at a time to ride in cowboy competitions."

"Cowboy competitions?"

"Some folks are beginnin' to call 'em rodeos, now. They are shows where you pay an entry fee to ride on bucking horses, 'n you compete with other cowboys for the prize money.

"My wife didn't like it. Emma said that I made enough money for us just by breakin' horses for the ranchers. And, like she pointed out, there was enough ranches in Wyoming to keep me more than busy. That way I wouldn't have to be gone from home all the time.

"I won a lot more often than I lost, the prize money was good, and I, well, to tell you the truth, I got a little full of myself.

"About three months ago, I came home from a trip I'd been on for a little over six weeks, and I found Emma dead. She'd been shot and, by the way it looked, with her clothes and all, whoever did it had had his way with her. The body was already—" Buster paused in midsentence, pinched the bridge of his nose, and blew out air for a few times before he continued. "The body was already beginning to . . . well, Emma must have been there for almost the entire time I was gone and nobody had come to check on her. It was my fault. I left her home alone so I could go out and have people applaud me.

"After that, Mr. Jensen, I sort of lost it. After the funeral, I just rode away.

"In the three months since then I've gambled and drunk away just about every cent I had from the prize money, which was a little over three hundred dollars. And about the only thing that's kept me away from bad women is that I can't get Emma out of my mind. It's like I said, I'm not the same person I once was."

"Can you still break horses?"

"Oh, yes sir. That I can do."

"Monte, are there any charges against Mr. Crabtree? Does he owe a fine or anything?" Smoke asked the sheriff.

"He's free to walk out right now."

"Buster, as it so happens I find myself in a situation where I need to break a lot of horses. Would you be interested in doing a job like that, for me?"

"Then, you will hire me?" Buster asked, his voice rising in hope.

"I generally leave the hiring and firing up to my foreman, Pearlie," Smoke said. "So we'll have to see what he says."

"Oh." Buster's voice fell.

"But, since he works for me, I do have a little influence with him," Smoke added with a broad smile.

"Oh, thank you, Mr. Jensen. Thank you."

"Do you have a horse?"

"Yes, sir, and that's about the only thing from my

past life that I do have. But he's been put up at the livery, and I don't have the money to get him out."

"You leave that up to me. I'll pay the bill and you can pay me back out of your first paycheck."

"Sheriff Carson?" Buster said.

"Yes?"

"I want to thank you for taking me on as a prisoner when I come in here this morning." Buster smiled. "And for feeding me lunch."

"Well, it's not often that bank robbers turn themselves in to me," Sheriff Carson replied. "Especially when they haven't even robbed the bank yet."

"I'll see you, Monte," Smoke called as he and Buster started toward the door.

"Smoke, tell Sally thanks for the lemonade," Monte replied. "It was real good."

There was part of the story Buster hadn't told Smoke. As he waited at the livery for Smoke to pay the bill on his horse, Buster took a piece of paper from his pocket.

It was Mar . . .

He showed the note to Smoke. "I found this note clutched in her hand. Emma didn't finish the note, but she didn't have to. I know who she was talking about."

"Who is Mar?" Smoke asked.

"Marvin Hayes, and like me, he is a bronco buster who breaks horses for ranchers. Also like me, he rides in cowboy competitions." Buster was quiet for a long moment. "We were friends once. As a matter of fact, Marv was as good a friend as I ever had."

"You say you were friends, and yet he did this?" Smoke asked, indicating the note. "What ended your friendship?"

"I took his girl from him."

"Your wife?"

"Emma Jean Malcolm. She and Marv were engaged when I met her. In fact, on the very day they were to be married, she ran away with me. Marv never forgave either one of us, but I never knew he would do something like this."

"Did you show the note to the sheriff?" Smoke asked.

"I showed him the note and told him who the *Mar* was, but by that time Marv was gone. The sheriff put out some wanted posters on him, and I took it upon myself to find him. It wasn't until I ran out of money and leads that I had to give up the search."

"He'll make a mistake someday and you'll find him," Smoke said.

"I sure as hell hope so."

After Buster told his tale, the two men rode for another fifteen minutes or so without talking.

It was Smoke who broke the silence. "Here we are."

They approached an arch that stretched over the road with the name of the ranch in wrought-iron script.

"This is your ranch?" Buster asked as they passed under the arch. "Damn, this is as big as Sky Meadow, and I didn't think there were any ranches anywhere bigger than that."

"Duff MacCallister," Smoke said.

"What? Yes, that's who owns Sky Meadow. You mean you've heard of him?"

"Duff is a friend of mine," Smoke said without further amplification.

As they approached, Pearlie was coming up from the barn to meet them.

"Who's the lost soul?" Pearlie asked by way of greeting.

"Pearlie, this is Buster Crabtree. He wants a job with us, and I told him that, as my foreman, you do the hiring."

"Smoke, to be honest, we don't have any real need for another man, right now," Pearlie said. "Sorry, Crabtree," he added.

"I also told him that I had some influence with you, and I would recommend him. I thought we might be able to use him to break horses," Smoke added, ameliorating his override.

"Well, actually we *could* use someone to break some horses for us. Are you any good at that?" Pearlie asked.

"Pretty good," Buster said.

"Just pretty good?"

"Well, I don't like to brag, but since my getting hired depends upon whether or not I'll be able to break horses, I'll tell you that I'm damn good. A lot better than most."

"Uh-huh. You're willing to prove that, are you?"

"Yeah, I'm willing to prove it."

"Cal!" Pearlie called. "Get a saddle on Punch and bring him here."

Smoke chuckled. "Punch, huh?"

"Punch? Strange name for a horse," Buster said.

"That's because he punches his riders out of the saddle," Pearlie said.

Buster smiled. "Uh-huh. I thought it might be something like that."

"Actually, I'm pulling a dirty trick on you," Pearlie said. "So far, nobody has been able to stay on Punch, and that includes Cal and me. I guess what I'm actually doing is seeing if you have the guts to try."

"If I get thrown, does that disqualify me?"

Pearlie smiled. "Not unless it disqualifies everyone else on the ranch who has ever tried, 'n that's just about everyone but the cook."

A moment later Cal brought up Punch, a dun quarter horse. Punch was moving his head up and down in nervous jerks, showing his agitation.

"Hand me the reins," Buster said.

Taking the reins, he stepped up close to the horse. Though it looked like he was about to whisper something, he actually bit the animal on the ear. Punch snorted in surprise and pain, then Buster swung into the saddle.

Punch instantly threw his hind legs into the air, but Buster leaned back in the saddle and pulled the horse's nose sharply to the left until it touched his leg. That maneuver stopped the immediate bucking, forcing Punch into an incredibly tight circle.

The horse tried to kick again, and Buster jerked Punch's head back so that he couldn't lower it. As he couldn't lower his head, he couldn't throw his hind legs up.

Punch leaped into the air then came back down on

four stiffened legs, but his rider remained glued to the saddle. Buster used his spurs to start Punch forward, and the horse began an explosive gallop in an attempt to unseat the rider. That attempt failed, so again he began to buck, but this series of bucks was as unsuccessful in dislodging his rider as the previous bucking had been.

Again Punch began to gallop, running all the way down the long drive to the archway. Eschewing the open arched entry, he sailed majestically over the fence. On the other side of the fence, Buster turned him around and started back with him. Punch was headed for the open entryway, but Buster directed him toward the fence and another graceful leap.

By the time horse and rider returned to where Smoke, Pearlie, Cal, and half a dozen other Sugarloaf hands were standing, staring in amazement, Punch was approaching at an easy, controlled, trot.

"Woah, boy," Buster said when they arrived.

Punch halted and stood there, calmly.

"Back up," Buster said, indicating what he wanted with the reins. Punch backed up for several steps.

"Turn to the left." Again, with the reins, Buster guided the horse as he turned in a complete circle, first to the left, and then to the right.

Buster dismounted, patted Punch on the forehead, then mounted again. He rode Punch down to the barn and back with Punch proceeding at a gentle walk. When he returned he dismounted and handed the reins to Pearlie.

"You want to try him?" Buster asked.

"I don't know," Pearlie said, hesitantly.

"Give 'em to me. I'll try," Herman Nelson said.

Pearlie handed the reins to Herman, who, after a moment of hesitation, climbed into the saddle. Punch just stood there.

"Why isn't he moving?" Herman asked.

"You haven't told him where to go," Buster said with a little chuckle.

Herman clucked at Punch, pulled his reins around, and rode down to the entry arch and back doing so in three gaits, at a gallop, trot, and for the approach, walking.

"Well now," Herman said as he swung down from the saddle. "I'd say Punch is going to be a good, gentle mount for someone."

"You're hired," Pearlie said.

CHAPTER FIVE

On the Dallas to Fort Worth road

The line of trees between the road and the creek not only shielded Catron from the road as he waited, the water in Cottonwood Creek kept his horse quiet and satisfied. He had been there for about fifteen minutes when he heard the distant shout of the stage-coach driver.

"Heah, heah! Giddap, now!"

Catron also heard the pop of the whip, but he knew the driver had merely snapped the whip over the team and hadn't actually struck them. He peered around a tree, not making himself visible, but leaning out just far enough to look down the road to the east. He could see dust roiling up, and just in front of the dust, the coach and the team, which was coming at a rapid trot.

Shortly after Catron arrived, he had chopped nearly all the way through a small tree. The trunk wasn't more than four inches in diameter, but the tree itself was tall enough to completely cover the road when felled, and would provide enough of an impediment to passage that the coach would have to stop. He took about four more chops, the tree fell just as he intended, and the road was blocked.

Catron remained out of sight until the coach approached.

"Whoa, hold on there! Whoa!" the driver called, hauling back on the reins. "Lookie there, Dennis. Just how 'n the hell do you think that tree got across the road like that?" he asked his shotgun guard.

"Damn if it don't look to me like it was cut," the shotgun guard answered.

"What is it? Why have we stopped?" one of the passengers called.

"Allow me to answer that question for you," Catron said, stepping out and onto the road. "I have impeded your progress so that I might relieve the driver of a money pouch he is carrying."

"What makes you think we're carryin' any money?" the driver asked.

"Oh, I don't think, Mr. Peterson. I *know* you are carrying a thousand dollars."

"What? How the hell do you know my name?"

"It is called preparation," Catron replied. "Your name is Mitch Peterson, and the gentleman beside you holding the shotgun is Jesse Brubaker. You are carrying one thousand dollars in a special species transfer from the Dallas Bank of Savings to its sister bank in Fort Worth. Now, if you would toss down the pouch, I'll be on my way, and you can continue your journey."

Suddenly and unexpectedly, a man jumped from the coach and shot at Catron, the bullet passing by so close that Catron could hear it pop.

Catron returned fire, and the man grabbed his

stomach and doubled over. From the corner of his eye, Catron saw the guard lift his shotgun, but before he could fire, Catron swung his pistol around and fired a second time. The guard fell from the coach.

In panic, the driver threw up his hands. "Don't shoot no more, mister. Please, don't shoot no more!"

"You others in the coach, step outside please."

"Mister, there ain't no more passengers in there but one old man and one old lady."

"Step outside, or I will start shooting into the coach."

An old man with white hair and a white beard stepped down through the open doorway and, reaching back, helped an old woman down.

"I'm sorry to have inconvenienced you, Mr. Peterson, but you do understand, don't you, that if you had thrown down the money pouch when I first asked, that none of this . . . unpleasantness . . . would have been necessary? Now unless you want this old gentlemen to have to drive the coach the rest of the way, you will give me the money."

"Here!" the driver said tossing down the pouch.

"Thank you."

The old man shouted a vulgar word, and to Catron's surprise, he grabbed the gun of the deceased passenger and pointed it at Catron.

Catron fired twice, killing the old man and the woman, then he turned toward the driver and fired again.

When Catron rode away a moment later, the coach remained immobile in the middle of the road. Blocked from any farther passage, the team couldn't negotiate the downed tree. He left behind him three dead passengers, a dead shotgun messenger guard, and a dead driver.

From the *Fort Worth Messenger:*

CATASTROPHE !

On the Dallas–Fort Worth Road

Yesterday Dr. David Vivian, while on the way to Dallas, had his trip interrupted by a most horrendous sight. The good doctor came across the Dallas to Fort Worth stagecoach stopped in the middle of the road. There, he discovered the driver, Mitchel Peterson, age 42, and the shotgun guard, Jesse Brubaker, age 31, were both dead.

Even more terrible was the fate of the three passengers, all of whom were killed in an apparent stagecoach robbery. The dead passengers were Neil Vincent, 39, owner of the Vincent Meat Packing Company, Boris Schumacher, age 76, former owner of the Lone Star Saloon in Dallas, and his wife Pearl, who was 73.

It would appear that the robbers had prior information about the money shipment, though it is not known how they may have come by such information, as the stagecoach company had taken precautions to keep such information secret. The amount of money taken was $1,250.00 and the identification of the robbers is unknown.

Hell's Half Acre, Fort Worth

When Eb Lattimore stepped into the Waco Tap Saloon, he saw Delbert Catron standing at the end of the bar, farthest from the batwing doors .

Lattimore walked down to stand beside him. I see by the newspaper that my information was good."

Catron slid an envelope across the bar. "Take it and leave."

"I thought we might have a drink together and—"

"Take your money and leave," Catron repeated.

"All right," Lattimore said. "Maybe some other time."

"Yes, some other time."

After Lattimore left, Catron finished his drink, then slid the glass across the bar as a signal that he wanted another one.

"Say, ain't you the one they call the Professor?" the bartender asked as he poured the drink.

"I have been addressed as such," Catron replied. "Why do you inquire?"

"Oh, I ain't got no particular reason. I was just curious, is all."

"You are familiar with the phrase *curiosity killed the cat,* aren't you?"

"What? Uh, no. What does that mean?"

Catron lifted the refilled glass to his lips. "It means it isn't safe to be too curious."

"Yes, sir, well, I didn't mean nothin' by it," the bartender said. "No, sir, I didn't mean nothin' by it at all. You want somethin' else, you just lift your finger 'n I'll be here right away."

Catron didn't reply. He set the glass back down on

the bar and began to study it. None of his past associates would ever imagine him as he was today, standing at a bar in a western saloon, wearing a pistol on his hip. What would have been even more shocking to them would be to know that, so far, he had used that same pistol to kill seventeen—that number only recently reached with the five he had killed during the stagecoach robbery.

As was wont to happen from time to time, Catron allowed the memories of Manchester, Missouri, three years ago to replay in his mind.

"It isn't just Catron's standoffishness that sets him apart from everyone else," Dr. Shelby said. "Have you ever seen him draw and shoot a pistol? He practices constantly."

"Good Lord in heaven, where does he think he is? In the Wild West somewhere? Why would he do such a thing that is so out of sorts for a college professor?" Dr. Parish asked.

"He says it is his hobby," Professor Cumby replied.

"Perhaps so, but you must concede that a quick-draw artist is at best strange, and at worst inappropriate for a professor of English. Especially here at Derbyshire College, a school with a student body from only the wealthiest and most elite families. Why, he almost takes on the persona of one of those infamous gunfighters from the West," Dr. Parish said.

"The faculty meeting is about to start, and Catron isn't here yet," Cumby said.

"He is never on time and often misses them entirely," Shelby said.

"I wonder where he is." Cumby asked.

At that exact moment Professor Delbert Catron, wearing trousers but no shirt, was standing at the bedroom window, looking out over the beautifully maintained campus lawn. "I need to be going."

"Why?" asked the naked woman on the bed behind him.

"There is a faculty meeting."

The woman chuckled. "Then that's all the more reason you don't need to leave yet. After all, my husband is conducting the faculty meeting. I don't expect him to come barging through that door."

"Nevertheless, I am expected at the meeting."

Two days later, Professor Catron was lecturing his class on Charles Dickens, considered one of the most influential writers. "Although Dickens is known for his social commentary on the prevalent conditions in England, his literary works have gained popularity amongst readers, editors and publishers far beyond England. As your assignment, I would like for you to write an opinion on—"

"Damn you, Catron! You have been with my wife, and I'm going to kill you!" This loud shout came from Julian McClain, the Dean of Derbyshire College. The challenge was immediately followed by a gunshot as McClain fired at Catron.

The bullet slammed into the blackboard behind Catron. Against the screams and shouts of the students, Catron, jerked open his desk drawer, took out his pistol, and returned fire. A black hole appeared in the middle of McClain's forehead, and he fell, dead before he hit the floor.

Professor Catron was immediately suspended from his teaching duties while he awaited the trial. Although Sue McClain reached out to him during his suspension, he thought it best to avoid her. When the hearing was held a week later, there were twenty-three witnesses to the shooting, and their accounts resulted in a finding of nolle prosequi, by virtue of self-defense.

With the legal action having been removed, Catron answered the request of Donald Taylor, the president of the college, to come to his office. Catron assumed it was to tell him that his suspension had been lifted, but that wasn't the case.

"Mr. Catron, the board of directors has found that your indiscreet behavior with Mrs. McClain is what led to the fatal confrontation between you and the dean. Therefore, with effect retroactive to the date of your suspension, we are terminating your tenure as professor of English."

"I was not charged," Catron replied.

"I feel it incumbent upon me to tell you that, in addition to your termination, we have made public a report of your transgressions which, no doubt, shall preclude any other college or university hiring you. And should you apply, we will so inform the institution in question when they ask for references."

Realizing he'd always held a secret desire to go west, that desire seemed the motivation for his determination to become expert in drawing and shooting a pistol. With his career in education now permanently closed, he took the next train headed west from St. Louis.

He had no idea how he would make a living after arriving in Kansas, but that dilemma was solved two days after he got off the train in Kansas City when he learned that a messenger would be carrying over five hundred dollars for a cattle transaction. The messenger became his second victim. The fifteen since then included a few gunmen who simply wanted to test their mettle against him.

He was smart enough to keep his name off the wanted lists. His notoriety came from the shooting incidents in which *he had, so far, been able to prove the homicides justifiable for reasons of self-defense.*

"Hey you! What the hell are you doing standing in my place?"

The loud bellow jerked Catron back from his contemplations.

The angry shout also interrupted half a dozen conversations as everyone in the saloon looked toward the source. Nearly everyone recognized Orrin Talbot, a big man whose size intimidated all he encountered. He was staring at Catron, though it could best be described as an angry glare.

"Mister, you need to find yourself some other place to stand," Talbot said, the words coming out as a preemptive challenge.

"I do thank you for the invitation, but I don't see any need for moving from this place. As it so happens, I'm quite satisfied with this position," Catron replied in a cultured voice.

"I ain't *invitin'* you to move, mister. I'm *tellin'* you to move. Now, I'm goin' to give you a second chance 'cause I ain't never seen you before, 'n maybe you don't know who I am. But I'm Orrin Talbot. Ever'one knows that part of the bar where at you're a-standin' now is my own special place. Now, git."

"I'm sorry. Perhaps with your limited cognitive abilities you didn't understand. I shall attempt to speak more clearly."

"Cog . . . cog? What the hell did you just say?"

"I informed you that I have no intention to vacate this spot. I have grown quite comfortable with it, and

I intend to stay." Catron spoke so quietly that Talbot had to strain to hear it.

"Then let me tell you what I'm a-goin' to do to you, you fancy-talkin' lout. I'm goin' to knock you on that ass of your'n."

Catron smiled at Talbot.

Normally, just the suggestion of a physical confrontation was enough to intimidate people, but this man's reaction surprised Talbot. Why was he smiling?

"What the hell are you smilin' at?" Talbot asked, putting as much threat into his challenge as he could.

"Mister Talbot, I think I would be remiss if I didn't make you aware that should this unpleasant encounter between the two of us continue, it may become even more heated, in which case it could well result in your demise."

"It'll what?"

"You will be killed," Catron said. "But if you apologize to me now, and acquiesce to my right by previous domain to this position, I'm quite willing to let the matter pass."

Talbot laughed out loud. "If I apologize to you? Well now, is that a fact?"

"Am I to take that as a refusal to apologize?"

"You're damn right I ain't goin' to apologize."

"Then I'm afraid I must withdraw the offer to let it pass. Listen to me carefully. I'm telling you in front of all these witnesses present that if you will turn around and walk out of the room right now, I will let you live."

Talbot laughed out loud. "You will let me live? What the hell, mister? Are you crazy? I ain't goin' nowhere till you get the hell out of my spot."

"I'm afraid that was your last chance, Mr. Talbot. Your fate has been sealed."

"You sure are a-talkin' mean for someone who ain't near as big as me," Talbot said.

"Talbot, don't you know who this feller is?" the bartender hissed. "This here fella is Del Catron, the one they call the Professor."

The bartender's news brought an immediate reaction from Talbot, and the confident, mocking expression on his face changed to one of absolute terror. "You? You're the Professor?"

"Actually, a more correct title would be Professor Emeritus, as I no longer hold a teaching position anywhere."

In a world without guns, Catron would be a peripheral figure, submissive to all around him. But the West was a world with guns, and he had proven by numerous previous encounters that he was a man to be feared.

"I might add, Mr. Talbot, that I am pleased to make your acquaintance, brief though our relationship shall be," Catron said with his smile unrelenting.

"Wait a minute, now. Hold on here. There ain't no need to be a-takin' this any further," Talbot said, his voice quaking with fear.

A barroom fight was one thing—Talbot had been in many of those—but the possibility that it might develop into a shooting confrontation was new to him. "I tell you what. You can stand there as long as you want. I'll find me some other place to go."

"Oh, I'm afraid it is too late for that," Catron said. "Have you forgotten? You rejected my offer of a peaceful settlement. So, as I told you, the offer to let this pass has been withdrawn. Now, our enmity has been established, and it wouldn't be good for either one of us for it not to be resolved."

Something about Catron shifted then, an inexplicable change in his eyes. Though they were brown, now there was a flash of yellow in them. Looking at them, Talbot got the feeling that he was staring into the fiery pits of Hell, and he felt his knees growing weak.

"I-I don't want to draw against you."

"Oh, you don't have to draw against me. I'm quite prepared to let you extract your pistol before I go for my own gun," Catron said.

"Look here. I'm tellin' you now, there ain't no need in this a-turnin' into a shootin'," Talbot said, the fear very evident in his voice.

"As I said, Mr. Talbot, I have every intention of letting you draw first. Shall we open the ball?" Catron suggested.

Without further response, Talbot's hand suddenly dipped toward his gun.

The smile never left Catron's lips and he waited until Talbot's pistol had actually cleared the holster.

When Talbot realized that he was holding a gun in his hand while Catron's pistol was still in the holster, he had a moment, no longer than a heartbeat, of exhilaration. But even before he could pull the trigger, Catron's pistol was out and booming.

Talbot also managed to get off a shot, but it was muscle memory only, and the bullet plunged into the floor. A stain of red spread across Talbot's chest, and he gurgled a curse as the blood rose in his throat, then dribbled from the corners of his mouth, matting his beard. Talbot fell backward, his heavy body sending up a puff of dust as he hit the saloon floor. His arms flopped out to either side of him, the gun dangling from a crooked, but stilled finger.

CHAPTER SIX

Catron stood there looking down at the body for a long moment with smoke curling up from the barrel of his gun. Then he put his pistol away and turned to the bar. "Barkeep, I would like another drink, please. Beer this time," he ordered.

Catron had drunk less than half of that beer when a deputy sheriff, who had been summoned by a witness, came into the saloon. He walked over to the body that lay facedown.

"What the hell? Is that Orrin Talbot?" the deputy asked.

There was affirmation from several of the patrons.

"So, the big bully finally got his comeuppance, did he? Who done it?"

"I did," Catron said, turning to face the deputy.

"You?" the deputy said as if he were unable to believe that this mild-looking man could have gotten the better of someone like Orrin Talbot.

"Yes."

"Any reason for it?"

"I'm afraid it was forced upon me, Deputy. Mr.

Talbot started it by ordering me to move away from the bar. I refused to do so, and the resulting dispute continued until he went for his gun. At that point I had no choice but to respond, and as luck would have it, I was able to draw and shoot before he could complete the action he had initiated."

"Damn, the way you talk," the deputy said. "Wait a minute! You're the one they call the Professor, ain't you?"

"I have been called that," Del Catron said.

"And you say Talbot went for his gun first? He was actually dumb enough to draw against you?"

"You may inquire of any of the eyewitnesses if you wish."

"That's right, Deputy," the bartender said. "Talbot went for his gun first. The Professor didn't have no choice but to pull his own gun."

Several others verified the account.

"Why would Talbot be dumb enough to draw agin' someone like you? Unless maybe he didn't know who you was."

"Oh he knew all right. I told him," the bartender said.

The deputy looked down at Talbot's body and shook his head. "Well, Talbot always was a blowhard 'n a bully. I guess this time it just all come back on 'im. All right. Don't look like there's nothin' I can hold you on." The deputy turned to leave.

"Deputy?" the bartender called out to him.

"What?"

The bartender pointed to Talbot's body. "You ain't goin' to just leave 'im here, are you? I mean, they's folks drinkin' and eatin' here. It won't be good for business for 'em to have to step over a dead body."

"I'll get Ponder down here to pick 'im up," the deputy said as he left.

Turning back to the bar, Catron finished his beer. "I think I should like a—"

"Your finest brandy, and I'll pay for it. Make it two brandies," another man said, stepping up to the bar alongside Catron.

Catron looked toward the man who spoke to him. Men often tried to befriend him for one reason or another, and normally Catron dismissed them out of hand. But something about this man intrigued Catron, though he couldn't put his finger on it. "May I inquire as to the name of my benefactor?"

"The name isn't important. What is important is the business opportunity I would like to offer you."

"What kind of business opportunity?"

"One that can make you a lot of money. Actually it will make both of us a lot of money as I intend to be your silent partner if you agree to take the job. Would you join me at one of the tables? I'll be happy to share all the details with you."

As soon as the bartender poured the two brandies, Catron picked up one of them, then followed the man over to the most isolated table. "Before we begin our discussion, I think you should know that while circumstances have resulted in the frequent employment of my gun, I am not a professional assassin, and I will not kill for hire."

"Oh, now, hold on here, Professor Catron. I'm not asking you to kill anyone in particular," the man said.

"In fact, if everything goes right, you won't have to kill anyone at all, and I hope that's the way it turns out."

"If everything goes right," Catron repeated. "But of course, to quote the late poet Robert Burns, 'The best laid schemes o' mice an' men gang aft a-gley.' You said a lot of money. How much money are you talking about?"

"I'm talking about a good deal of money. Several thousand dollars, in fact."

"Several thousand dollars, you say? Very well, you have piqued my interest. What do you want?"

"It so happens that I know that one hundred very expensive horses are about to come to Fort Worth. And I know where we can sell those horses for a lot of money."

"Don't tell me that it is your idea that we buy those horses, then sell them somewhere else at a substantial profit," Catron replied. "That would require my participation in the initial purchase, and I have neither the interest nor the funds for such a thing."

"No, what I want is for you to steal those horses," the man replied, then he laughed. "Consider this. If we paid nothing to acquire them, when we sell them every cent we get will be profit."

"Oh, so you and I are to steal the horses, are we? Let me ask you this. Have you ever stolen horses before?"

"No, and I won't be stealing these horses, either. You will steal them. I will sell them. As I told you, I already have an outlet for them."

"I hardly think that you would expect me to steal one hundred horses all by myself."

"Of course not. I would expect you to have some

help, but who, and how many helpers you acquire, is up to you. My role in our partnership will go no further than providing information and planning."

"Once I have my organization assembled, how will I get in touch with you?"

"You won't have to worry about that. I'll get in touch with you."

"How soon will that be? I shan't be able to hold them for long, unless I can make it a financially viable endeavor for them."

"I'm sure you'll find some way to hold them together." The man stood and walked away.

After his mysterious partner left, Catron remained sitting at the table contemplating the people he would be able to gather for his larcenous enterprise. The first name that came to mind was Eb Lattimore, the man who had given him the information for the stagecoach robbery.

"Yeah, hell yeah, I'll do it," Lattimore said. "I'm plumb tard of workin' for the stagecoach line anyhow."

"No, keep your job for now," Catron said. "It's best not to bring any unwanted attention to yourself. I'll contact you when I need you."

Catron's next stop was in Red Oak. There, he would find Jory Gibbons and Dooley Evans. The two men were half brothers, raised by the same mother, a part-time prostitute who had never married either of their fathers. She wasn't even sure that their names had actually been Gibbons and Evans, though those were the names she had been given.

Catron had used the two men once before, and they had followed orders well. That was important to him. He dismounted in front of Duncan Livery and stepped inside. The two men were mucking out one of the stalls.

"Gentlemen, I have need of your services," he said.

Gibbons looked around at him. "Professor, what are you doin' here?"

"I have come to see if you two would like to come with me and make a little money"—he interrupted his sentence with a little chuckle—"or if you would rather stay here and continue to shovel horse patties."

Gibbons and Evans looked at each other for a moment, then both tossed their shovels into the ooze they were shoveling.

"We'll come with you," Evans said.

Catron smiled. "I thought you might."

With his first three men signed on, Catron continued his recruitment.

He found Dan Parker and Merlin Dawkins in jail in Springtown, Texas. "Why are these two men in jail?" Catron asked the town marshal.

"They were fined thirty dollars for indecent exposure, 'n they don't have the money to pay it, so they'll be spendin' thirty days in jail."

"I beg your pardon. Did you say indecent exposure?"

"They were drunk, and they were caught pissing on the wall of Sikes's Hardware Store."

"Who saw them?"

"Nobody saw them but my deputy. It was about two o'clock in the mornin' when they was doin' that. But it don't matter none whether anyone else seen 'em or not. It's still agin' the law to piss out in public like that."

"I would like to speak with them for a moment or two, if you don't mind."

"Sure, go ahead. I don't care."

The first thing Catron did when he stepped back into the cell area was to see if anyone else was in jail at the time. He wanted his conversation with the two men to be private.

Catron stepped up to the cell. "So, the two men who are still wanted for their daring holdup of the Kansas Limited now find themselves incarcerated for the dastardly crime of urinating on the wall of Sikes's Hardware. Tsk, tsk, tsk. As David's lament over Saul and Jonathan states, 'How the mighty have fallen.'"

"Professor, what are you doin' here?" Dawkins asked.

"I'm here to pay your fine and ask if you would be interested in entering into an endeavor with me that holds the promise of a significant amount of money."

"I think I can answer for both of us when I say hell yes!" Dawkins said.

"I'll pay your fines, and you can come with me now," Catron said.

Jory Gibbons, Dooley Evans, Dan Parker, and Merlin Dawkins remained in the saddle and Catron dismounted in front of Boyce's Blacksmith Shop in the small town of Risco. They could hear the ringing sound of hammer on steel, as well the hiss of red-hot metal being immersed in water.

"What the hell are you doing?" someone shouted

from inside the shop. "I told you to do the Emerson job first. Emerson!"

"Cooper was here first."

Catron recognized Murry Morris's voice.

"Let me ask you this, Morris, you dumb turd. Who the hell do you work for? Cooper or me?"

Catron was standing in the doorway and saw Morris wearing a full-length apron and holding a glowing horseshoe in a pair of blacksmith tongs. The man doing the yelling was an older man with a red face, bulbous nose, and unruly gray hair.

"Actually, he doesn't work for either you or Mr. Cooper," Catron said. "He works for me."

"What?" the older man said. "Who the hell are you?"

Morris had looked toward Catron and smiled when he walked in. He laid down the tongs and began to take off his apron. "Like he said, he's the man I work for."

Catron's gang was now formed.

CHAPTER SEVEN

Big Rock

"Seven cars? You need seven stock cars?" the railroad dispatcher said in reply to Smoke's request.

"Yes," Smoke replied. "I have one hundred horses to ship."

"Well, actually you won't really need seven cars. Six will do. Each car is divided into two separate compartments, and each compartment contains eight individual stalls. That means you would only have four horses left over, but you could double up on four of the stalls."

"No," Smoke said. "I don't want to take any chances on injuries during the trip down. Besides, we are also taking our own individual mounts so that would be eight extra, instead of four."

The dispatcher chuckled. "You're the boss, Smoke. Seven cars it is. You do know, though, don't you, that if you have that many cars you will also have to have a dedicated engine. And with that much of a consist, you will have an entire train."

"Yes, I well understand that. And since we'll be going along with the train, I'll need to hire a Pullman car."

"May I suggest a caboose instead? A Pullman car, or a private car, will cost you as much as all seven of the cattle cars combined. But a caboose would serve your purposes quite well, and it won't cost any more than one of the cattle cars. That is, if you don't find the conditions in a caboose to be too Spartan."

Smoke chuckled. "Good idea, George. A caboose it will be, and thanks for the suggestion. Now, what is this going to cost?"

"The total cost will be sixteen hundred dollars for the seven cattle cars and the caboose, plus an additional four hundred dollars for the engine. Two thousand dollars in all."

"How soon can we get the train assembled?"

"Oh, I think we can put one together for you within ten days or so. Have your horses here a week from next Monday."

"A caboose? We're going to go all the way to Fort Worth, Texas, in a caboose?" Sally asked after Smoke told her of the arrangements he had made for transporting the horses to Big Jim and Live Oak Ranch."

"Sally, the caboose is two hundred dollars. A Pullman car would be fourteen hundred dollars."

Sally smiled. "It's just as I said, Smoke, we're going all the way to Fort Worth in a caboose, and what a brilliant idea that is."

"Just as you said, huh?" Smoke replied.

Cal laughed. "I heard her say that, Smoke. I sure did."

"All the horses are ready to go, aren't they?" Smoke asked.

"I'll say they are," Pearlie replied. "Hiring Buster Crabtree is the best hire you ever made. I've never seen anyone who could handle horses like him."

"Uh, the best hire Smoke ever made?" Cal asked.

"Hey, don't get all upset, Cal. As I recall, Miz Sally is the one that hired you. And you're the best hire she ever made."

Cal smiled. "Yeah, that's right. She is the one who hired me, and I am the best hire she ever—" He paused in midsentence. "Wait a minute. I'm the only one she ever hired."

"Ha!" Pearlie said.

"Cal, consider this. Pearlie just said that Buster was the best hire Smoke ever made. I suppose he forgot that Smoke hired him." Sally grinned.

"Ha! Yeah!" Cal said.

Smoke chuckled. "Tell me, Sally, would the term *hoist by his own petard* fit Pearlie here?"

"Very good, Smoke. Very good," Sally replied with an approving laugh.

"Ah, I was just teasing anyway," Pearlie said.

The four were having lunch in Lambert's Restaurant, and their discussion was interrupted by a shout from the kitchen door.

"Hot rolls!" Lambert shouted. "Hot rolls!" Hot rolls began flying around the restaurant as quickly as he took them from the deep pan he was holding and throwing them to the customers.

Pearlie reached up and snatched one out of the air,

then handed it to Sally. Cal was next, then Smoke and then Pearlie caught a second roll that he kept for himself.

"When do we leave?" Pearlie asked as he put butter on his roll.

"Next Monday," Smoke replied. "Before we go back home today, I'll send Big Jim a telegram giving him our schedule."

Douglas, Wyoming Territory

Marvin Hayes was standing at the bar of the Lonesome Cowboy saloon. He had ridden over from Tie Siding when he heard that Buster Crabtree might be in Douglas.

"Would you like another beer?" the bartender asked.

"Yeah, I think I would," Hayes said, sliding his beer mug across the bar. "Say, I'm lookin' for an old pard of mine. Me 'n him used to ride in cowboy competitions together. Some folks back in Tie Siding told me he might be here."

"What's your pard's name?" the bartender asked as he drew a mug of beer from the beer keg.

"His name is Buster Crabtree."

"You mighty damn right he was here," the bartender said as he set the mug of golden liquid before Hayes. "You tellin' 'bout the cowboy competition is what made me think of it."

"Why, did you have a competition here?"

"Well not so's you could call it a competition. I mean it warn't nothin' really organized." The bartender chuckled. "But I'll tell you true, that Crabtree feller won 'im two hunnert dollars by ridin' two of the meanest mounts in all of Sweetwater County."

"Is he still here?"

"No, he left town. Oh heck, must've been two weeks or more, now."

"You're sure he's gone?"

"Mister, did you get a good look at this town when you come in? We ain't got but about a hunnert 'n fifty people in the whole town. Ever'body here knows ever'body else, 'n we know when someone new comes in, 'n when someone leaves. Crabtree ain't here no more."

"Since you seem to know the business of ever'body, mayhaps you can tell me where at he went to," Hayes suggested.

"I heard 'im talkin' to Strayhorn, 'n seems to me like he told Strayhorn he was goin' to go down into Colorado."

"Where in Colorado?"

"Now that, I can't tell you. You might ask Strayhorn. He owns the livery that's just down the street."

Hayes took a swallow of his beer, then set it on the bar and started toward the door.

"Mister, you ain't drank hardly none of your beer," the bartender called out to him.

"I don't want no more right now," Hayes said.

The bartender watched him leave, then, picking up the beer, he looked around the saloon, and when he was certain nobody was watching, he poured the rest of the beer back into the keg.

* * *

Strayhorn was pitching some hay into the ten stalls when Hayes stepped into the barn.

"Your name Strayhorn?"

"That's right. What can I do for you?"

"I'm told you might know where I can find Buster Crabtree."

"What are you lookin' for him for? You the law? A bounty hunter or somethin'? 'Cause if you are, you're barkin' up the wrong tree. Crabtree ain't the kind of man who'd get hisself crosswise with the law."

"No, it ain't nothin' like that. Me 'n Buster is old friends is all, 'n I've kinda lost track of 'im."

"Well sir, I don't, for sure, but he was talkin' some about Boulder, Colorado, afore he left. You say you 'n him's old friends. Where did you know him at?"

"Oh, I've knowed 'im all over. We used to ride together in cowboy competitions."

"You!" Strayhorn said, the expression on his face changing from one of curiosity to anger. "Would your name be Marvin Hayes?"

"What of it?"

"You're the one. You're the one that kilt Buster's wife! What are you lookin' for him for? Iffen I was you, I'd stay as far away from him as I could."

"Is that what he told you? That I killed his wife?"

"Anyone that would kill a woman, let alone it bein' another man's wife, is lower than a snake. He's lookin' for you, mister, —n when he finds you—"

Strayhorn saw the evil smile on Hayes's face and stopped in midsentence. "Damn! You're lookin' to kill him, too, ain't you?"

"You're smarter 'n you look, Strayhorn."

Strayhorn was still holding the pitchfork, and lifting it, he thrust it, tines first, toward Hayes.

Hayes slipped by the pitchfork thrust, grabbed a hammer off the shelf, and brought it down hard on Strayhorn's head. The hammer blow put a hole in the side of his head, exposing some of the brain. Hayes looked around, and seeing that he was alone, he dragged Strayhorn's body into the stall with one of the horses. Knowing horses better than most men, he knew how to get a horse agitated. A moment later, the frenzied horse began kicking, and Hayes saw with some satisfaction that one of the kicks further crushed the side of Strayhorn's head.

He returned to the saloon.

"Strayhorn warn't there?" the bartender asked.

"I don't know," Hayes said. "There's a man lyin' in one of the stalls. Looks like his head has been half bashed in by the horse. I don't know if that's Strayhorn or not, seein' as I don't know 'im. I thought I should tell you about it so's you can let the others know."

"Damn!" the bartender said in shock when he saw the man lying in the stall. "Who woulda ever thought Strayhorn would get kilt by a horse?"

"This here is how I found 'im," Hayes said. "I come into the livery 'n I heard the horse makin' quite a racket, so I come back here to see what was goin' on, 'n this is what I seen."

There were at least six men with Hayes, drawn by the news of what had happened to one of their own.

"Somebody needs to put that horse down," one of

the men said. "Once a horse gets a taste of man killin' they likely to do it agin."

"Who's goin' to tell Nellie that her husband has been kilt?" someone asked.

"We'd best get Pastor Owens to do that. He'd prob'ly be able to make it easier on 'er than any of us would."

Five minutes later, with the citizens of Douglas still lamenting the death of their friend, Hayes rode out of town, heading south. If Buster Crabtree was in Boulder, Hayes would find him and kill him.

CHAPTER EIGHT

"The first thing we must do is find a place for us to hole up between jobs," Catron told the others after he had completed recruiting his gang.

"Wait a minute now," Dawkins said. "You ain't talkin' 'bout findin' a cave or somethin' like that, are you? I don't like bein' outside all that much. I don't like the skeeters, 'n I don't like snakes."

"Oh I think we can be a little more comfortable that that," Catron said.

"I got a place to stay," Lattimore said.

"Yes, and I intend for you to maintain your current residence," Catron said. "It will be good to have eyes and ears among the people. This will be for the rest of us, but I want you to come with us now, so you'll know where it is."

"You got somethin' in mind?" Morris asked.

"As a matter of fact, I do have such a place in mind. I found us a nice cabin that has a good supply of water and, perhaps even more important, is sufficiently out of the way to preclude the likelihood of any accidental visitors."

"Well great. Let's go there then," Dawkins suggested.

"That's where we *are* going. Of course, I neglected to tell you that before we can take possession, we must dispossess the current occupants."

"We gotta what?" Morris asked.

"Some people are living there now. We are going to take it from them," Catron said.

West Fork of the Trinity River, Texas

The cabin was about five miles from Azle, on the West Fork of the Trinity River. Somewhat bigger than the one-room cabins that were so ubiquitous in this remote areas of Texas, it was the residence of Gus Belford, his wife Joanna, and his two sons, Amos, who was twelve, and Hugh, ten. Gus had built the house not with the intention of ranching, but of growing corn in the rich soil.

A nearby stream was a year-round supply of fresh water and was filled with fish—a source of food until the farm was established and he could begin augmenting their income and their food supply by raising hogs and chickens.

Gus was fishing with his two sons when Amos saw the riders approaching. "Poppa, looks like we got company a-comin'," he said.

After watching them for a moment, Gus felt a sense of foreboding, though he couldn't put a finger on the reason for his apprehension. "Go into the house, boys."

"What for?" Amos asked. "There sure ain't no way Mama can cook for this many people."

"Go into the house," Gus repeated, more forcefully. Realizing by the sound of his voice that their father was serious, the two boys returned without further question.

As the men approached, Gus wished that he had brought his shotgun out with him, though he realized that with at least seven men, it would have been a useless gesture. The shotgun would have to be reloaded after each shot.

"Hello, gentlemen. Come to water your horses, did you?" He forced a smile, hoping to portray a calmness he didn't feel, and pointed to the river. "Well, as you can see, there's plenty of it here."

"Would you mind telling us the proximity of your nearest neighbor?" one of the men asked.

"What?"

"How close is your nearest neighbor?"

There was nothing immediately frightening about the man who asked the question. He was of normal size, well groomed, and soft spoken. But something about his eyes, a flame of yellow overpowered the brown.

"I'm not sure."

"Now why would you tell us that you aren't sure? You do live here, don't you? How do you expect us to believe that you don't know any of your neighbors?"

"I don't know what business that is of your'n, mister, but I'm tellin' you the truth. Me 'n my family just come here from Tennessee no more 'n four months ago, 'n we been so busy with a-buildin' this cabin 'n all that we ain't met nobody yet. Hell, I ain't even *seen* nobody else since we come here except for you folks. You're the first ones that has ever come around."

"Did you hear that, gentlemen?" the dandified man

said to the others. "Absolute isolation. This house will be perfect."

"Perfect? Perfect for what?" Gus asked, even as his apprehension turned to abject fear.

The well-groomed man smiled, though the smile projected more evil than humor. He drew his pistol and shot Gus.

"Poppa!" someone shouted from the house.

"Dawkins, I would like for you and Morris to see if there is anyone in the house other than the two boys we saw as we approached," Catron ordered.

"If there is, what do you want to do with 'em?" Dawkins asked.

"I want you to kill them," Catron replied.

"Kill them?" Morris asked, surprised by the order. "If there's two kids, there's likely to be a mama, too. Are you sure you want to kill a woman 'n some kids?"

"I'm afraid we have no choice. It would not serve us well to have extraneous people in our new, secret quarters."

"Damn. For a professor, you sure got a mean streak about you," Parker said.

"On the contrary, Mr. Parker," Catron replied. "I am neither purposely cruel, nor gratuitously compassionate. I am in fact, quite dispassionate, governing my actions on the principles of practicality."

Big Rock

"Hell, I'll bet you this here new feller you got out at Sugarloaf ain't no better rider 'n James True is," said Eddie Webb, the cow boss for the Double Tree Ranch.

"I don't know about that," Pearlie replied. "I've seen True ride and I admit that he's pretty good. But I've seen Buster ride also, and in my book Buster has True beaten hands down."

"What are you talkin' about? Earl Prescott can out-ride James True on the best day True ever had," said Ray Underhill, who rode for the Straight Arrow ranch.

The spirited discussion was taking place in Long-mont's Saloon, and at least three other names were mentioned as perhaps warranting the title of best rider.

"There's one way we can find out," Webb said. "Why don't we have a contest?"

"Yeah," Underhill said.

"I don't believe you're goin' to get all them boys to ride agin one another just for the fun of it," Luke Kelly said. "There's goin' to have to be some reward or somethin'."

"Hey, why don't we have it out at the baseball park? They's seats there 'n we can charge folks to come watch 'n give the winner the money."

"No," Pearlie said. "We'll only give the winner half the money. The rest of it we'll give to the volunteer fire department. If we do that, we could probably get the firemen to sell tickets for us."

"Yeah, that's a good idea!" Webb agreed.

"Pearlie, do you really think Buster is going work out here breakin' horses all day, then want to go into town and break another horse?" Herman Nelson asked.

"How many horses has he broken since he started working here?" Pearlie asked.

"I don't know, ten, fifteen maybe?"

"Let's say he's broken ten horses. Divide what he's being paid by the number of horses he has broken, and that comes out to three dollars a horse. By riding in the competition, he could make as much as a hundred dollars."

"If you don't think this will delay us getting mounts ready to take down to Texas, I don't have any objections to it," Smoke said when Pearlie told him what he and some of the other ranch foremen were putting together.

"And I think the idea of giving money to the volunteer fire department is a really good one," Sally said. "Almost as good an idea as giving the money to the school."

"Gee Miz Sally, I wish I had come to you first," Pearlie said. "But the others are planning on giving money to the fire department, and they're going to get the firemen to sell the tickets."

"Oh, I'm not talking about money from the ticket sales," Sally said. "I'm talking about money from the pastry sales. I'll get some of the other women together and we'll bake pastries and have coffee and lemonade."

It was decided that the rodeo would be on the following Saturday morning.

Seven men signed up to participate, and ten "difficult" horses had been donated by the area ranchers. Louis Longmont, Sheriff Carson, and Phil Clinton would be the judges, making their decision upon the difficulty of the horses and the skill of the riders.

"It's too bad you broke Punch," Herman said to Buster as they were discussing the event. "He would be a good one."

"There are a couple I haven't broken yet," Buster said. "I've been holding them back because they are going to be hard, as hard as Punch or maybe harder. We can put them in."

"I'm goin' to bet twenty dollars on you, Buster, but I'm having to give odds, so don't you go getting your neck broken and letting me down," Cal said.

Pearlie laughed.

"What is it? What are you laughing at?"

"I'm just trying to figure how Buster getting his neck broken is going to let *you* down."

"Oh, yeah. Well, Buster, I don't want to lose my twenty dollars, but I don't want you to get your neck broken, either."

Buster smiled and put his hand to his neck. "I appreciate your concern."

Sidewinders' hideout

The six outlaws that Catron had recruited were now calling themselves the Sidewinder Gang.

Dawkins had come up with the name. "There ain't nothin' that scares folks more 'n a rattlesnake. 'N them sidewinders is 'bout the worse there is of all the snakes."

"Why not just call ourselves the Catron Gang?" Morris asked.

"No, thank you," Catron said. "I don't care to have my name spread all over the state in such a way. The name Sidewinders will be quite acceptable to me."

"Where's Lattimore?" Gibbons asked.

"He's with his woman, I reckon," Evans replied.

"She ain't just his woman. She's his wife. They're married," Dawkins said.

"Yeah, they may be married, but she's still what she is on account I was with her myself warn't no more 'n a month ago," Evans said.

"Does Lattimore know that?" Dawkins asked.

Evans laughed. "Hell, I reckon he does know it, seein' as he's the one that got it set up for me."

Fort Worth

"You goin' to be able to stop whorin' pretty soon," Lattimore said.

"What if I stop now?"

"I ain't ready for you to stop yet, but pretty soon you can. I got somethin' I'm workin' on."

"What is it? Are you goin' to start drivin' the coaches instead of workin' in the stable?" Maggie asked.

"No, it don't have nothin' to do with that. But I've hooked up with some other fellas 'n one of 'em is just real smart. He's so smart they call him the Professor, 'n he's got some good ideas as to how we can make some money. 'N not just some money, but a lot of money."

"Eb, did you say you'll be working with the man they call the Professor?"

"Yeah."

Maggie shook her head. "I've heard of him. You don't need to get hooked up with someone like that."

"What do you know about him?"

"I don't know no more than what I've heard, but they say he's a killer."

Lattimore thought of their encounter with the family that once occupied the cabin they had taken over.

"I reckon he is when he has to be. But I ain't none too interested in that, seein' as how if I'm on his side it'll be somebody else that's gettin' kilt. But it's like I told you, we're goin' to find some ways to make a lot of money 'n when I can do that, why, they don't nothin' else count. 'N oncet I start makin' a lot o' money, why, you'll be able to quit your whorin'. That is, if you're really a-wantin' to."

"What do you mean, if I really want to?"

"I don't know. Sometimes I get the idea that maybe you're a-likin' it a bit more 'n you let on."

"I really want to quit," Maggie said resolutely. "So, when do you expect to start making all this money?"

"Soon."

"How about if I stop now?"

"No, you need to keep on a-whorin' 'til I tell you you can stop. We ain't made no money yet, but I 'spect we will be makin' some just real soon."

Sidewinders' hideout

A couple of days after acquiring the hideout on Crooked Creek and the West Fork of the Trinity River, Catron called a meeting. "Gentlemen, I think it may be time for me to share with you the reason I have assembled this group. I was recently approached by someone who is in a position to provide me with information that will be quite profitable to us."

"Who is he, and what kind of information are you talking about?" Dawkins asked.

"It is not necessary that you know who our informant is, nor need you be aware of the nature of just what we are planning until the time comes. It is in our best interest, at the moment, for me to keep this information to myself. However, when the conditions are right, I'll let you know. And I assure you, the wait will be quite profitable."

"When will that be?" Lattimore asked. "The big money, I mean."

"It will be when it is," Catron replied. "But before our major undertaking, I have decided that we need to do something immediately so that we may raise enough funds to buy provisions such as food, ammunition—"

"And maybe get us some whiskey?" Gibbons interrupted.

"Any whiskey that is bought will be bought on your own. Whatever money we get from this first job will be split in two. Half of the money will be to establish an operating treasury for our enterprise, and we will make an equal division of the remaining half."

"Where at are you plannin' on gettin' this money?" Dawkins asked.

"We are going to rob the bank in Dido."

"Dido?" Parker said. "Iffen we're goin' to rob a bank, ought it not to be one bigger than that little bank in Dido? I mean, Dido is such a little town, how much money can their bank have?"

"At this point we don't need a large amount," Catron said. "We only need enough to sustain ourselves until a better opportunity presents itself. And it is a matter of risk and return. There are two advantages in striking the bank at Dido—it won't be guarded, and there is no local law."

"When do we do it, and shall I come here, or meet you somewhere?" Lattimore said.

"When is your next day off?" Catron asked.

"We don't have no coach runnin' on Saturday."

"Meet us at Wahite Creek just outside Dido on Friday night."

CHAPTER NINE

Big Rock

Like many small towns throughout rural America, Big Rock had an amateur baseball team, and during the summer spirited games were held between such towns as Big Rock, Hermitage, Steamboat Springs, Eagle Park, Dixon, and others.

This Saturday morning, though. the stands were filled to capacity. Some three hundred people had paid a dollar apiece not to see a baseball game, but to see area cowboys compete against each other in riding untamed horses. Sally was in charge of the concession stand. She and four other ladies from the town, including the schoolmarm, were doing a brisk business with bear sign, cinnamon buns, and apple turnovers.

The riders had drawn their horses by lot, but the three judges, by mutual agreement, had decided the order in which they would ride. Deciding to leave what they perceived as the best for last, the order was posted on a portable chalkboard.

> *Jonas Perkins – Twin Peaks Ranch*
> *Dudley Stewart – Back Trail Ranch*
> *August Hagen – Pine Tree Ranch*
> *Isaac McAfee – Doubletree Ranch*
> *Earl Prescott – Straight Arrow Ranch*
> *James True – Doubletree Ranch*
> *Buster Crabtree – Sugarloaf Ranch*

Perkins and Hagen were thrown in less than ten seconds. Stewart and McAfee were on for longer than ten seconds but both were eventually thrown. Earl Prescott, James True, and Buster all three rode their horses until they quit bucking. They were the three riders remaining.

The three most difficult horses had purposely been left out of the original draw and they were matched, by lot, with the remaining three riders.

Prescott was the first rider, and he stayed with his mount until it quit bucking, receiving the applause of the crowd as he rode it around the field at a gallop, waving his hat triumphantly.

James True was the next rider and to the surprise of everyone, he was thrown as soon as he mounted. The crowd, many of whom had bet on True, was stunned.

"Well, it looks like it's between you and Prescott," Cal said.

"No, wait a minute," Buster said, holding out his hand. "Something's not right here."

"What do you mean? What are you talking about?"

"Smoke!" Buster called. "Stop that horse!" He pointed to the horse that had just thrown True. The horse was being led out by the wranglers who had been working the rodeo.

"Hold on there," Smoke called, stopping them before they were able to lead the horse away.

"What do you mean? We got to get the next horse ready," one of the wranglers said.

"Just hold it up, right there," Smoke said.

"I ain't goin' to do nothin' o' the sort," said another of the wranglers.

"Hold the horse there, Creech," Sheriff Carson ordered.

Creech started, "Sheriff, we need to get the next horse out here 'n—"

"I said hold it right there!" Carson interrupted and looked over at Smoke. "What is it, Smoke? Why are you holding up the horse?"

By then Buster had reached them. James True had recovered from his fall and had come over to see what was going on as well.

"Take the saddle off," Buster said.

"Well, yeah, that's what we're fixin' to do," Creech said, "soon as we get 'im back to the paddock."

"Take it off now," Buster insisted.

"Look here. You got no right to order me to do that," Creech insisted.

"What difference does it make whether we take the saddle off here or back there?" asked Dace, the first wrangler.

"It's just that they ain't got no right orderin' us around like this," Creech insisted.

"What is it, Crabtree?" True asked, made curious by Buster's strange reaction.

"I noticed something about this horse just before

you mounted. I might be wrong, but I don't think I am."

"Take the saddle off now," Sheriff Carson ordered.

"I'll do it if Creech won't," Dace said and quickly removed the saddle.

"Look there," Buster said, pointing to blood on the horse's back. The blood was coming from a small puncture.

"Let me see that saddle," Smoke ordered.

Without hesitation, Dace handed the saddle to him.

"Look. I thought something was wrong." Buster pointed to a nail that had been driven through the saddle so that, as soon a rider's weight was applied, it would push into the horse.

"I think maybe we should take a look at the saddle we're about to put on Buster's horse," Smoke said.

As Smoke suspected, a nail had been driven through this saddle as well.

"It ain't my fault," Creech said. "Prescott give me five dollars apiece to do it."

"Creech, you squealin' bastard!" Prescott shouted angrily.

"Prescott, you're disqualified," Sheriff Carson said. "True, you get another ride."

"I don't know," True said. "With that nail hole in 'im . . ."

"Take my horse," Buster offered. "We can put some liniment on this one and by the time I'm ready to ride, I think he'll be okay."

Both True and Buster gave the crowd a good ride, but in the end, based perhaps more on the horse than the rider, the judging panel was unanimous in awarding first place to Buster Crabtree.

"Buster," True said afterward, "I got no quarrel with the judges, 'n I thank you for noticin' somethin' was wrong with my first ride."

The two men shook hands, and though they were too far away from the crowd to be heard, seeing the competitors shake hands caused another round of applause.

Wahite Creek, Dido, Texas

It was Saturday morning and the Professor, as well as the members of the Sidewinders gang of outlaws had spent the night on Wahite Creek. They had just eaten breakfast and were waiting for the bank to open in the little town of Dido.

"Ha, lookie here," Morris crowed. "I just pissed a grasshopper offen that stick there."

"Morris, you dumbhead, some of us is still eatin' breakfast," Lattimore said. "Ain't you got no more sense than to take a squirt where folks is eatin'?"

"Yeah, well it ain't like I peed in anyone's coffee. Besides, I'm all peed out, now anyway," Morris said.

"Gentlemen, may I suggest we get saddled?" the Professor said a short while later. "We have to attend to some financial business."

"Financial business. Yeah, I like that," Gibbons said.

It was a typical Saturday morning in Dido, a small town twenty-two miles northwest of Fort Worth. Main Street was crowded with area ranchers and farmers who generally came into town on Saturday to take advantage of the two general stores, a leather goods store, a livery, stagecoach depot, two restaurants, and three saloons.

Precisely because it was a particularly busy day, nobody paid any specific attention to the seven men who came riding in just after ten o'clock in the morning. Besides, it wasn't unusual to see that many ranch hands coming in together. Saturday was a day that allowed the cowboys and farm hands, as well as the ranchers and their families, to enjoy some time in town.

Catron and the others rode down Main Street until they reached the Dido Bank and Trust, a squat adobe building at the far end of the street. Four of the seven men dismounted, while the remaining three remained in the saddle, holding the reins of the horses of the other four.

"Shouldn't we ought to put on masks or somethin'?" Evans asked as they started toward the bank. "I mean, what if someone recognizes one of us?"

"That won't a problem," Catron replied. "No one will be left alive to identify us."

When Catron and the others stepped into the bank four people were present—two customers, a man and a woman; a teller behind a window; and a man sitting at a desk off to one side. The male customer was at the teller's window transacting business, while the woman stood patiently behind him.

The man sitting at the desk looked up, somewhat surprised to see so many come in at the same time, then he had a quick intake of breath when he saw that all four men were holding pistols. "What . . . what do you want?" he asked in a frightened voice.

The panic in his voice got the attention of the teller and the two customers.

"We would like to make a withdrawal," Catron said.

"A withdrawal?" the bank manager replied, confused by the strange comment. "I don't understand. I know every account holder, and you aren't one of them."

"Oh, whether or not we have an account here is of no consequence. You see, we plan to withdraw all the money from the accounts of all who do bank here."

"You mean this is a robbery?"

"That is a most astute observation sir, for yes, this is a robbery."

"Mr. Dempsey, what will I do?" the bank teller asked.

"Give them the money, Mr. Benton," Dempsey replied. He was standing with his hands raised.

"Put your hands down, would you please, Mr. Dempsey?" Catron said in a conversational voice. "I would not care to have someone walking by outside look in and see you with your hands up."

"You're . . . you're the one they call the Professor, aren't you?" Dempsey asked as he lowered his hands.

"I am indeed." Catron turned his attention to the teller. "You heard your employer, Mr. Benton. Turn all the money you have over to my associate."

A moment later Benton, with shaking hands, held out a small packet of bills."

"What's this?" Dawkins growled, indicating the money in Benton's hand.

"It's the money," Benton replied in a shaky voice.

"We said all the money!" Dawkins demanded.

"That would be all the money," Dempsey said. "As of this morning our cash on hand was eight hundred and twenty four dollars and fifty-seven cents.

"Are you tellin' me that this here bank don't have

no more than eight hunnert dollars?" Lattimore asked. "Who the hell ever heard of a bank that didn't have no more money than that?"

"We are not actually an independent bank. We are an adjunct to the First Trust of Fort Worth," Dempsey explained. "And because of that, we do most of our banking by draft, keeping only a limited amount of cash here for the convenience of our customers. We get cash from the First Trust once a week, but I'm afraid that we never have more than a thousand dollars on hand at any given time.

"I must say I really can't understand why you men would bother to rob an institute with so little return," Dempsey said.

"What'll we do, Professor?" Dawkins asked.

"Take the money, little though it may be," Catron replied.

Dawkins took the money, then as soon as he had it in his hand, Catron shot Benton, then Dempsey.

The woman screamed, but her scream was cut short when the other three men opened up.

The citizens of the town heard the gunfire and for a moment they were confused as to where it was coming from. Then looking toward the bank they saw four men come out and swing up into the saddles of the horses that were being held for them.

"Damn, I think them fellers just held up the bank!" someone shouted.

The town-crier-like announcement wasn't really needed. By now everyone on the street, from the clerk sweeping the porch in front of Rafferty's Store, to the pedestrian shoppers, to the four men playing horseshoes, knew what was going on.

"Everyone, out of the way. Get off the street if you don't want to get shot!" Catron shouted loudly, and he punctuated his shout by firing a couple of unaimed shots down the street. The shooting had the effect he wanted.

Everyone scattered, leaving them with a totally unopposed departure.

Sidewinders' hideout

Jory Gibbons, Dooley Evans, Dan Parker, Merlin Dawkins, Murry Morris, and Eb Lattimore were sitting around the table in the house that Gus Belford had built for his family, the family that the outlaws had killed.

"Sixty dollars apiece? That's all we get?" Gibbons complained.

"Sixty dollars apiece, and four hundred dollars in our treasury," Catron said.

"Who woulda thought a bank wouldn't have no more money 'n that?" Lattimore said.

"This here ain't workin' out like I thought it would," Evans said. "I figured that joinin' up like I did, I'd be able to make a lot o' money. 'N to my way o' thinkin', sixty dollars ain't a whole lot o' money."

"Leastwise there ain't nobody a-huntin' us, 'n we got us a good place to hide out," Morris said.

"Yeah, but we're near 'bout out of the food that was left here," Dawkins said.

"And that, gentlemen, is why a corporate treasury is necessary," the Professor said. "I intend to go to town to make purchases that will restock our armament needs and our pantry."

"Yeah, well, I intend to go into town 'n get drunk."

"Any of you who wish may go into town, and you may enjoy yourself within limits," the Professor said. "But if any of you get drunk, or if any of you get into trouble with the law, even to the most minute degree, I will eliminate you from our group."

"Eliminate us? What does that mean?" Parker asked.

The Professor stared at Parker and as he did so, there was a flash of yellow in his eyes. Parker felt his knees grow weak, and a hollowness in the pit of his stomach.

"It . . . it don't matter none what that means, on account of I ain't goin' to get drunk or get into no trouble neither."

"I'm glad that you understand," the Professor said, just before he left.

"You know what I think he meant?" Gibbons posed to the others. "I think he meant he'll kill us if we get drunk."

"Yeah, well, I don't know 'bout the rest of you, but I don't plan on gettin' drunk or gettin' into no trouble that's liable to get the Professor pissed off none," Dawkins said.

CHAPTER TEN

Monday morning found Smoke, Pearlie, Cal, Herman Nelson, and Buster Crabtree standing at the holding corral at the Denver Northwestern and Pacific Railroad depot, waiting for the stock cars to be put in position to be loaded. Neither the engine nor the hired caboose had arrived yet, so the stock cars were being brought up by a switch engine that was a permanent fixture of the railroad yard in Big Rock.

Sally came out to watch.

"There's no need for you to be here, Miz Sally," Cal said. "Why, you could be waitin' in the depot, reading newspapers and drinking coffee and such."

"I've read the papers and had my coffee," Sally replied. "I began to worry about whether or not you could get all the horses successfully loaded without my supervision."

"Lord, Miz Sally, you sure are—" Cal stopped in midsentence.

"I sure am what?" Sally asked pointedly, tapping her foot as she stared at Cal.

"Uh, I was just going to say that you sure are a good supervisor."

Smoke laughed out loud. "Cal, my boy, it looks to me like you managed to get yourself out of that one."

"Here come the cars," Pearlie said and all looked up the curved sidetrack to watch as the line of cars was being pushed into position.

"How do you want to load them? Do you want to go from front car to back, or back car to front?" Buster asked as the cars arrived.

"Load from front to back," Sally said.

Buster looked at Smoke.

"Don't look at me, Buster," Smoke said with a little laugh. "You heard the lady. Load them front to back. Sally's in charge."

Once all the horses were loaded, there was no longer a need for Buster or Herman, so they took their leave.

"It's like I said. Buster has been a good hire," Pearlie said after the two men left.

"Yes, and he is such a nice man," Sally said. "But there is something about him. It is as if he has some secret sadness from his past."

"He does," Smoke said, and as they waited for the engine and caboose to arrive, Smoke told them the story of Buster's wife being killed while he was away riding in the cowboy competitions.

"Oh, Smoke," Sally said. "I know this reminds you of Nicole."

"Yes," Smoke said, thinking of his first wife, who, like Buster's wife, had been murdered in his absence.

* * *

"You've come along real good," Herman said as he and Buster rode side by side back to the ranch. "You should stay here at Sugarloaf. You've already seen how easy Smoke 'n Pearlie are to work for."

"I have to admit this is the best job I've ever had. And I would like to stay here but"—Buster paused before he continued—"I have a job that's still undone."

At that very moment the "job undone" that Buster referred to was dismounting in front of a remote store just on the Colorado side of the Colorado–Wyoming border. No horses were tethered near the store, though a team of horses was nearby in a lean-to barn and a wagon sat just outside. Marvin Hayes looked up and down the road and saw no one. He pulled his pistol from his holster before he stepped inside.

The store was redolent with familiar aromas— ground coffee, molasses, smoked meats, and peppermint stick candy. The man behind the counter was wearing a stained apron, and a pair of wire-rim glasses was perched on his nose. He had tufts of white hair above his ears, though he was otherwise bald.

"Have a look around, mister. Anything you see that you want, let me know and I'll get it for you," the man, probably in his late fifties, called out to him.

"What I want is all your money," Hayes said, lifting his pistol.

"All right, all right. Yes, sure, you can have it," the man replied nervously.

"Hand it over," Hayes demanded.

The store owner took a box from under the

counter then opened the lid. The money in the box was mostly coins, though there were a handful of dollar bills."

"Is this it?" Hayes asked frustrated by the small amount.

"We're a small country store, mister. We don't do that much business."

"Then this will have to do," Hayes said, picking up the box with his left hand, while still holding the pistol pointed toward the store keep.

"Mister, drop that gun!" a woman called out.

Looking toward the sound of the voice Hayes saw a woman. Her gray hair was done up into a bun and like the store keep, she was wearing a stained apron. She was also holding a rifle.

Hayes moved his pistol toward her, pulling the trigger before the woman had time to react. His bullet struck her right in the middle of her chest.

"Millie!" the store keep shouted, fear and horror reflected in his voice.

Hayes turned the pistol toward him and shot him in the forehead. Then he walked over and looked down at the woman, intending to finish her off, but no second shot was necessary. She was already dead.

Sticking a peppermint candy cane in his mouth and taking the money box with him, Hayes walked back out to his horse. A quick perusal assured him that he was still alone, so he remounted, and started south.

If Buster Crabtree was in Boulder or anywhere else in Colorado, he intended to find him.

Big Rock

The engine and caboose arrived within another hour after Herman and Buster left, and with the train assembled, Smoke and the others boarded the caboose. The front third of the caboose was taken up by a bedroom. In the middle third were long leather cushioned benches on either side, which would provide seats during the day, but could be made into beds for Pearlie and Cal at night. The last third of the car had a table with seating for four and a kerosene stove that could be used for cooking and heating, though it would not be needed for heating during this trip.

Because this train was not part of the regular Denver and Rio Grande schedule, they had to wait until the dispatcher cleared them before they could actually leave the station. They weren't able to leave until the middle of the afternoon.

Shortly after the train pulled out of the depot in Big Rock, Sally made a pot of coffee. As she began preparing for supper, she laughed out loud.

"What is it?" Smoke asked.

"I was just thinking about Professor Spivey."

"Who?"

"William Spivey was the professor in my methods of education class when I was in college. I wonder what he would think now, to see me cooking dinner at a kerosene stove in a railroad caboose."

"He would want us to make room for him," Cal said, and the others laughed.

After dinner Cal helped Sally clean up while

Smoke sat at the table doing some figuring on a tablet. After computing all costs, he determined that he would net just over sixty-five hundred dollars from this operation. It would be a very satisfying trip, not only because of the money he would make, but also because of the opportunity to visit with old friends.

Pearlie was sitting alone reading a newspaper. "Well how about this? Just what in the world will they think of next?"

"What has so aroused your curiosity, Pearlie?" Sally asked.

"Listen to this," Pearlie said, and he began to read. "'All are aware of Alexander Graham Bell's telephone, and all equally aware of Thomas Edison's talking machine. And while these two instruments are the wonders of our age, suppose some clever person figured out how to join the two, to wit'"—he stopped reading and looked up at Sally. "Miz Sally, what does *to wit* mean?"

"It means that you are about to explain something," Sally said.

"I am?"

"Read on, Pearlie," she said.

"Oh, yeah. 'What would be the purpose of some clever person joining the two? Consider this. Grandmother wants to invite the family over to her house for dinner on Sunday, but when she calls there is no one to take her call. She must wait and try again and again and continue to call until she succeeds in making the connection.

"But if some clever person could design a method whereby when the telephone rings, it is answered by the talking machine, the machine can tell the caller that you aren't home. Ah, you say, but if the phone is not answered, will the caller not already know that?

"But wait. Suppose the talking machine could not only answer the call, but engage its marvelous capacity to record voices. If so, Grandmother could leave the message on the machine that she wishes to invite you to dinner.

"Although no such answering machine now exists, there is certainly within the capability of current equipment to devise and implement such a wonderful device.'"

Pearlie looked at his friends. "What will they think of next?"

"A picture that moves," Cal said.

Pearlie laughed. "That'll be the day."

Having switched to the Union Pacific Track, Smoke's train was shuttled aside in Dodge City long enough to allow a couple of scheduled trains to pass. During those two hours, Smoke sent a telegraph to Big Jim. They were due to arrive on Thursday, but because of such things as being shuttled aside, he had no accurate estimate as to what time of day they would arrive.

CHAPTER ELEVEN

Live Oak Ranch

"How are you coming with moving out the fence so we can hold more horses?" Big Jim asked.

"We haven't started it yet," Clay said.

"Why not?"

"Well, sir, Dalton has come up with an idea that I think is a pretty good one. I thought maybe he had already discussed it with you."

"No, he hasn't discussed anything with me. What are you talking about?"

Clay was the foreman, but Dalton, being Big Jim's son, was technically Clay's superior, though the two men had such a symbiotic relationship that the matter of who was in charge had never become an issue.

"The reason we're gettin' new horses is because most of the horses we have is pretty much wore out. Dalton was sayin' that maybe we should sell the ones we got now, and just use the new ones. If we do that, why there won't be any need in making the corral any bigger."

"Dalton might have a point there, but I sort of hate to sell them. So often they wind up in a glue factory."

"Couldn't you talk to Mr. Miller 'bout that?" Clay asked. "He handles horses, too, doesn't he?"

Big Jim smiled. "Clay, that's a good idea. Yes, sir, that's a very good idea. As a matter of fact, I think I'll ride into town and see Preston today."

A few minutes after Big Jim rode away, Dalton came walking toward the corral. A young boy, no more than five years old, was trailing along behind him. Dalton reached up and pushed back the low-crown black hat he was wearing. The boy, who was wearing a smaller version of the hat, mimicked Dalton's move.

"Who's your helper?" Clay asked.

"Why, he's a new cowboy who just signed on," Dalton said.

"Manny, don't you be getting in Mr. Dalton's way now," Clay said to the boy.

"I ain't gettin' in Dalton's way, Pop. Din't you hear him say that I'm the new cowboy that just signed on?"

"Mr. Dalton," Clay admonished.

"Mr. Dalton," Manny corrected.

"Don't be hard on 'im, Clay. As I recall there was a time when you had someone following you around."

"Yes, but you were never a pest," Clay said.

"Never?"

Clay chuckled. "How could you be? You were the boss's son."

Dalton laughed as well. "I just saw Pop ridin' out. You told him about my idea of getting rid of the extra horses?"

"Yeah, he thinks it's a good idea, if he can keep 'em from winding up in a glue factory."

"Hah! What did I tell you? I told you he would think that. Did you suggest that he see Mr. Miller?"

Clay nodded. "That's where he's going, now."

Fort Worth

A gleaming white building was set apart from neighboring buildings by the large window in front. The name of the business was painted on the window in dark blue cursive letters, shadowed with yellow.

TARRANT COUNTY LIVESTOCK, INC.
Preston Miller, *Broker*

Big Jim dismounted in front of the building then walked inside.

"Hello, Colonel," greeted Leonard McGee, Miller's clerk.

"Hello, Leonard. Ask Preston if he has time to have lunch with me, would you, please?" Big Jim said.

McGee stepped into the back office, but it was Preston who came back out. With a broad welcoming smile, he extended his hand. He was wearing a gray jacket and dark trousers, a high-wing-collar shirt and a bow tie. "I've always got time to have lunch with you, Jim. Uh, you *are* buying aren't you?" he added in a lilting tone.

"That's how you got rich, isn't it? Cadging meals and drinks from your friends?" Big Jim teased.

"Yes, now that you mention it, a drink would be nice, too," Preston said with a little laugh. "Thanks for offering."

"If we go to Frank's Saloon, we can have both," Big Jim replied.

Frank's Saloon defied any conventional description. It was neither saloon, nor restaurant, but it was both. It had a spacious dining room with white covered tables and cushioned chairs. Walking through the dining room into the back was like Alice passing through the looking glass, for there was a bar and bartender just as in most saloons and tables where bar patrons could order meals from the dining room if they wished.

"How many head will you be shipping this year?" Preston asked.

"It looks like I'll be moving about five thousand head. What's the market price now?"

"It's close to sixty dollars a head," Preston replied with a smile. "That's up a little from last year."

"What are my costs?" Big Jim asked.

"I'll get my cut of three dollars a head, and right now shipping costs are ten dollars a head." Preston took a pencil and small notepad from his jacket pocket and began to figure. "It looks like two hundred thirty-five thousand dollars net for you."

"Burgess has made an offer of handling my herd for five dollars a head."

Preston chuckled. "Poor Drew, he won't give up."

"What puzzles me is why he would think I'd be willing to go with him for five dollars a head, when you're only charging three dollars."

"Well, to be honest, Jim, Trinity River is charging six dollars a head for processing the cattle. I'm sure Burgess thought he was offering you a good deal, and in fact, he was."

"Wait a minute, Trinity is charging six, Burgess is charging five, and you're only charging three? How can that be?"

Preston smiled. "It's called a friendship investment. I'm going to do the best I can for you because you are my friend, but also because I want to keep your business in the long run."

"But what good will it do you to lose money?"

"Oh, believe me, I'm not losing money. And if you look at it this way, I'm getting fifteen thousand dollars for handling your cattle, while Burgess and Trinity are getting nothing."

Big Jim chuckled. "Well, I suppose if you put it that way, it does make sense. And I'm glad to be getting the best deal I can. My expenses are a little higher this year. I've bought a hundred new horses, I built a new machine shed, I had to put a new roof on the barn, and I've raised everyone's wages, even for the part-time hands."

"Yes, I heard about the one hundred horses. Now, Jim, don't get me wrong, I'm not going to be hurt, or anything, but, I know you didn't buy those horses through me. Did you buy them through Burgess or Trinity?"

"No, I bought them direct from the rancher."

"You bought them direct from the rancher? Oh, Jim, why didn't you come through me? I know I could beat whatever price you're paying."

"I'm sure you could, Preston, but it isn't a matter of price as much as it is the quality of the horseflesh. I'm buying them from Smoke Jensen. He not only has a reputation for turning out the very best quarter horses, he also happens to be a very good friend."

"Well, I suppose I can understand that, especially the part about doing business with your friends," Preston said easily. "I generally tend to look at the price of the horses I manage more than I do their quality, but of course you understand that for livestock brokers like Burgess and me, it's all about money."

Big Jim chuckled. "Oh yes, I understand businessmen and money."

"When are the horses getting here?" Preston asked.

"I don't know for sure, but I expect Smoke will send me a telegram as to when I can expect them. There is another reason I have come to see you."

"Something else, you say?" Preston replied, the expression on his face reflecting his curiosity. "What is it, if not the new horses?"

"Well, it does have something to do with the hundred new horses. You see, I'm going to have to get rid of about eighty of the horses I have now so that I can make room for the new mounts. And I don't care how much I'm paid for the mounts I'm selling."

"Oh, then you've come to the right man," Preston said. "I can handle getting rid of the old horses for you quite easily, especially if you're not all that particular about what you'll have to get for them."

"Yes, but it may not be as easy as you think. I am particular about one thing."

"Oh? And what would that be?"

"Preston, I've grown attached to these horses. Even though I ride Shiloh as my personal horse, I've ridden every one of the others more than once, and they have been very good workhorses. I care what happens to them, and I don't want to see them to go to the glue factory."

"Hmm, you're right. That *will* make it a little more difficult," Preston said. "But for you, my friend, I will find an outlet for your horses where you can be assured they won't be killed for glue."

"Thanks, Preston. I knew I could count on you," Big Jim said with a broad smile.

"How's the gather going?"

"I'm leaving it in Dalton's hands this year. Of course, he has Clay to help him."

"Dalton and Clay are getting along pretty well, are they?"

"Yes, they are. Of course, Clay and Dalton have known each other since Clay was twelve and Dalton was no older than five or six." Big Jim chuckled. "Dalton followed Clay around like a little puppy dog. And now, Clay's little boy, Manny, is doing the same thing with Dalton."

"I'll bet Dalton likes that," Preston said.

"I know he does. I'm an old man, Preston. I don't have that much longer left, and I'm glad to see that, with Dalton and Clay at the helm, Live Oak will be in good hands when I'm gone. And of course, I'll be counting on you to help them with anything pertaining to the cattle business."

"Here now," Preston said. "Let's not be talking about you being gone. You're one of my closest friends, Jim, and I don't give up my friends that easily."

Big Jim chuckled again. "Well, don't put on your funeral suit just yet."

* * *

Although Boone Caulder and Big Jim had not come to town together, it just so happened that both were in town at the same time. Boone was in the Waco Tap Saloon. A cowhand, Boone would, if asked where he worked, answer the question by saying that he rode for the Live Oak brand.

That "brand" was a simple line depiction of a live oak tree, representing Live Oak Ranch. Clay Ramsey had given Boone permission to ride into town when his tasks were done for the day.

Unlike many of the cowboys who came into town in the same clothes they had been working in all day, Boone was considerably more fastidious. He was wearing blue twill trousers, an orange shirt, and a blue kerchief. A turquoise-studded silver band encircled the crown of his hat.

"Oh, honey, you aren't like all the other cowboys," said Cindy, one of the bar girls who worked in the Waco Tap Saloon. "You always look so nice when you come in."

"There's no reason why a fella can't look nice when he comes into town," Boone said.

"Did the rest of you men hear that?" Cindy asked, addressing the others in the saloon. "If Boone can look nice, the rest of you can, too."

"And maybe if some of you would take a bath every now and then, you wouldn't stink so," one of the other girls added, holding her nose. Her comment drew laughs.

"Hey, Boone, that ain't the horse you normally ride, is it?" one of the patrons asked when Boone took his drink over to join three men at a table.

"The Colonel said I can't ride Buttermilk anymore,"

Boone replied, the tone of his voice showing his displeasure.

"Why not?"

"I don't know. It's just one of his stupid rules, is all. He said something about him not wanting the horses and the men to get to liking each other too much. He says if a horse likes one rider too much that he might not do as well for another rider."

"I suppose that makes some sense. So, what's going on out at Live Oak?

"Oh, Charley, have I told you we're getting in one hundred new horses?"

"A hundred new horses? That's quite a few. Who's the Colonel buyin' them from, Swain Bird?"

"No, sir. He's getting them from Colorado."

"Wait a minute. The Colonel is buying one hundred new horses, and he's getting them all the way from Colorado?"

"Yes."

"Why in the hell is he gettin' 'em from Colorado? I don't understand why he wouldn't buy them right here in Texas. I know Mr. Bird has that many to sell."

"These Colorado horses are supposed to be something special," Boone said. "They're sayin' that the Colonel is paying ninety dollars a head for them."

"Ninety dollars for one horse? Damn, that's a lot of money for a horse, isn't it? Hell, you could get two horses for that much money."

"I'll say," Boone said. "And there are a hundred of them. That's nine thousand dollars."

"Nine thousand dollars." Charley let out a low whistle. "I don't think all the money I've seen in my whole life would come out to nine thousand dollars."

"It does make a person think, doesn't it?" Boone said.

"Think about what?" one of the others asked.

"Money," Boone answered. "Nine thousand dollars is a lot of money."

"Caulder?" someone called out.

"Yeah, what do you want?" Boone recognized Bud Summers, who worked for Western Union.

"Oh good. I just took a chance that someone from Live Oak might be in here, and here you are. I have a telegram for Mr. Conyers and you could save me a trip out there if you would take it to him."

"Why should I do your job for you?" Boone asked.

"Well, you'll be goin' back anyway, 'n I almost always get a two-dollar tip for taking one out. He'll probably give it to you."

"Yeah, all right," Boone agreed, holding out his hand. "Do I have to go now?"

Bud Summers chuckled. "Well, sir, the way I read this here telegram, you'll be fine as long as you get it to him sometime before Thursday."

After Summers left, Boone noticed that the envelope wasn't sealed, so he removed the telegram and read it.

WILL ARRIVE ON THURSDAY WITH ONE
HUNDRED HORSES IN GOOD SHAPE STOP
WILL PROBABLY BE VERY LATE IN THE
DAY STOP

SMOKE JENSEN

Damn, I'm holding nine thousand dollars in my hand, Boone thought.

CHAPTER TWELVE

Big Jim had returned to the ranch and was out by the corral talking to Clay Ramsey when Boone Caulder came riding up. Boone dismounted and approached the two men.

"You're back early, aren't you, Caulder?" Clay asked.

"Yeah, but what happened is, Western Union gave me a telegram for the Colonel, 'n I figured I should deliver it quick as I could."

Boone held out the telegram, Big Jim read it, then looked back toward Boone. "Thank you, Boone."

"Yes, sir, I, uh . . ."

"Yes?"

"I, uh, just thought you might want it right away is all," Boone said, realizing that he wasn't going to get a tip. "Clay, if you don't mind, I'll be going back into town now."

"As long as you're back here in time to roll out with the rest of us tomorrow mornin'," Clay said.

Big Jim held out the telegram. "This says the horses will be here Thursday.

* * *

Back in the bunkhouse, Boone Caulder was sitting cross-legged on his bunk playing solitaire.

"You know why Boone's always playin' solitaire, don't you?" John Moll asked. "It's on account of because he cheats so much that he can't get nobody else to play cards with 'im." He laughed. "Look at 'im. He's cheatin' his ownself right now."

"What makes you think that?" Boone asked.

"On account of last week I seen 'im throwin' punches at hisself because he caught himself cheatin' in solitaire. Why if I hadn't broke up the fight between him, there ain't no tellin' what he woulda done to hisself," Bert Rowe said.

"Bert, you're so damn windy you'd blow down a barn," Boone said, joining the others in laughing.

Andy Dunlap came into the bunkhouse then. "I know you fellas is havin' just a real good time partyin' 'n all, but we have to round up some horses that the Colonel's gettin' rid of."

"Is he getting rid of all of 'em?" Boone asked.

"No, just eighty from what I've heard."

"I hope he isn't getting rid of Buttermilk."

"Buttermilk ain't your horse, Boone," Andy said. "You know damn well that ever' horse on the place belongs to the Colonel, and I reckon that gives him the right to get rid of any horse he wants to get rid of. Besides which, it wouldn't make no difference to you iffen he got rid of Buttermilk or not. The Colonel has done said he didn't want you bein' the only one to ride 'im anymore."

"Yeah, well, whenever Dalton takes over the ranch,

I don't think he'll be as stubborn about some things as the Colonel is. And I don't mind telling you that can't come fast enough for me," Boone said.

"Why would you say somethin' like that?" Andy asked. "You know damn well that the Colonel ain't never goin' to quit runnin' the ranch while he's alive. By sayin' you'll be glad when that happens is the same thing as sayin' you'll be glad when he's dead."

"I didn't say anything of the sort," Boone insisted.

"Yeah, well, maybe you didn't come right out 'n say nothin' like that in so many words, but it sure as hell sounded like that. 'N I wouldn't say nothin' like that 'round the cow boss. You know what store Clay puts in the Colonel."

"Yes, but I didn't say that, so don't go putting words in my mouth."

"I'm sorry. I didn't mean nothin' by it," Andy said. "I guess I just took it wrong."

"Hey, Boone, you're the one that brung the telegram to the Colonel 'bout them horses, ain't you?" Billy Lewis asked.

"Yes, I'm the one that brought to him. Why do you ask?"

"Well, I was just a-wonderin' if that telegram said 'nything 'bout when them horses was goin' to get here?"

"They'll be here by late in the day come Thursday, and they're coming by their own private train. That should give you a hint as to how important they are," Boone said. "And to tell you the truth, I'm looking forward to them getting here and riding one of those special horses."

"Ha, the Colonel will probably keep you on one of

the old horses we have now, after he sells Buttermilk," Gimlin teased.

Big Jim went back into town the next day to see Preston Miller, and when he stepped into the office, Leonard McGee looked up.

"Good afternoon, Colonel. Can I help you?"

"Is he in?" Big Jim asked, nodding toward the door of Preston Miller's office.

"Oh, I believe he has decided to take a libation at Winders' Cattle Exchange Saloon," McGee replied.

"Thank you, Leonard. I'll just join him there."

Big Jim stepped into Winders' Cattle Exchange Saloon a couple of minutes later and saw Preston and Drew Burgess sharing the same table. He approached them with a smile.

"Well, fancy seeing the two of you together. If Lee and Grant could meet at Appomattox, I suppose a couple of enemies like you two can meet here"

"I've told you before, Jim, we are competitors, we aren't enemies," Preston said.

Big Jim waved him off. "I know, I know. I was just teasing, is all."

"Drew, it might interest you to know that Jim has just bought one hundred horses from the Sugarloaf Ranch. I don't know if you are aware of them or not, but Sugarloaf horses are among the best in the West."

"Oh yes," Burgess said. "I know all about Sugarloaf horses. What cattle and horse broker doesn't know about them? On average, horses go for seventy to eighty dollars, but Sugarloaf horses can bring as much as a hundred and ten to a hundred and twenty dollars. If you don't mind my asking, Colonel, what are you paying for them?"

"I'm paying ninety dollars apiece for them," Big Jim said

"Ninety dollars?" Burgess said in surprise. He looked at Preston. "Preston, did you put that deal through for him? Ninety dollars for horses that could bring as much as a hundred and twenty dollars?"

Preston shook his head. "I wish I could take credit for it, but Jim did that deal all by himself."

"How did you get such a good deal?" Burgess asked.

"Smoke Jensen is a good friend of mine, so he gave me what he calls his 'friendship' deal."

"Well, it is good to be friends with such a man," Preston agreed. "By the way, what brings you back into town so soon? You aren't going to try and make me pay you back for the dinner you bought for me yesterday, are you?"

"Ha! Preston, you are as tight as the bark on a tree. I know damn well that would be a huge waste of time, so I'm not even going to try. The reason I'm here is to make arrangements for my horses."

"You mean the eighty you're getting rid of? No worry. I've already found a buyer. Luckily, a freight dealer in Dallas needs fresh horses for his teams. I'm getting thirty dollars apiece for them. That'll be two hundred and forty dollars, minus my ten percent."

"Thank you, Preston, and I especially thank you for finding them a home that will keep them out of the glue factory. But it's the new horses I'm talking about. The train is going to arrive on Thursday, and as it isn't a scheduled train, there's no telling when it will actually get here. It may be too late to take them directly out to the ranch and if that is so, I'm going to need a place to keep them overnight. I was wondering if I might be able to use one of your holding pens down at the depot. I'll be glad to pay whatever fee is required."

"Of course you can use them, and I wouldn't think of charging you anything. I'm not using the holding pens now. It's no inconvenience for me to have them there."

"Thank you very much, Preston. I'll have some of my men pick them up Friday morning."

"There is no rush. Leave them there as long as you need," Preston offered.

That night, music from half a dozen pianos poured out onto Calhoun Street, each piano player banging his keyboard louder than the other.

Boone pushed through the swinging batwing doors of the Waco Tap Saloon and after a quick perusal, saw the man he was looking for. Drew Burgess was sitting alone at a table and gave Boone an invitational nod.

"You said you wanted me to bring you some information when I could," Boone said, joining him at the table.

"Yes, I did," Burgess replied.

"Well, I've got some information for you. It's about the horses that the Colonel is buying."

Burgess shook his head. "I already know about the horses. I met with Conyers and Miller earlier today."

"Yes, but do you know that they'll be comin' in on Thursday, 'n more than likely they'll be spendin' the night right here in town, in Mr. Miller's holding pens down at the depot?"

"Yes, I know that as well. I also know that Miller isn't charging Conyers anything to keep them here. Ol' Miller has a golden goose in Conyers, and he doesn't plan on letting it go. Hell, I hear he has even cut the cost of handling Live Oak cattle into half of what everyone else is chargin'."

Boone shook his head. "Well, I can't tell you anything about that on account of things like that ain't nothin' I can ever get involved in."

"Tell me this, Caulder, if you know. If the horses spend the night in Miller's holding pen, will there be anyone there to guard them?"

Boone shook his head. "No, there ain't goin' to be nobody guardin' 'em. We'll have some folks meetin' the train to help off-load the horses, then we'll be comin' in the next mornin' to pick 'em up. Clay ain't said nothin' 'bout puttin' anyone up here to watch 'em. 'N if he was plannin' on doin' that, I'd sure know about it."

"All right. Enough about the horses. How many cattle are being shipped, do you know?"

"Four or five thousand head. I'm not exactly sure. I do know we plan to leave at least two thousand head behind. Clay has been working out the gather schedule, and he's figuring in the ones that won't be shipped out."

"He's leaving behind two thousand head?" Burgess asked.

"At least that many. Maybe more."

"I had no idea he'd be leavin' that many behind," Burgess said. He gave Boone a twenty-dollar bill.

"Thanks, Caulder. If you get any more information you think I might want to know, bring it to me."

"Mr. Burgess?" Boone asked.

"What?"

"What I'm doin', I mean, givin' you information like this, you don't think that's doin' the Colonel wrong, do you? I mean, I sort of feel like I'm spyin' on him, 'n I don't really want to do that."

"You can put your mind at ease, son. This has nothing to do with Big Jim Conyers. This is between Preston Miller and me. You can spend your twenty dollar bill in good conscience."

"Thanks!" Boone said. "I'm goin' to put this with the other twenty you gave me 'n I know exactly what I'm goin' to spend it on."

Clay and Dalton went into town the following day and after taking care of some business, stepped into the Emerald Saloon for a drink.

"Dalton, you've come along just fine since you come back to the ranch. You're as good a man in the saddle as any hand we've ever had work here, 'n you've got good business sense. I know for a fact that the Colonel is real proud of you. You don't seem nothin' at all like the little sprout that used to follow me around all the time. I know it's more 'n likely out of place for me to be sayin' anything like this, seeing as you're actually my boss 'n all. I just wanted it said, is all."

"Clay, I don't think it's out of place at all. Coming from you, those words mean a lot to me. By the way, the reason I followed you around like I did when I was a little sprout was because you were my hero."

Clay cleared his throat, then glanced down at the table. "You know, there's somethin' in the Bible about a hero havin' clay feet. I'll be keepin' that in mind."

"That's a good thing to know. Since I've got my own little person following me around now, maybe I had better keep that in mind as well."

"Ha! You think Manny thinks you're his hero? No such thing. He's just keepin' an eye on you for the Colonel."

Dalton laughed. "Yeah, I thought it might be something like that."

Andy and Boone came into the saloon then and joined Dalton and Clay at their table.

"Did you get nails and baling wire?" Dalton asked.

"Yeah, we got it," Andy said. "By the way, ever'one in town is talkin' 'bout the new horses we're gettin'. They're all lookin' forward to them gettin' here, seein' as horses from Sugarloaf have a reputation of bein' such good horses."

"Well, they're supposed to be here tomorrow, and I don't mind saying that I'm looking forward to them myself," Dalton said.

CHAPTER THIRTEEN

"Uh-uh, you're a-lyin'. They ain't no horses that's worth a hunnert 'n ten dollars apiece except for maybe racehorses, 'n they're worth a lot more 'n that," one of the saloon patrons said.

"Sugarloaf horses is, 'n they's a hunnert of 'em comin' into town."

Catron was sitting at a table by himself, but he was close enough to overhear the conversation.

"All right. Let's say they is some horses that's worth that much money. Why would they be comin' to Fort Worth?"

"On account of Big Jim Conyers has bought 'em, that's why."

"Are you tellin' me that he has bought a hunnert horses for a hunnert 'n ten dollars apiece?"

"Well, I don't rightly know what he paid for 'em, but I just know that he bought a hunnert of 'em to replace his remuda what he said was some wore out. 'N the new horses is bein' brought in by train. From what I've heard, they'll be here tonight."

That was what Catron wanted to hear. He had

already been told that the horses would be there tonight, but he was the kind of person who liked to be very sure of his information. He had not only learned that the horses would be arriving tonight, he had been told specifically where they would be and that no one would be present to watch over them.

Catron had agreed to steal the horses. He knew they had already been sold and would have to be moved only a very short distance.

The transaction with the horses, though they would bring in some money, was little more than a test for a much bigger payday. And while the operative with whom he was working might be testing how things were going to go, Catron was conducting his own test. If everything didn't go as smoothly as promised, he had no intention of complaining to the man he would be working with. He would just kill him.

One-room house, Grove Street

"How much money will it be?" Maggie asked.

"I'm not sure, but I know it'll be more 'n anythin' I've made lately, 'n more n likely more 'n anythin' you can get from a month of sellin' yourself," Lattimore replied.

"Yes, well speaking of that, I have a gentleman who is paying to stay all night with me," Maggie said.

"How much will you make from that?" Lattimore asked.

"Ten dollars."

"Ten dollars? Hell, you get five dollars from someone who don't may stay for more 'n ten minutes."

"Yes, but anyone who is goin' to spend the whole

night with me can't get in my bed until one o'clock in the mornin', and by then the regulars have all left. This will let me entertain my regulars till after midnight, then make some more money after midnight."

"Yeah, well, you can go ahead with what you're doin' now, but soon as the big money comes in, I'm goin' to buy me a saloon 'n then, when you 'entertain,' why, ever'thing you make will belong to us."

"Yes, wouldn't that be just . . . wonderful," Maggie said, but Lattimore failed to grasp the sarcasm in her tone.

He had no idea that her all-night engagement would start much earlier than midnight, and that the one she was meeting was more than just a casual customer.

Texas and Pacific depot, Thursday evening

Once Smoke's special train reached Fort Worth, it was shuttled away from the high iron, as the railroad people called the main track. A dedicated track had been reserved for the train so it took more than a few minutes for it to pass through the various switch tracks, sometimes requiring it to back up before proceeding forward again. That was done several times until finally their train came to a stop.

"This is it. This is our track," Smoke said.

"How do you know?" Sally asked.

He chuckled. "Because this is the last track in the yard. If we are switched again, this train will wind up taking a dirt road."

Sally looked out the window and laughed. "I would say that you have a point."

Pearlie and Cal were looking out the opposite side of the car.

Cal spoke first. "Look, there's Dalton standin' out there."

"Yes, and Clay is with him," Pearlie said. "I don't know who the other man is, though."

"Well, it's good to be met," Sally said.

"Smoke, hello!" Dalton called as Smoke and the others stepped down from the caboose.

"Hello, Pearlie, Cal, Miz Sally," Clay added.

"Who's this fella?" Cal asked, nodding toward the third man.

"That's right. He wasn't here when you were before. This is Boone Caulder."

"Hello, Boone. I'm Cal and this is Pearlie. That's Smoke Jensen and Miz Sally. Miz Sally is the one standing nearest the car."

Dalton laughed. "I'm pretty sure Boone can tell the difference."

"How? He's never met . . . oh," Cal said, the expression on his face showing his embarrassment.

"We're here to take you home with us soon as you arrive," Dalton said. "Ma's having Filipa fix up quite a supper for you."

"What about the horses?" Smoke asked.

"We're goin' to leave 'em here till tomorrow," Clay said.

"Oh, I don't know. I hate having to leave the horses in the cars one more night," Smoke said. "It's pretty confined in there, so you know damn well they can't be very comfortable."

"There's no need for you to be worryin' any about

that. Pop's made arrangements with Mr. Miller to board them here for the night."

"Board them here?"

"Yeah, Mr. Miller told Pop it would be all right. Preston Miller is a cattle and horse broker and has some rather large holding pens right here on the depot grounds. This is where he keeps his animals just prior to shipping them out. The horses will be just fine here. Clay and Boone and I will help you get them down from the cars."

As they were working, a tall, dignified man approached them.

"Hello, Mr. Miller," Dalton said, noticing him. "Smoke, this is Mr. Miller. He's the one who told Pop we could use this holding pen."

"Preston Miller," the man said, extending his hand. "And you would be the esteemed Smoke Jensen, I presume?"

"I'm Smoke Jensen, but I don't know anything about the esteemed part."

"By esteemed I'm talking about your relationship with Jim Conyers. He considers you an esteemed friend, and as I consider Jim an esteemed friend, I would like to think that his friend is my friend."

Smoke chuckled. "Well, I'll tell you the truth. You've gotten off to a good start by letting us keep our horses here. The trip itself was hard enough on them. I wouldn't want to keep them cooped up for another night."

"You may use my holding facilities for as long as you wish," Miller said magnanimously.

* * *

Preston Miller wasn't the only one present for the off-loading of the horses. Several railroad workers, as well as a handful of cowboys, were moving cattle into an adjacent pen. Nearby was someone who, at first sight, might be taken as one of the cowboys, but he was not working.

Drew Burgess watched the off-loading of the horses from about fifty yards away, protected from view. He was standing behind the corner of one of his own holding pens.

It was the first time he had ever seen Smoke Jensen. Burgess had heard tales of Jensen's prowess with the handgun, and he wondered what the result would be if someone like Jensen and the Professor ever got into a shooting confrontation. He was fairly certain that the Professor could beat Jensen, but he didn't overlook the possibility that Jensen might prevail. He had a feeling that question might be answered, as he was sure events were now in play that might well bring about a confrontation between the two.

Burgess didn't consider himself a violent man, but if Smoke Jensen and Del Catron were ever to meet, he would love to have a ringside seat to the program.

Clay had driven a wagonette in from the ranch, but Smoke and the others had brought their own horses, so between Fort Worth and Live Oak Ranch they rode alongside the open wagon. Bench seats faced each other along each side in the back and could accommodate several passengers. While Clay was carrying no passengers, the wagon did come in handy for carrying the luggage of the four.

"So tell me, Dalton, how is married life?" Sally asked the young man who was riding alongside her.

"It's wonderful," Dalton said. "Marrying Marjane is the best thing I've ever done."

"There is nothing better than a happy marriage," Sally said with a loving glance toward Smoke.

"Oh, and wait until you see Clay's little boy, Manny," Dalton added.

"Manny?"

"Don't you remember the baby Tom delivered on Christmas Eve?"

"Oh, heavens. How could I ever forget that? Little Emmanuel was a miracle baby," Sally replied. "The more so because the drover that performed the delicate cesarean delivery turned out to be not a common drover at all but one of the nation's leading surgeons. You'll never convince me that God didn't put Dr. Tom Whitman there for just that purpose."

Dalton chuckled. "Well, my sister certainly believes that. She married him."

"Yes, and a beautiful wedding it was, too," Sally said. "Does Rebecca still like Boston?"

"She says she does, but I know she misses Texas."

"We are a nation of displaced people, Dalton. I wouldn't be surprised if four out of any ten people you might meet are from somewhere else."

"Like you?" Dalton asked.

"I'm quite happy here, but yes, I am a prime example of a displaced person."

* * *

"Sally, how good to see you again!" Julia greeted gushingly, opening her arms in an embrace after the little entourage arrived.

Big Jim's reception of Smoke, Pearlie, and Cal was just as effusive.

"By the way, Dalton, the last time I saw you, you were wearing a badge in Audubon," Pearlie said. "So, how do like ranching? Have you taken to it yet?"

"I'm really enjoying it, but I reckon it's up to Pop as to how good a job I'm doin'."

"He's doing fine," Big Jim said. "So well, in fact, that I'm thinking about moving a rocking chair out to the front porch and just sitting there for the rest of my days, drinking coffee and eating peaches from a can while Dalton runs things."

"Ha," Dalton said. "I think you'd better talk to Clay before you do that. He's still teaching me how to find my way back to the house when we're out on the range."

"Don't listen to him, Colonel," Clay said with a little laugh. "I've been working with Dalton ever since he was a pup, and he's turned into as fine a rancher as I've ever seen."

"Dalton, seems to me like you said somethin' about your ma havin' supper ready for us," Pearlie said. "So if you two would quit tellin' each other how great you are, maybe we could go inside 'n get somethin' to eat."

"Pearlie!" Sally gasped. "How rude!"

"I'm sorry, Miz Sally, but I'm really hungry."

Julia laughed. "I don't consider it rude, Sally. I

consider it practical. Supper is goin' to get cold if we don't eat. Filipa?"

"*Sí, señora?*" A squat, rather rotund woman answered the call.

"Is dinner ready?"

"*Sí señora, la cena está lista.*"

"*Gracias.*"

The southern half of Rusk Street passed through a district of Fort Worth known as Hell's Half Acre. The Red Light Saloon was only one of an unruly collection of bordellos, cribs, dance houses, saloons, and gambling parlors. When Boone stepped into the saloon, four men were standing at the bar, and most of the tables were full. The piano was banging out a discordant rendition of an almost recognizable song, and four bar girls were moving from table to table, flirting with the men customers.

Boone knew the bartender and greeted him by name. "Hello, Mitcham. Do you have anything for me?"

Mitcham drew a beer for Boone and set the mug before him.

Boone saw that the beer mug was sitting on a key and gave Mitcham a dollar for the beer. None of the other customers seemed to notice that Mitcham returned no change.

Fifteen minutes later Boone walked through the lobby of the Mansion House Hotel and climbed the stairs to the second floor. After two short taps on the door, he put the key in the lock and opened the door.

"Hello, Boone. I wasn't sure you would be able to come today."

"Hello, Maggie."

She was about six inches shorter and six years older than Boone. At thirty she was still an attractive woman, though no one would call her beautiful. Also, unlike the girls who worked the bars, Maggie used few paints and artifices to enhance her looks.

"I'll have to get back before breakfast tomorrow," Boone said.

"You are busy with the roundup?"

"Yes."

"How many cows will Live Oak be shipping out this year?"

"I head Clay say we would be sending at least five thousand head to market."

"That's a lot of cows."

"Yes, and don't forget they are Angus. Five thousand Angus are worth a lot more than Longhorns, or even Herefords."

"I wonder how much money five thousand head of Angus cows would be worth?" Maggie asked.

"Three hundred and seventy-five thousand dollars," Boone said, answering instantly.

"My, are you a genius in arithmetic? How did you come up with that answer so fast?"

"I already knew the answer. When I found out how many head we would be shipping, I figured it out."

"What would five hunnert head be worth?" Maggie asked.

"That's easy. All you have to do is divide by ten,

so five hundred head would be worth thirty-seven thousand, five hundred dollars."

"Oh, what would it be like to see that much money at one time?" Maggie asked. "Just think, if we had that much money, Boone, we could leave here. We could go to Memphis or California or New Orleans or some such place where nobody knows us, and we could live like a king and queen."

"Yes, if we had that much money," Boone said.

Live Oak Ranch

After supper they gathered in the parlor and Jim, Julia, Smoke, Sally, Dalton, and Marjane visited, while Pearlie and Cal went out to the bunkhouse where they would be staying. There, they met all the men who rode for the brand—Andy Dunlap, Billy Lewis, Bert Rowe, John Moll, Donnie Webb, Dub Wilkerson, Dewey Gimlin, Gene Finley, Roy Baker, and Ron Scobey.

"Hey, where's Boone?" Dub asked.

"He went into town right after supper," Bert said.

"Damn, I wanted him to show Pearlie 'n Cal that picture-lookin' thing he's got."

"It's not a picture-lookin' thing, it's a stereoscope," John said. "Anyhow, it's right up there on the shelf over his bed."

"Boone has a stereoscope?" Pearlie asked, surprised at the revelation.

"Yeah, you want to look through it?" John replied.

"Yes, I'd love to."

"What if Boone was to come in here now 'n see somebody usin' that thing?" Dub asked.

"He ain't goin' to be back tonight," Bert said.

"How do you know he won't be back?" Dub asked.

"On account of I think he's made him a girlfriend outta one o' them saloon girls downtown. Anyhow, he wouldn't mind if Pearlie 'n Cal look at it. Heck, we do it all the time."

"That's true," Donnie said.

Pearlie and Cal began viewing pictures through the stereoscope.

"Wow, look at that picture of the Grand Canyon," Cal said. "Looks like you could just fall down into it."

Pearlie put his hand on Cal's shoulder. "Don't worry. I'm not goin' to let you fall."

The others laughed.

CHAPTER FOURTEEN

Seven miles away from where Pearlie and Cal were visiting with their new friends, seven men were making their way through the dark at the Texas and Pacific Depot stock-holding pens.

"Damn, this place stinks," Dawkins said.

"Yeah, well when you have this many cows penned up, you're goin' to get a lot of shit all piled up together, so it's goin' to stink," Dooley Evans said.

"Cows? I thought we was here after horses," Dawkins said.

"We are here after horses, and they're down in the last two pens," Catron replied.

The moon was exceptionally bright, and it provided enough light for Catron and the Sidewinder Gang to be able to see what they were doing. That had a negative effect as well. It also made them visible to anyone who might happen to look in their direction.

"There they are," Parker said.

"Damn," Morris said. "Them is some fine-lookin' horses. Hey, Professor, why ain't we keepin' seven of 'em for our ownselves?"

"We will stick to our original plan. We'll take fifty horses and sell them for sixty dollars apiece," Catron said.

"Sixty dollars? I thought you said they was worth a hunnert 'n ten dollars," Lattimore said.

"On the market they are worth a hundred dollars apiece, but I'm sure you understand that as we are dealing with stolen horses the traditional market is closed to us. We must get rid of them as quickly as possible, and we must accept whatever we can get for them.

"In our case we already have them sold, which means we won't have to have them on our hands for long, and sixty dollars apiece will net three thousand dollars. You may recall that this is much more than we got from the bank in Dido."

"Iffen we was to take all of 'em, we'd have twice as much money," Evans suggested.

"As it turns out our . . . business . . . connection was able to sell only fifty of them, and fifty is what we'll take," Catron said, setting the word *business* apart from the rest of the sentence.

"Why don't we let him sell fifty 'n we sell the other fifty?" Lattimore asked.

"Consider this," Catron said. "We will have these fifty horses delivered to our contact before sunup. Then we are through with them. If we had fifty more to deal with, it could take days, maybe even weeks, before we would be able to sell them. The contingency would mean that we would wind up with much less than sixty dollars a head.

"In addition, we would have to find food and water

for the horses, as well as keep them contained. That would prolong our exposure and increase the chances of our being discovered."

"The Professor's right. This here is the best way to handle it," Parker said.

"Parker," Catron said to the man who had just spoken. "I need no affirmation. From now on it will not be necessary to say that I am right. The mere fact that I am saying it is all the verification that will be required."

Quietly, and unobserved, the Sidewinder Gang took advantage of the darkness and the distance from the depot building to shield them from any observation as they cut out fifty horses. Then, with their pilfered herd, they disappeared into the night.

The next morning Smoke was standing out on the porch of the big house. He had already had breakfast and was drinking his second cup of coffee when he saw Dalton coming toward him, followed closely by a little boy. "Good morning, Dalton. I see you've got yourself a pard, there."

"This is Manny," Dalton said, running his hand through the boy's dark hair. "Why, I don't think we could run the ranch without him."

"They can't run the ranch without me," Manny repeated.

"I'm sure they couldn't, and I know that I wouldn't even try." Smoke went down the steps, then squatted in front of the boy.

The boy seemed a little startled, and he looked down at Smoke's boots."

"What are you looking for, Manny?"

"Grandpa says a cowboy should never squat if he's wearing spurs," Manny said. "I just wanted to see if you were wearing spurs."

Smoke chuckled. "That's good advice. That's why I would never do it."

"You know what else you should never do?" Manny asked.

"No, what is that?"

"You should never kick a cow pile on a hot day," Manny replied with a giggle.

"You need to listen to Manny," Dalton said with a little laugh. "He's just full of advice."

"I know all about ranchin'," Manny said.

Clay came up from the bunkhouse. "Dalton, have you seen Boone anywhere this morning?"

"Boone? No, I haven't seen him. Why do you ask?"

"I was going to take him along with us to get the horses, but he isn't in the bunkhouse. Dub said he left just after supper last night and nobody has seen— Wait. Never mind. There he is."

The subject of Clay's concern was coming up the road at that very moment.

"Boone, where've you been?" Clay asked.

"Why do you ask? I was here until everyone went to bed last night. I'm here before breakfast ended this morning. I haven't missed anything, have I?"

"No, I suppose not," Clay said. "We're going into town to pick up the new horses that came in last night. Since you were with us to help off-load them, I figured it would be good to have you come along with us to pick 'em up this morning."

Boone smiled. "Yeah, I'd like that. The sooner the horses get to know me, the easier it will be when I start riding them."

Believing that four men were all that would be needed to bring the one hundred horses back, Clay chose Andy Dunlap, Ron Scobey, and Boone Caulder.

"Are all the horses broke?" Andy asked Pearlie, who along with Cal had come to see the men off.

"They've been broken by 'bout the best bronco buster I've ever seen," Pearlie said. "But they haven't been broken to cattle."

"Actually, I didn't expect they would be broken to cattle," Clay said. "And the truth is, it will work better if we train 'em to cattle ourselves."

"Let's go get 'em," Scobey said. "I'm anxious to see them."

Just over half an hour later, they reached the holding pens at the depot.

"What the hell?" Clay said, the tenor of his voice shocked and angry. "Where'd they all go?" His explosive comment came as soon as he and his men arrived at the holding pen to pick up the horses.

"What is it, Clay? What's wrong?" Andy asked.

"What's wrong? Look in there. Does that look like a hundred horses to you?"

"Damn, you're right! It don't look like a hunnert," Andy said.

"There are fifty of 'em," Boone pointed out.

"Fifty? How do you know?" Scobey asked.

"I just counted them."

"What'll we do, Clay?" Andy asked.

"We'll do what we came to do," Clay said. "We'll take the horses back to the ranch."

"But they ain't all here."

"Then we'll take the ones that are here."

"What are we goin' to tell the Colonel 'bout some o' the horses not bein' here?" Andy asked as he rode alongside Clay while they were taking he horses back.

"I don't reckon we're goin' to have to tell him anything. He's goin' to know as soon as we ride up," Clay said.

"No, I mean what are we goin' to tell him about how it happened?"

"How *did* it happen, Andy?"

"I don't know."

"Then that's the only thing we can say," Clay replied.

Dub Wilkerson and Dewey Gimlin held the corral gate open as Clay and the others brought the horses under the arch and up the road leading to the corral where they'd be held. Big Jim had come out to welcome them, and his satisfied smile was replaced by a look of confusion.

"Clay, why didn't you bring all of them in? Where are the rest of the mounts?" he asked as he made a quick count of the horses that were being turned into the corral.

"I don't know where they are," Clay said.

"You don't know?"

"Colonel, I know that we off-loaded a hundred of them last night but when we went to pick 'em up this morning, there was only fifty of 'em."

Big Jim watched until the last horse was behind the closed gate, then he returned to the house where Smoke, Sally, Dalton, and Marjane were visiting in the parlor.

Smoke looked up. "So tell me, Jim, what do you think of your new mounts? I would say I picked out the best one hundred for you that I could."

"There are only fifty of them," Big Jim said.

"They only brought in fifty? Why didn't they bring all of them?"

"Clay said that was all that were in the pen."

"What? I don't understand. We brought a hundred down. I don't have any idea what happened to the other fifty."

"It seems rather obvious that they were stolen. Clay asked at the depot and nobody saw a thing. It would appear that I'm out fifty horses," Big Jim said.

"No, you aren't out any mounts. You may be fifty short from what you wanted, but I'm only going to charge you for the fifty that you got."

"Smoke, you don't have to do that. You delivered one hundred horses to me, so I'll pay you for all one hundred," Big Jim said.

"No, that's just the point, Jim. I delivered them to the holding pens in Fort Worth. I didn't deliver them to you at the ranch. The way I look at it, I'm responsible for them until you actually take delivery. You can pay me for fifty now, and the other fifty when I find them and get them delivered."

"When you find them? You mean you're going after the horses?"

"I am," Smoke said.

"All right. If you feel that you must," Big Jim said. "But regardless of whether you are able to recover them or not, I have a roundup to complete. In the meantime, you're welcome to use the ranch as your base of operations."

"I appreciate that."

"No, with you going after those horses, I'm the one who should be appreciative, and believe me, I am."

"Do you want me to send anyone with you?" Clay asked when he learned of Smoke's intention.

"No, Pearlie and Cal are all I'll need, but thanks for the offer."

Dido

A piano player was banging away on the upright piano in the back of the Long Trail Saloon. The bartender was wiping the bar where three men stood, holding a conversation over their drinks. As it was midafternoon, only two of the bar girls were working, though in truth, neither one of them could actually be called a girl anymore as age and the dissipation of their profession had put to lie that appellation. Nor could it really be said that they were working. Lola was standing with her back to the bar, leaning against it, while the other girl, Belle, was standing by the piano.

Six men, who were so frightening in appearance that neither Lola nor Belle made anything but a half-hearted approach to them, had, without asking, pulled together two of the tables. The six men were the Sidewinder Gang.

All six men had felonious backgrounds, and two of them, Evans and Gibbons, had WANTED DEAD OR ALIVE posters all over Kansas, while not-very-accurate drawings of Dawkins were closer to home in Texas.

"The Professor's gettin' the money right away, ain't he?" Evans asked.

"Yeah, he said for us to meet him in the Long Trail today, which is why we're here," Dawkins said.

Gibbons looked around. "I'll say this. This here was about the easiest job I ever done. It didn't take us much more 'n a couple of hours from start to finish."

"I wonder how much it'll be," Parker said.

"How much money you got 'n your poke now?" Dawkins asked.

"I got seventeen dollars, which is all I got left from the last job we done."

"I'm guessin' that when Catron comes in here, he'll be carryin' more 'n seventeen dollars."

The others laughed.

"There he is," Lattimore said and the six men looked toward the batwing doors.

Catron was carrying a cloth bag with him, and he smiled at the others as he walked over to the table. "Gentlemen, today is payday." He took a seat at the table then emptied the contents of the bag.

"Look at that," Lattimore said, indicating the bound stacks of greenbacks.

"Fifty horses brought in three thousand dollars. One thousand dollars is committed to our treasury, which leaves two thousand dollars for us to split, equally. That comes to two hundred and eighty-five dollars each."

"Where at did we actual sell all them horses?" Lattimore asked. "Last I seen of 'em was when we left 'em in a holding pen back in Cambridge."

"As long as we received our agreed-upon payment, where the horses wind up is none of your concern," Catron said. "As a matter of fact, the less any of us know about the operation beyond our own participation, the safer it will be."

"I thought when we all got together that we was goin' to be makin' a lot of money," Evans said. "Now, I'll admit that two hunnert 'n eighty-five dollars is more money 'n I've had in a long time, but it ain't exactly what I was thinkin' of when we was talkin' about big money."

"I would suggest, Mr. Evans, that you just enjoy the money you received from this job and let our cooperative friend and me make arrangements for the next one. From our preliminary discussions, I can assure you that our next operation will be much more lucrative."

"That's another thang. Who is this friend you keep talkin' about? Who is it that we're a-workin' with?" Gibbons asked.

"The fewer people who know the identity of our accomplice, the safer it will be for all of us," Catron said.

"But think about this, Professor. What if somethin' was to happen to you? I mean, if we didn't know who it was that we been a-workin' with, how could we keep on a-goin' with you bein' gone 'n all?"

Catron's chuckle was without humor. "Well, now, Jory, if I am deceased, what makes you think I would care whether the rest of you can go on or not?"

Gibbons forced a chuckle.

"You said the next job we do. Have you 'n him, whoever he is, got somethin' in mind for our next job?" Dawkins asked.

"We do indeed, and with proper planning it will be as easy as this one was, but the payoff will be much, much greater."

CHAPTER FIFTEEN

Fort Worth

When Drew Burgess stepped into the White Elephant Saloon, he saw Preston Miller sitting at a table with Steve Richardson, editor of the *Fort Worth Messenger*. The two were so involved in their discussion that neither noticed Burgess until he was practically upon them.

"Do you gentlemen mind if I join you?" he asked, pulling out a chair and sitting before either of them could even respond. He knew it would be easier for them to object before he sat down than to ask him to leave once he was seated.

"No, join us. Please do," Richardson said.

"So, tell me, Miller, everyone is talking about the fifty horses stolen from you. Do you have any idea what happened to them?" Burgess asked with a disdainful smile on his lips.

"They weren't my horses," Miller replied pointedly.

"Oh no, that's right. They were Conyers's horses, weren't they? You were just allowing him to use your holding pen. And I understand you weren't even charging him, were you?"

"No, I wasn't. Why should I charge him for one night, when the pen wasn't being used? It's called working with your customers. You should try it some-time. If you would, you might do more business."

"Yes, maybe I will try it," Burgess said. "Though if I do such a thing, I'll try not to lose half of the stock I'm holding."

"I'm sure that you know I have expressed my re-grets. Jim Conyers is my friend. I would go so far as to say that he is my best friend," Preston said. "I have no idea what happened to those horses. But yes, Drew, as the loss occurred while the horses were technically under my control, I can't help but feel responsible."

"Fifty horses, for which he paid ninety dollars apiece and which he entrusted to your safekeeping, would amount to four thousand, five hundred dollars. Do you feel responsible enough to make up the loss for your good friend?" Burgess asked.

"I . . . I feel a moral responsibility, not a fiscal re-sponsibility," Preston replied.

"Moral responsibility, not fiscal," Burgess said. His laugh was mocking. "Yes, that's a very good one."

"Actually, I feel rather sorry for the perpetrators," Steve Richardson said.

"Why would you say that?" Burgess asked, surprised by the newspaper editor's comment.

"Smoke Jensen has taken it on himself to bring the guilty ones to justice. The type of justice he normally dispenses leaves no room for appeal."

"Jensen?" Burgess asked.

"Yes, Jensen. The man who sold the horses to the Colonel," Richardson replied.

"Why would he go after the horse thieves? Once he got them here, they were no longer his responsibility were they? What is he doing? Hiring Pinkerton or something?"

Richardson chuckled. "Believe me, Drew, Smoke Jensen has no need for help from the Pinkerton Detective Agency. As a matter of fact, they would more likely be looking for help from Smoke Jensen."

"Smoke Jensen?" Burgess gasped in surprise. "Wait a minute. Are you telling me that the Jensen who delivered the horses is Smoke Jensen? The famous gunman?"

"Well, I don't exactly like the term *gunman,* as it has a rather dark connotation," Richardson said. "But yes, that is the same Jensen."

"Damn, I had no idea," Burgess lied. "I wonder if the thieves knew."

"They will know now," Richardson said. "I'm about to publish the story."

"What is there to publish?" Burgess asked. "Is not everyone already aware that the theft took place?"

"Well, for one thing, Big Jim has empowered me to let the public know that he has offered a reward of one thousand dollars for information leading to the arrest of the men who did this."

"That is a reward that will never be paid," Burgess said.

"Why do you say that?" Richardson asked.

"The way the horses have just disappeared? No, whoever planned this was a genius, and the people who did it will never be found."

* * *

From the *Fort Worth Messenger:*

Cowardly Theft of Horses

Late in the day on Thursday most recent, a private train arrived at the Texas and Pacific Depot carrying a valuable cargo. The cargo consisted of one hundred blooded quarter horses raised on the Colorado Ranch of Kirby Jensen. The horses from Sugarloaf Ranch are known far and wide for their strength, speed, endurance, and intelligence and are reputed to make the best cow ponies in the entire West.

Shortly after the train arrived, deeming it too late to drive the horses out to Live Oak Ranch, the animals were placed in a holding pen belonging to Preston Miller. When riders from Live Oak arrived the next morning to take the horses to their new owner, they found that fifty of them had been stolen during the night previous.

Mr. Conyers, to whom the horses were to be delivered, has offered a reward of one thousand dollars for anyone who can come forth with information that may lead to the arrest of the perpetrators.

At the moment there are no clues as to who the villains may be. However, by word of this newspaper, I am putting them on notice. Kirby Jensen, who raised the horses and personally delivered them to his friend, Big Jim Conyers, has taken on the task of tracking down the missing horses. If the name Kirby Jensen isn't familiar to you, perhaps you know him as Smoke Jensen, one of the most feared gunmen of the West. Gunman, yes, but he has never been known to employ his weapon except in the defense of right and the destruction of evil.

Mansfield, Texas

Jared Dixon lay the newspaper aside, then looked over at Amon Gates and Lem Delaport. The three men were in the Penhook Saloon. Petty criminals, they supported themselves by any means they could. Their last job, robbing a country store, had netted only one hundred and seven dollars. They were down to less than nine dollars between the three of them.

"Hey, Amon, didn't you say that Dawkins was braggin' to you 'bout some horses they stoled?" Dixon asked.

"Yeah. He 'n Parker has both joined up with the Professor."

"I know where we can get a thousand dollars," Dixon said, tapping his finger on the paper."

"Where? How?" Delaport asked, responding before Gates could.

"They's a thousand-dollar reward that's bein' give for anyone that would tell on who it was that done it."

"Are you crazy?" Delaport asked. "Do you really want to double-cross the Professor?"

"How is it we would be double-crossin' *him* when he wouldn't even let us come into his gang after we asked 'im?" Dixon asked.

"Hey, it says Smoke Jensen is after 'im," Gates said. "Maybe instead of tryin' to get a reward for tellin' on the Professor, we could tell him that Smoke Jensen is after 'im. The Professor might give us a reward his ownself for tellin' 'im about it."

"How did you find out Smoke Jensen was after them?" Delaport asked.

"What do you mean, how did I find out? It's right here in the paper," Gates said.

"In the paper," Delaport said slowly.

"Yes, right here. Hell, anybody can read it an'—" Gates stopped in midsentence then grinned sheepishly. "Anybody can read it," he finished.

"Well, we need to come up with somethin'. We're down to our last few dollars," Gates said.

Fort Worth

"Let me see those," Boone said, pointing to a pair of boots on display in Chip's Shoe Alley.

"Are you sure those are the boots you want to look at?" the proprietor replied.

"Yes, I want to see them. Why do you ask? Is there somethin' wrong with them?"

"No, they are fine boots. It's just that someone like you, well, the truth is I don't think you'll be able to afford them. These aren't the kind of boots a cowboy normally buys. Now, I do have some fine working boots that you might—"

"I said I want to see those boots," Boone said, raising his voice to a harsher level.

"Yes, sir, if you insist." The proprietor reached for them and handed them to Boone.

"Damn, these are sure enough some pretty boots," Boone said, holding them in his hand for a closer examination.

The store owner saw that his customer might actually be interested in buying them and switched his attitude from of one of skepticism to that of a businessman intending to close the sale. "These boots are a work of art. The leather was worked by Enrico Sanchez, who, almost anyone will tell you, is the best there is. And the silver inlay was done by Julio Cortez."

"I'll take them."

"You . . . you haven't even asked how much they are," the proprietor said.

"I'll take them," Boone repeated.

As Smoke, Pearlie, and Cal rode into town, they passed by a sign.

WELCOME TO
MANSFIELD
POPULATION 921

The three men rode south into town on Matlock Road. They heard the sawing and hammering of a new house that was being built. Two wagons were backed up to the dock of a freighting company. One of the wagons was being loaded, and the other was being unloaded. Four young boys, barefoot and in coveralls, were playing a game of marbles.

It had been a full week since they began their search for the missing horses, and so far they had had no luck at all. As unlikely as it seemed, the horses had simply disappeared. They had reached this place simply by the processes of search and elimination.

"This is a busy little town," Cal said.

"It's a good place to get some provisions," Pearlie suggested. He pointed to a saloon. "And if we'd like to get some information, seems to me like that would be a good place to start."

"You just want information?" Smoke said. "I was thinking we might also got a beer there, but if you'd rather not."

"A beer would be good, too," Pearlie said quickly, and Smoke and Cal chuckled.

They dismounted in front of the Penhook Saloon then walked inside with the eager anticipation of taking care of a trail-induced thirst with a beer.

"Horses can't just disappear. They have to be some-where," Cal said.

"Besides which, they've got to get rid of 'em. And we've let ever'one know that we're lookin' to buy some horses. You'd think someone might get word to us that they had some horses for sale," Pearlie said.

"Yes, and that makes me think they might already have sold the horses," Smoke said.

"This quick? You think they sold 'em this quick?" Cal said.

"No, I think they had them sold before they ever took them. That's why they only took fifty of them."

"Damn, if that's the case, this is a slicker operation than I thought," Pearlie said. "Smoke, do you think—"

"Do I think this might have been an inside job? Smoke interrupted. "Yes, I think it is very possible, but until we get something definite that points to that, I'd like for us to keep it among ourselves."

"Why?" Cal asked. "Don't you think we ought to tell the Colonel about it?"

"If Jim thought someone he trusted had betrayed him, I think he would be hurt, and I don't want to put that on him until we are sure. Also, if it got out that we suspected someone on the inside, that might give whoever it is the opportunity to run."

"Yeah, I see what you mean," Cal said.

The saloon was like hundreds of others they had seen over the years and throughout the West, and as a result it was comfortable and welcoming. Ordering a beer for each of them, the three men chose a table by the potbellied stove, which was cool, though there still lingered a faint aroma of its last use.

"I wouldn't be surprised if those horses were in Mexico by now," Pearlie said.

"I don't think so," Smoke said. "News of them has gotten out, and I don't think they could be moved that far without someone seeing them. Word would get back."

"Then where are they?" Cal asked.

"I don't think they went any farther than the thieves could have taken them on the night the horses were stolen. That's why I believe they were sold before they were stolen."

"One of the other ranchers, do you think?" Pearlie asked.

"I don't know, but it may be worth looking into," Smoke said.

"But aren't all the other ranchers here about friends of the Colonel?" Cal asked. "I don't think Big Jim would take too kindly to us doing something like that."

"Maybe someone isn't as much of a friend as Big Jim thinks," Smoke said.

"Smoke, if we're goin' to be out any longer we're goin' have get some more vittles," Pearlie said. "Coffee, bacon, and such. Seeing as this is a nice, busy little town, I think it would be a good place for us to get our vittles restocked. Maybe I should go get a few things."

"I'd better go with you," Cal said. "There's no tellin' what you'll come up with if you go by yourself."

"I'll be right here," Smoke said, lifting his beer to emphasize his point.

CHAPTER SIXTEEN

Lem Delaport had been standing at the bar when the three men came in, and during the time they were here, he used the mirror behind the bar to study them. He knew there was something familiar about them when they'd first stepped into the saloon, but he couldn't put his finger on it. Then, when he heard the name *Smoke,* he knew exactly who it was. They were talking about horses being stolen, and Lem believed he could use that information as well as the knowledge that this was Smoke Jensen for an advantage.

When two of the men left the saloon, Delaport set his empty mug down, wiped his mouth with the back of his hand, and turning away from the bar, took one more look at the man who remained alone at the table.

Yeah, that was him.

"That feller in the Penhook Saloon ain't none other than Smoke Jensen," Lem Delaport said to Amon Gates and Jared Dixon a few minutes later.

"How do you know?"

"On account of I seen 'im last year when I was up in Audubon. Then I heard one of them that was with 'im call 'im Smoke. How many men do you reckon there are that's called Smoke?"

"What's he doin' in Mansfield?" Dixon asked.

"You read the paper same as I done. He's lookin' for them horses that got stoled."

"Wait a minute," Gates said. "Them's the horses Dawkins said that him 'n the Professor 'n the others stoled, ain't they?"

"Yeah, I'm sure it is."

"Maybe we should tell Dawkins," Dixon suggested.

"Why should we tell 'im?" Delaport asked.

"I bet they don't know how close Jensen has got to 'em. More 'n likely they'd give us a reward," Dixon said.

"I've got a better idea," Gates said. "Instead of a reward for tellin' 'im about Smoke Jensen, how 'bout we use this information to get took into the gang?"

Delaport shook his head. "Catron didn't take us in before, 'n he ain't likely goin' to be takin' us in for not doin' no more than just tellin' 'im somethin'."

"So what you're sayin' is he won't be givin' us no reward, 'n he won't be takin' us in neither?" Dixon asked disappointedly.

"It depends on whether we tell him before or after," Delaport suggested.

"Before or after what?" Gates asked.

"Before or after we kill Smoke Jensen."

"Kill 'im, huh? Are you serious? Smoke Jensen ain't all that easy to kill. Fact is they's been a awful lot of folks that's tried it, 'n damn near ever' one of 'em as has tried has wound up gettin' they ownselves kilt," Gates said.

"That's 'cause he nearly 'bout always has them two men with 'im, 'n they're nigh as good with a gun as he is."

"So you want the three of us to go up agin the three of them?" Dixon asked. "Well now, that don't make no sense a-tall. Fact is, that's a damn good way o' gettin' our ownselves kilt, iffen you was askin' me."

Delaport smiled and shook his head. "No, it's a good way for the Professor to take us into his gang, on account of we're goin' to be the ones doin' the killin'. There ain't neither one o' them other two in there with 'im right now, 'n the reason I know this, is, 'cause I seen 'em leave. He's in there all by his ownself."

"All right. What do you think we should do?" Dixon asked.

"I'm goin' to go in first, 'n I'll be standin' at the bar. Gates, you come in through the back door, Dixon, you come in through the front. As soon as both of you is inside, look at me. I'll give the signal, 'n when I do, we'll all three draw at the same time 'n commence a-shootin'. If we time this right, he'll be dead afore he even knows what's goin' on."

After Pearlie and Cal left, Smoke remained seated at the table, and at the moment he was idly making circles on the table from the condensation at the bottom of the glass. Whoever stole the horses had to have some inside information. They had to know that the horses were coming. They had to know the horses would spend the night in the holding pen, and that there wouldn't be anyone watching over them. That knowledge was absolutely necessary in order to have presold the horses, probably to someone within no more than an hour's ride from where they were taken.

Smoke didn't want to blame any of Big Jim's hands, but at the moment he couldn't come up with any other idea as to how—

In the glass Smoke saw the reflection of a man standing just inside the back door of the saloon. That alone wouldn't have been of particular interest to him, except for the fact that the man at the back door was holding a gun in his hand. At that precise moment the gun was down by his side, but Smoke didn't like the looks of it.

Standing quickly, Smoke turned to face the man holding the gun. "Mister, is there any reason you're holding that gun in your hand?" he challenged. Pointedly, Smoke's pistol remained in the holster.

"Shoot 'im, shoot 'im!" Gates shouted, bringing up his pistol.

Smoke drew and fired before Gates was even able to bring his pistol to bear. Hearing "shoot 'im, shoot 'im" told Smoke there must be a second shooter. Spinning quickly, he saw that there *was* a second man who had come in through the front door. He, too, had a gun in his hand, not by his side, but pointed at Smoke. The second gunman was already thumbing back the hammer on his pistol and was able to get a shot off.

Dixon and Smoke fired at the same time, but Dixon missed, and Smoke didn't. As a result of the exchange of gunfire, Dixon, like Gates a second earlier, went down with a bullet in his center mass.

Delaport, who had come back into the saloon a moment before either Dixon or Gates had entered, was caught completely by surprise by the sudden and unexpected outbreak of shooting. His plan had been for all three of them to shoot at the same time, but when he saw how quickly Smoke had reacted, as well as the fatal results, Peabody left his gun in his holster.

With his pistol still in hand, Smoke perused every other patron in the saloon. Counting the bartender, there were seven other men and two bar girls in the saloon. Four of the six customers were standing at the bar, two more were at another table, and the bar girls were beside them. All six saloon patrons and the bartender were looking on with shock and disbelief. None of the men appeared to represent a threat to him at the moment, so Smoke put his pistol back in its holster, returned to his table, and waited for the law, which was sure to come.

"Mister?" one of the men at the table asked. "Do you know them two?"

Smoke took the opportunity for a closer examination of each of the bodies, then he shook his head. "No, I don't know either one of them."

Delaport, realizing that he had been seen with the two men, and fearing that some connection might be made, spoke up. "The one up there by the front door is Jared Dixon. That one in the back is Amon Gates."

"Yeah, that's right," said one of the other men. "You would know them at that, on account of I've seen the three of you together a few times."

Smoke wasn't surprised when a moment later a man wearing a badge rushed into the saloon with gun in hand.

"Ain't no need for you now, deputy," the bartender said, speaking around the match he had in his mouth. "All the shootin' is over."

The deputy looked at the two bodies on the floor. "Who did this?"

"That feller that's a-sittin' at the table over there by the stove is the one that done it," the bartender said, taking the match from his mouth to use as a pointer. "But a-fore you get all flustered 'n anxious, I'm tellin' you that he didn't have no choice, on account of them two on the floor come at him with their guns already drawed."

"Who are you, mister, and why would they want to kill you?" the sheriff's deputy asked.

"I'm Smoke Jensen, and you might ask that man over there why they wanted to kill me. He knows them."

The deputy looked over toward Delaport. "Do you have any idea why they were trying to kill Mr. Jensen?"

"He said he was Smoke Jensen. You don't recognize the name, Deputy Kuntz?" Delaport asked.

"Smoke Jensen," a couple of the others said in awe.

"Are you a wanted man, Jensen? Were they after some kind of a reward? It won't do you no good to lie, on account of I can telegraph back to Sheriff Maddox 'n find out."

"No, he ain't no wanted man," the bartender said. "You mean you ain't never heard of Smoke Jensen? Why, they's even been books that's been wrote about 'im."

"He's like a real famous gunfighter," Delaport said. "'N I heard Gates 'n Dixon talkin' 'bout how they could make a name for themselves iffen they was to kill Smoke Jensen," Delaport said.

"If you knew they were goin' to try that, why didn't you stop 'em?" the deputy asked.

"I thought they was just talkin' betwixt themselves. I sure didn't think they would actual try such a thing, elsewise I woulda tried to talk 'em out of it."

"What are you doing in Mansfield, Mr. Jensen?" Deputy Kuntz asked.

"My two friends and I—"

"Your two friends?"

Smoke nodded toward the door where Pearlie and Cal were standing, having just entered the saloon.

"As I was saying, my two friends and I are looking for some stolen horses."

"You talkin' 'bout them horses that was stoled from Big Jim Conyers? I read in the paper 'bout them. What do you have to do with it?"

"I'm the one that sold the horses to Big Jim, and I would sort of like to see them wind up where they're supposed to be."

"And you think they might be here?"

"They aren't here," Smoke said. "Our search just sort of brought us here."

"You think these two men had anything to do with stealing your horses?"

"I don't know," Smoke said, staring pointedly at Delaport. "It could be, but I have no real reason to suspect them."

One of the things that had emboldened Delaport to implement his plan was the fact that he had seen Dawkins in town no more than an hour before the shooting occurred. He knew that Dawkins liked to visit Señora Bustamante's Casa de la Felicidad, and that's where he found him.

"I have some news for the Professor," Delaport said.

"Tell me what it is, and I'll take to him," Dawson answered.

"No, I want to tell him myself, 'n I don't know where he is. You take me."

"He don't want nobody comin' out there."

"He's goin' to want to know what I got to tell 'im," Delaport said. "It could maybe even save his life."

"All right. But this better be good," Dawkins said. "I don't think the Professor likes you all that much, on account of he ain't let you join up with us when you asked."

"What is Delaport doin' out here?" Catron asked Dawkins. "You know better than to bring an outsider here."

"Yeah, well, he ain't exactly an outsider. I mean, seein' as he's tried to join up with us before," Dawkins said.

"What do you want, Delaport? I am in no more of a mood to accept you into our group than I was the last time you asked," Catron said.

"I've got some information you would like to know," Delaport said. "I'll give it to you if you'll let me join up with you fellers."

"What is the information?"

"Have you ever heard of Smoke Jensen?"

"Of course I have heard of him."

"Well if you've heard of 'im, you know how good

he is with a gun 'n all. 'N he's comin' after you on account of you stole them horses."

"That information was in the newspaper," Catron said. "You have told me nothing I didn't already know."

"Yes, but I know where he is. I know 'cause Dixon 'n Gates tried to kill him. Onliest thing is, he wound up killin' them."

"Where is Mr. Jensen now?"

"Well sir, when I left Mansfield, that's where he was."

"I didn't ask where he was. I asked where he *is*," Catron said.

"Well, I don't rightly know where he is right now, but I thought maybe tellin' you this news that you'd let me join up with you," Delaport said.

"I don't think it is in our best interest to take on another member at this point, nor do I think it is in our best interest for someone to be privy to the location of our hideout, and to know of our association with the missing horses. I'm afraid the answer is no."

The smile on Delaport's face faded when he saw Catron draw his pistol.

"Hey, what are you—?"

Catron pulled the trigger. "Bury him where we buried the family that built this cabin," he said as he holstered the still-smoking pistol.

CHAPTER SEVENTEEN

"I don't think there is any way to recover the stolen horses," Smoke told Big Jim when he, Pearlie, and Cal returned to Live Oak. "It seems pretty clear now that whoever stole them had some sort of plan in mind beforehand, and may well have been able to get rid of them the same night they stole them."

"I wouldn't be surprised. But despite what you said, I'm going to pay you for one hundred horses," Big Jim insisted.

"Suppose we come up with a compromise," Smoke suggested.

"What sort of compromise?"

"Suppose I go back to Sugarloaf and get another fifty horses ready for you? That way you can pay me for a hundred, and I'll deliver a hundred."

The two men were having coffee in the dining room, and Big Jim drummed his fingers on the table for a moment as he considered Smoke's offer. "Well, I *would* like to have another fifty horses."

"Then it's done," Smoke said. "I'll bring fifty more

horses down here, and that will fulfill our original contract."

"I'll go along with that proposal on one condition," Big Jim said.

"What's that?"

"If you won't let me pay for fifty more horses, then at least let me pay all the expenses of getting them here. I'll pay for the cars, and this time," he added with a smile, "I think you should get a private car instead of a caboose. I'm sure Sally would appreciate that, wouldn't she?"

Smoke laughed. "I'm sure she would."

Texas and Pacific depot, Fort Worth

The northbound train had arrived a few minutes ago and was sitting on the track, venting steam and making a clanking sound as the journals cooled. The departing passengers stood alongside, awaiting the conductor's boarding call.

"Sally, you know you are very welcome to stay here with us until Smoke comes back, don't you?" Julia asked. She and Big Jim, as well as Dalton and Marjane, had come down to the depot to see Sally and the others off.

"Oh, I thank you for the offer, but somebody needs to go along with these three, if for no other reason than just to keep them out of trouble," Sally teased.

"You're right, Miz Sally, and I'll be glad to help you with Pearlie," Cal said.

"Cal, you couldn't even find your way onto the car if someone didn't show you how," Pearlie replied.

"Heavens, do they always talk to each other like that?" Marjane asked.

"Always," Dalton said with a smile. "But you just let someone threaten one of them and they'll learn real fast what good friends they are."

"All aboard!" the conductor called.

"We have to go," Sally said, and she exchanged hugs with Julia and Marjane, while Smoke shook hands with Big Jim and Dalton.

Drew Burgess had just made some arrangements to ship out twenty horses to a buyer in New Mexico when he saw Big Jim Conyers and his family in the depot. "Going somewhere, are you, Colonel?"

"No, we were just here to tell some friends good-bye."

"Would that be Smoke Jensen?"

"Yes," Big Jim replied with a smile. "Do you know Smoke?"

Burgess shook his head. "I've never met him, but I've heard of him. He's the one who lost fifty of your horses for you, isn't he?"

"No, that isn't right. That isn't right at all," Big Jim protested. "Why would you even say such a thing?"

"Well, according to what I heard he brought a hundred horses that you had purchased down from Colorado. But instead of delivering them to your ranch, he left them here, unprotected, in one of Miller's holding pens. Then, during the night, fifty of them were taken."

"That is true, but I'm the one who suggested that

the horses stay here overnight. I thought they would be secure in one of Preston's holding pens."

"You should have left them with me," Burgess said. "If you had, you wouldn't have lost any of them."

"How can you be so sure of that?"

"Because, unlike Miller, I wouldn't have let them stay here for free. I would have charged you fifty cents a head to keep them here, and I would have had guards watching over them all night."

"Yes, well, I left them with Mr. Miller because we have always done business together, and he is my friend. But hindsight is always good, isn't it, Mr. Burgess? You can say now, after the fact, that you would have kept a guard all night but I really doubt you would have been any more aware that the horses could be stolen than Preston was."

"Except that everyone in town was aware that you had bought the horses, and everyone knew they were particularly valuable. No, Mr. Conyers, in addition to hindsight there is also foresight, and knowing what I know about human nature, I could have almost predicted that if left unguarded they would be stolen. I'm just saying that had you boarded the horses with me for fifty dollars, you would have saved yourself forty-five hundred dollars."

Big Jim sighed. "I don't know, Mr. Burgess. Perhaps you are right. But it does no good to shut the barn door after the horse is gone, does it? What is done is done, and I have learned an expensive lesson."

"By the way, I understand that you are letting Miller broker your cattle again this year."

"And why not? He is only charging me three dollars a head. You wanted five dollars a head."

"Have you ever considered, Mr. Conyers, that you get what you pay for?"

"What do you mean?"

"You paid nothing to have your horses kept overnight, and you got nothing in return. Miller provided you with no protection at all, and you lost fifty horses. Now you are paying only three dollars a head for your cattle to be booked. How safe will your cows be?"

"I'm sure they will be very safe. Now, Mr. Burgess, if you will excuse me, I must rejoin my family. Have a good day, sir."

Burgess watched Big Jim walk away then, speaking so quietly that nobody could hear him, he said, "Just wait, you crazy old fool. Your cattle aren't nearly as safe as you think they are."

On the northbound train Smoke sat with his folded fist held against his chin and stared, not at the passing scenery, nor even at anything in the car. He was, in fact, staring at the back of the seat in front of him.

"Smoke?" Sally said.

He didn't respond.

"Smoke?" she said again.

Her second summons got his attention and looking at her, he smiled. "Yes, my love?"

"You can't win them all."

"What do you mean, I can't win them all? What are you talking about?"

"You know exactly what I'm talking about. You're blaming yourself for not being able to find those horses."

Smoke shook his head. "It's as if they just disappeared into thin air. I've never seen anything like it."

"Given the circumstances of their disappearing, do you think it was possible for you or anyone else to find them?"

"No," Smoke admitted.

"Then tell me, what good are you doing by sitting there and moping over something that you can do nothing about?"

"I'm not doing any good at all," Smoke admitted.

"Then please stop thinking about it. It's doing nothing but keeping you depressed, and when you are depressed, I'm depressed."

"All right. I'll quit thinking about it," Smoke agreed. He smiled. "Suppose I think about eating? Why don't we check out the dining car?"

"Did someone mention the dining car and eating?" Pearlie asked from the seat just in front of Smoke.

"I swear, Pearlie has ears that can shut out thunder, but if someone whispers something about eating he is instantly alert," Sally said

"Why are we talking about eating?" Cal asked. "Is it time to eat?"

Smoke chuckled. "Cal, since when have your eating habits been connected to a clock?"

"Oh, I don't reckon they ever have," Cal replied, giving a serious answer to a sarcastic question.

"What do you, say, Smoke, that we get these two poor, malnourished people to a place where they can get some sustenance? I would hate to see them expire of malnutrition when the dining car that could save them is only three cars ahead," Sally said.

"I guess since we took them to raise, we can't do anything else. All right. Let's go have dinner."

One-room house, Grove Street

"Two hundred dollars?" Maggie said when Lattimore showed her the money. "I thought you said you were about to do something that would make you a lot of money. You think two hundred dollars is a lot of money?"

"Do you have any idea how long I would have to work at the stage depot to earn two hundred dollars?" Lattimore replied. "I make thirty dollars a month there. Two hundred dollars is half a year's work. Besides, how much have you made on your back? Four, five dollars a night? Sometimes ten dollars on a good night?"

"Don't get me wrong, Eb, I'm not complainin' it's just—"

"You're not complainin'? I'd like to know just what the hell it is you're a-doin' if you ain't complainin'?"

"I'm a little disappointed is all. When you was talkin' about makin' a lot of money, I thought maybe you meant as much a thousand dollars or such."

Lattimore smiled. "Don't worry. We got somethin' planned that will make us that much money. What we just done was practice for it is all. You might say we was gettin' paid just for practicin'."

"What do you have planned?"

"Do you think I would tell you before we done it?

Like as not you'll get to blabbin' away 'n you'll wind up tellin' either another one of the girls, or maybe one o' the men that's beddin' you. I ain't a-tellin'."

Part of Lattimore's indignant reaction to Maggie's question was to cover the fact that he had no idea what their next job would be.

Sugarloaf Ranch

Unlike many of the other ranches in the area, Sugarloaf enjoyed an ample supply of water. The dozen or more streams and tributaries that branched off from the Gunnison River weren't natural offshoots; they had been created when Smoke dammed up the river. Normally, such a dam would have backed the water up until a large lake was formed, but that was prevented by a system of sluices and gates that rerouted the water to where it was needed. It also allowed enough of the river to pass through so that the ranches downstream from Sugarloaf weren't deprived of water. If fact, some of the streams Smoke had created continued on so that they, too, provided water to the downstream ranches.

This elaborate water system was good for Sugarloaf Ranch, for it brought water to even the most remote part of the ranch. Pearlie and Cal, who had been rounding up another fifty horses to take back down to Texas, stopped by one of the tributaries to let their own horses drink.

"I've been thinking about those horses disappearing like that, and I just can't get it out of my mind," Cal said. "Smoke said they were more 'n likely sold on the same night they were stolen. Pearlie, I just don't see how that's possible unless it was one of the Colonel's own men that set that whole thing up."

"Yeah, I've been pretty much thinking the same thing. The only way that could be is if somebody on the inside was taking care of it, and that has to be one of the Colonel's own hands."

"That sure would be bad if was happenin' here, wouldn't it? But it can't never happen here," Cal said.

"How do you know it can't ever happen here?" Pearlie asked.

"Well come on, Pearlie. You know all our hands. We know everyone here."

"We don't know Buster Crabtree all that well, because we just hired him. And don't forget, he 'n Smoke had that little run-in back in town just before we went down to Texas."

"Yes, and I once tried to hold up Sally, and you were once an outlaw. We can all change, 'n I figure Buster can too."

Pearlie chuckled, then poked Cal on the shoulder. "You've certainly got that right, friend. Truth to tell, I expect ever one ridin' for the brand more 'n likely has somethin' in his past that he would just as soon keep in his past."

"Including Smoke," Cal added.

Back at the big house, unaware of the speculation of his two top hands, Smoke was standing in the kitchen drinking a cup of coffee.

"How many horses do we have ready now?" Sally asked.

"We have half of them broken already."

"My, that's very fast, isn't it?"

"Yes, thanks to Buster." Smoke chuckled. "Buster is a good name for him. He's one of the best I've ever seen when it comes to bronc bustin'. Once he's on a horse he stays on it like he's glued to the saddle." He lifted his cup of coffee to his lips, then smiled across the brim. "I'm glad I didn't kill him. He's been really good at getting the horses ready."

"Kirby Jensen," Sally said sternly, "are you actually saying that the only reason you are glad you didn't kill someone is because he can break horses for you?"

"Well, it isn't the *only* reason," Smoke teased.

"Oooh, you are incorrigible," Sally said in resignation, though she ameliorated her reaction with a smile.

Smoke laughed, drained the rest of his coffee, then set the empty cup on the table. "I see Pearlie and Cal coming back with a few more horses. I think I'll go to see what's going on."

By time Smoke got there, the horses they had brought in were already in the corral, and Buster was closing the gate on them.

"We've only got fifteen more to bring in to have our fifty," Pearlie said.

"Good. At the rate we're going, I can take these fifty down to him by the end of next week."

"So *you* can take them down. You think Miz Sally's goin' to let you go alone, do you?"

"I don't know. I haven't thought of that. She might want to go."

"Smoke, I learned a long time ago there is no difference between Miz Sally *wanting* to do something, and her actually doing it."

"Really, you think so?" Smoke replied.

"Do I think so? I—" Pearlie stopped in midsentence when he saw the big smile spreading across Smoke's face. "It isn't nice for you to be teasing me like that," he said with a little laugh and a playful punch to Smoke's shoulder.

Chapter Eighteen

Live Oak Ranch

Boone Caulder was sitting on his bunk in the bunkhouse polishing his new boots.

"Lord a' mighty, look at them boots Boone's a-polishin' there," Andy said.

"Hold 'em up there, Boone. Let us get a good look at 'em," Bert Rowe said as he and Andy Dunlap and John Moll went over for a closer look.

Proudly, Boone held out his boots. Although they were brown in color, he had polished them to such a bright shine that they were glistening almost gold. They were trimmed with a white filigree and within the swirls at the top of each boot shank was a little silver decorative piece.

"Where in the world did you get them boots?" Bert asked.

"I got em in town, at Chip's Shoe Alley."

"Them there is one fancy pair o' boots, I'll say that," John said.

"How much would a pair of fancy boots like that set you back?" Andy asked.

"What do you mean?"

"How much did you have to pay for 'em?"

"Thirty-five dollars," Boone said.

"Thirty-five dollars?" Andy replied in an explosive response. "Good Lord, man. That's damn near a whole month's wages, 'n you're spendin' all of it on one pair of boots?"

"I want to look good to the ladies when I go into town."

"Ha, you don't need to be a-wearin' them fancy boots to look good. All you have to do is go into the Red Light or the Waco Tap or the Cowboy Saloon or some such place 'n hold up a couple o' dollar bills 'n you'll look good enough to the ladies," John Moll said.

"Anyway, why are you polishin' them boots like that?" Andy Dunlap asked. "We're right in the middle of the spring roundup now. You'll get them boots all polished up, then the next thing you know, you'll go out 'n step in a big pile of cow dung. Hell, it don't make no sense."

"Now tell me, Andy, do you really think I'd pay thirty-five dollars for a pair of boots like this, then wear 'em while I was chasin' cows? I got other boots for that."

"Yeah, well, you're crazy to pay that much for a pair of boots no matter what they look like," Roy Baker said. "Why, you don't have to pay no more 'n four or five dollars for a good, sturdy pair of work boots."

"You aren't listening to me." Boone held out the boots so all could see them. "These aren't work boots. It's like I told you, these are boots for dressin' up 'n lookin' good." Boone went back to brushing them.

"Hey, Boone, tell me somethin', will you? How come it is you have money to buy boots like that 'n that silver band you wear 'round your hat? Hell, you don't get paid no more 'n the rest of us, but you get them new boots, that silver band 'round your that 'n that picture-lookin' thing. Where does the money all come from?" Dewey Gimlin asked.

"Dewey, have you ever seen me get drunk and lose all my money in a poker game?" Boone asked. "Have you ever seen me have more than one beer when we go into town?"

"But you was in town most all night, the other night. That had to cost you somethin'."

"Yes, but like I said, I save my money to spend it on what I want. I don't go into town every payday and drink half of it away in one night."

"Ha! He's got you there, Dewey," Billy Lewis said.

"Yeah, well, Boone, you can put them fancy boots down for now, 'n the rest of you stop your palaverin'. It's time to go to work," Andy said.

As the cowboys out at Live Oak were getting ready to go to work, back in town, Drew Burgess was standing at the counter in the Western Union office, listening to the instrument. As the key clacked, Paul Noble, the telegrapher, made rapid marks on a yellow tablet, keeping up with the flow of information. When the clacking finished, Noble made a few clicks in return, then walked away from his instrument.

"Here are the figures you asked for, Mr. Burgess," Noble said, shoving the paper across the counter so Burgess could see it.

"As you can see, longhorns are bringing forty-five dollars and Herefords are bringing sixty dollars a head. Though, you won't be dealing with any longhorns, will you? I think the last longhorn rancher here in Tarrant County went over to raisin' Herefords last year."

"Angus," Burgess said.

"Angus? What about them? There's only one Angus rancher in Tarrant, Dallas, Wise, Jack, and Pinto counties all combined."

"That doesn't stop me from bein' curious. What are Angus bringing?"

"As of today, Angus are bringing seventy dollars a head."

Burgess did a rapid calculation. "Damn, that means Jim Conyers has nearly half a million dollars on the hoof," Burgess said.

"Half a million dollars?" Noble asked, clearly surprised by the number. "That's a lot of money."

"Yeah," Burgess replied in a quiet, almost covetous voice. "It's a hell of lot of money."

"Are you going to be booking any Angus cattle this year?" Noble asked.

"I've tried to get Conyers to let me handle his cattle transactions this year, but he's sticking with Miller."

"Well, you can't really blame him, I don't suppose," Noble said. "The Colonel and Preston Miller have been friends from the time Big Jim got here. I expect that he 'n Miller will continue to do business with each other until one of 'em dies."

"Yeah," Burgess said. "Until one of them dies."

* * *

Preston Miller's surrey was pulled by a matched pair of duns, and they were trotting smartly as he passed under the arched gate at Live Oak that same morning. As he pulled up to the Big House, Boone Caulder met his surrey. "If you'd like, Mr. Miller, I'll unhitch your team so they won't have to stand in the same place while you're visitin' with the Colonel."

"Why, thank you, Boone. That's quite nice of you," Miller said, passing over the reins as he climbed down.

A very pretty young woman stepped out onto the front porch. "Mr. Miller, the Colonel asked me to greet you and make you feel welcome."

Miller smiled at Tamara, Big Jim and Julia's daughter, as he climbed up the steps. "Well, thank you, my dear. Nothing can make a man feel more welcome than to be greeted by a beautiful young woman."

Tamara led Miller into the parlor, where Big Jim, Julia, Dalton, and Marjane were waiting.

"Preston, thank you for accepting my invitation," Big Jim said.

Preston glanced toward Julia. "Now, Jim, what kind of fool would turn down the opportunity to enjoy one of Julia's meals?"

"Filipa's meals," Julia corrected.

"Yes, and we'll just see how much you enjoy it. She's had Filipa prepare leg of lamb. Can you believe it? A cattleman's wife serving leg of lamb to a guest?"

"I like leg of lamb, and Filipa does such a wonderful job with it," Julia said. "And Jim, don't you pretend that you don't like it, because I know that you do."

"Shh," Big Jim cautioned, raising his finger to his lips. "If you said such a thing in front of anyone other than Preston, I could be ruined. But Preston is a good enough friend that I know he won't give me away."

Preston laughed. "Well now, Jim, I guess we'll just have to keep each other's secret. Here I am a cattle dealer, but I also like lamb."

After lunch, the six of them returned to the parlor to visit for a while before Preston went back to Fort Worth.

"Tell me, Tamara, how is it that some young swain hasn't captured you?" Preston asked. "Why, if I were ten years younger I would be camped outside this very door."

Tamara blushed and flashed a shy smile.

"She has turned into a beautiful young woman, hasn't she?" Julia said. "Of course she was a beautiful young girl, so it certainly isn't surprising."

"I have no doubt that the time will come, and soon, that I'll be beating young men off with a stick."

"Ha, and how did that work out with you beating Tom away from Becca?" Dalton asked.

"Well, Tom is almost as big as I am, so what did you expect?" Big Jim teased, referring to his son-in-law, Dr. Tom Whitman.

"Jim, I want to tell you again how sorry I am about the loss of your horses," Preston said. "I should have hired a guard to watch over them."

"That's what Burgess tried to tell me," Big Jim said. "But you ask me, he was just trying to make trouble. I see no reason to have a guard there. Why, I've kept cattle there many times, waiting to be shipped, and so have other ranchers, and we haven't lost any stock. We had no reason for us to think we would lose anything this time. Besides, if there had been a guard there, who is to say he wouldn't have been killed? I wouldn't want to think I was the cause of that. The loss of a few horses is certainly better than the loss of someone's life."

"You're a good man, Jim," Preston said. "Yes, I suppose I hadn't thought of that. By the way, how soon will your cattle be ready for shipment?"

"Not too much longer. We're working now, pulling out the ones we're going to keep and gathering the others."

"Good. I'm going to start marketing them now. I guarantee as soon as you consign your cattle to me, they are my responsibility. If any of them are stolen from my holding pens, it will be my loss, not yours."

"I would hope that neither of us loses," Big Jim replied.

"Tell me, Jim, have you ever heard of the Sidewinder Gang?" Preston asked.

"Sidewinder Gang? No, I can't say that I have."

"Why do you ask, Mr. Miller?" Dalton asked.

"They are as evil a bunch as have ever ridden the outlaw trail," Preston said. "I have heard that they are the ones who recently held up a bank in Dido. From as much as I can understand, they got away with less than a thousand dollars, but they killed three men and one woman in the process. It is said that the head of the gang is Del Catron, the one they call the Professor."

"The Professor. Yes, I have heard of him. They say he is the most deadly gunman since Wes Hardin. They also say he is particularly evil, which I guess he proved by killing three men and a woman for such a small amount of money," Big Jim said. "But tell me, Preston, why did you bring them up?"

"Have you considered the idea that they might have been the ones who stole your horses?"

"No, I hadn't thought of it. Why do you suggest that? Have you heard something?"

"No, but some organization had to be behind it. After all, they came in the middle of the night and drove off the horses without being discovered."

"That's true, yes, but they took only fifty head. Why would some outfit headed by the Professor take only fifty and leave fifty?" Dalton asked.

"It depends," Preston said. "If they already had a specific number of horses sold they could have taken them then gotten rid of them so quickly there would be very little likelihood they would ever be discovered."

"But if someone around here bought fifty of the horses, don't you think it would show up?" Big Jim asked.

Preston shook his head. "Not if they found someone who would broker the horses for them."

"Broker the horses for them? Why, that would take someone like—"

"Someone like me," Preston said.

"Someone like you?" Dalton asked, surprised by the comment.

"Burgess?" Big Jim suggested.

"I'm not accusing Drew Burgess, but I am accusing Del Catron and his gang of cutthroats that call themselves the Sidewinders. The question, of course, is how did they know the horses were there in the first place? I mean they had to know they were coming so they could broker the horses with whoever brokered them."

"It's pretty easy to figure how they knew that the horses were coming," Big Jim said. "It got out pretty quick that I was bringing in a hundred head of prime quarter horses."

"Yes, Andy and Bert both said they heard people talking about it in some of the saloons in town."

"And don't forget, Burgess knew about it because you and I and he discussed it one day in Winders Cattle Exchange Saloon, remember?" Big Jim said.

"Yes, now that you mention it, I do remember that conversation," Preston said. "As I recall, that was when you told me the day they would be arriving and made arrangements to keep them in my holding pens."

"But surely Drew Burgess wouldn't be involved in such a thing, would he?" Dalton asked. "I mean he is a well-known businessman, not only in Fort Worth, but Dallas as well."

"No, I wouldn't think it was him," Preston said. "But it had to have been someone with specific knowledge of all the details."

"Specific knowledge? Preston, are you saying it's an inside job? One of my men?"

"It isn't necessarily one of your men," Preston said. "But don't close your mind to that possibility."

"Oh, I hope that isn't the case," Julia said.

Preston smiled. "I just wanted to give you something to think about, but I talk too much. In this part of the country, riding for the Live Oak brand is as prestigious a job as any cowboy can have. It almost beggars belief that one of your own men would be responsible for this. Please, just forget that I said anything."

"No, I won't forget," Big Jim said. "You have given

me something to think about, Preston, and even though I know it was difficult for you to say such a thing, I appreciate that you are enough of a friend to tell me."

There was a knock on the door, and Marjane answered it.

"Mr. Miller wanted me to have his surrey in harness by two o'clock, 'n it's two o'clock," Boone Caulder said.

"Yes, thank you, Boone," Preston said, rising from his chair. "Jim, Julia, Dalton, Marjane, and Tamara, you have treated me as a member of the family today, and I thank you for that. Good-bye."

Big Jim walked out onto the front porch with Preston and bade him good-bye one more time as his friend climbed into the surrey.

"Good-bye!" Preston called back as, with a snap of his reins, he got the surrey underway.

"Mr. Miller is such a nice man," Julia said when Big Jim went back inside.

"Yeah, he's been a friend of yours for as long as I can remember," Dalton said.

"Longer than you can remember, Dalton, since he has been my friend since before you were born. When I first came here, he was a good man to know. He was already an established broker, and I was trying to start a ranch."

"He certainly seems comfortable with you," Marjane said.

"It may be because he has never married. He has no family of his own, so he has sort of adopted us."

"Jim, this business about who stole the horses. Do you think it was this man they call the Professor?" Julia asked.

"It could very well be," Big Jim replied. "But even if it was him, he still had to get rid of them."

"Burgess?" Dalton suggested.

"I don't know," Big Jim replied. "It could be, but I just don't know."

After taking care of the surrey for Preston Miller, Boone Caulder went back to the bunkhouse, where he put on his best jeans, his newest shirt, and his new boots.

"Woowee, Boone, I'm goin' to need you to stay away from me whenever we go into town," Dub Wilkerson said. "You're shinin' so much, there won't none of the girls in town that'll even see me."

It was late Saturday afternoon, so the roundup was halted for the day and wouldn't be picked up again until Monday morning. Because of that, Boone wasn't the only one who would be taking the day off. At least half a dozen of the men were planning an afternoon and night in Fort Worth.

"You don't need to worry none about that," Boone said. "I've got my own place to be going to."

"Yeah, you haven't been runnin' with the rest of us, have you?" Donnie Webb asked. "Where is it that you go when we go to town?"

"Don't you know? Boone has fell in love with one o' them soiled doves down in Hell's Half Acre," Gene Finley said.

"Woowee, damn! That's how come Boone's always got money. He's fell in love 'n she gives it to him for free. He don't have to pay nothin' for women like the rest of us do," Roy Baker said.

"That true, Boone?" Donnie Webb asked.

"Well now, if I told you, it wouldn't be a secret any-more, would it?" Boone replied, smiling at the teasing.

"I could follow you just to see whereat it is that you go," Donnie said, "but I don't plan to take away from my time just to see where it is."

CHAPTER NINETEEN

Sidewinders' hideout

"I've got another job for us," Catron said.

"More horses or another bank?" Dawkins asked.

"Neither. It's going to involve cattle."

"Oh, I don't know, Professor," Jory Gibbons said. "Me 'n Dooley has both cowboyed some. Hell, we even pushed a herd up into Kansas, 'n that's when I learned that me 'n cows don't get along all that good. 'N if we was to steal some cattle, we're goin' to have to drive 'em somewhere, that's for sure."

"When you made your foray up into Kansas, how much were you paid?" Catron asked.

"Thirty dollars a month and found. Took us two 'n a half months so when we was paid out, we drawed seventy-five dollars.

"The job I have in mind will pay you many times that, and you won't be directly involved with the cattle for any more than a couple of days."

"You're talkin' 'bout rustlin' cattle?"

"Yes."

"Yeah, well, I've done some rustlin' before," Gibbons

said, "'n when you rustle cows the first thing you got to do is get 'em away quick so's that no one sees 'em 'n sees where they come from. Then you got to find someplace to sell 'em. Any cows we steal here would more 'n likely have to be took as far away as San Antone, or maybe up to Dodge City or some such place. 'N that sure as hell takes more 'n a couple o' days. Then generally the folks you can sell 'em to will know they are stoled cattle, so they won't hardly give you nothin' for 'em."

Catron shook his head. "Do you remember how easy it was with the horses?"

"Yeah."

"Taking the horses was simply a test to see if the operational plan would work. It worked to perfection, so now all we have to do is apply those same procedures to rustling the cattle."

"So, what you're a-sayin' is, rustlin' these here cows you're talkin' about ain't goin' to be no harder than it was to steal them horses?" Gibbons asked.

"Only marginally so," Catron said. "And the reward will be significantly greater."

"You know what, Professor? Whenever you talk, most o' the time I ain't got no idea what it is that you're actually sayin', so's I'm goin' to ask you to say it in words that I can understand," Jory said.

"Because there will be several cows involved, this operation will be only a little more difficult than moving the horses was, but we won't go much farther than we went with the horses. And this operation will pay a lot more money to each of us than the business with the horses paid."

"You mean like maybe over a thousand dollars?"

"Quite easily so."

"Well, all right then," Jory said with a broad smile. "I'm ready to go. When is it, exactly, that we're goin' to take them cows? 'N where are we goin' to take 'em from?"

"We didn't take the horses until we had them sold. It will be the same thing with the cattle. We will take them when we have sold them. And it isn't necessary, yet, for you to know from where we will acquire them. You will be told when there is a need for you to know."

Jory shook his head. "There's somethin' I don't understand here. How can we sell somethin' that we ain't got yet?"

"It's what cattle brokers do," the Professor said.

"Cattle brokers? You mean like them highfalutin kind of men that works with ranch owners and the like?" Jory asked.

"That is exactly what I mean."

"Well, Damn. If we ain't in high cotton."

Fort Worth

When Big Jim stepped into the office building, Preston Miller greeted him with a wide smile. "My friend, we are going to have a drink to celebrate."

"What are we celebrating?"

"I have booked your herd of five thousand Angus for eighty dollars a head. Minus my cut and shipping charges, you will, quite easily, clear around two hundred and eighty thousand dollars."

Big Jim smiled. "Well now, I would say that does warrant a drink of celebration."

Preston poured whiskey into two glasses, then he

and Big Jim picked the glasses up and held them out in salute.

"How soon can we start shipping?" Preston asked. "With that many head, it would be easier to move the cattle is several shipments."

"I can get a thousand head to you this week," Big Jim said.

"Good, good. The sooner we get started, the quicker we'll get the money."

"I'll have Dalton and Clay bring in the first bunch tomorrow."

Drew Burgess was in the Palace Saloon when he overheard a couple of the city businessmen talking.

"Eighty dollars a head," Phil Puckett said.

"What? You have to be kidding me," Howard McGill replied. "Where did you hear that?"

"I heard it from Big Jim himself," Puckett said. "He ordered a wagonload of block salt to be delivered out to his ranch and told me then that he booked his cows for eighty dollars a head."

"Well, that's good," McGill said. "The better our ranchers do, the better it is for everyone.

Although Burgess didn't get involved in the conversation, he listened attentively, then after he finished his beer, he walked down to the Tarrant County Stock Broker office building.

Preston Miller was in the reception area talking to Leonard McGee, and he looked up in surprise to see his chief competitor. "Drew, what brings you here?"

"Is it true that you'll be getting eighty dollars a head for Big Jim's cattle?" Burgess asked.

"Well, I don't know as that is any of your business, but yes, I've booked his cattle at eighty dollars."

"I don't believe you."

"Oh? And why not?"

"I check the market by telegraph every day. This morning it was seventy dollars a head for Angus cattle, but you are telling Conyers that you have him booked at eighty dollars a head."

"Why would I say that if it weren't so?" Preston asked. "Do you really think I would take a loss of ten dollars per head?"

"No, what I think is you have told him that just to make certain he sells his cattle through you, then at the last minute you'll tell him that the offer has been reduced."

"Why would I have to lie to Jim to get his business? From the time Big Jim Conyers arrived here, he has dealt exclusively with me, not only because we are friends, but also because he knows I can and do get him the best possible prices."

"Yes, well, even if I could talk him into letting me handle his cattle I couldn't match your offer, let alone beat it."

Burgess left Preston, muttering to himself as he walked back to his own office.

Chapter Twenty

When Big Jim returned home from his visit with Preston, he went into the kitchen, where Julia was working with Filipa. Stepping over to Julia, he put his arms around her waist then lifted her up and swung her around.

"For heaven's sake, Jim, whatever are you doing?" Julia asked with surprise and a lilt in her voice.

"I'm celebrating with my sweetheart by swinging her around."

"You got the cattle booked!" Julia said.

"Not only booked, but for a record price," Big Jim said, setting her back down.

"Oh, Jim, that's wonderful!"

"Yes, well, it's thanks to Preston. He's the one who found the buyer and made the book."

"I'm so happy for you," Julia said.

"Happy for me? Be happy for everyone, Julia. For one thing, I'm going to give a bonus to every hand we have. Five hundred dollars for Clay, a hundred dollars for all the permanent hands, and fifty dollars for all the part-time cowboys we've hired."

"That's a great idea," Julia said. "And?" Almost imperceptibly, she made a slight nod toward Filipa.

"Filipa, if you were out there rounding up cattle, you'd be getting a one-hundred-dollar bonus. What do you think of that?"

"Oh, señor, I do not think I could round up the cattle," Filipa replied.

"Good, I wouldn't want you to do that, either. Besides, as a cowhand you would only get a hundred dollars. But as our cook, and all-round house helper, you are going to get two hundred dollars as a bonus."

Filipa gasped, and put both her hands across her ample chest. "Oh, señor, that is *maravilloso! Gracias, señor, gracias!*"

"Are you going to tell the men now or save it as a surprise?" Julia asked.

"I think I will save it as a surprise," Big Jim said.

"Good. I want to be there when you tell them. I want to see how they react."

"He wants a thousand head right away, so I'd better ride out and tell Dalton and Clay."

"A thousand head?" Dalton replied when Big Jim told him what Preston wanted. "Yes, sir, we can do that. When do you want it done?"

"First thing tomorrow morning," Big Jim said.

The following day, residents of South Fort Worth saw a large, black mass approaching them from the south. As it came closer, they were able to give substance and movement as the indistinct mass morphed into a herd of hundreds of cattle, the herd formation kept by cowboys riding alongside, whistling and shouting, sometimes breaking into a gallop to bring an errant stray back to the fold.

Dalton Conyers was leading the way, and he galloped out in front of the approaching herd to choose the best way to enter the city. He led the one thousand head of Angus cattle into town by crossing the railroad at the Cotton Compress, then moving west along Sixteenth Street to Houston Street and the Texas and Pacific Railroad yard. Many of the town's citizens had come down Houston, Main, Rusk, and Calhoun streets to watch the parade of cows along Sixteenth Street to where the cows would be turned into Preston Miller's holding pen.

The cattle had made an easy passage of the seven miles from the ranch to town, and were even docile during their passage down 16th, but when they reached the holding pen, they grew less docile. Ray, Gene, Andy, and Boone had to get more aggressive to force them into the pen.

Finally the last animal was pushed into the pen and the gate was locked.

"Good job, men," Dalton said. "We're twenty percent done."

Dalton gave the men the rest of the day off, and though they spread throughout town to the various saloons, where either by frugality or morality their time in town for the rest of the day was quite benign.

Live Oak Ranch

The next morning Andy Dunlap was working in one area of the ranch and Gene Finley in another.

Boone Caulder came riding up to the group Andy was heading.

"Did you find any that had strayed away?" Andy asked.

"No," Boone replied. "That is, I didn't really look."

"Why not?"

"On account of Clay wants me to go into town. He has some things he wants me to take care of."

"What sort of things?"

"I, uh, don't know yet. He said for me to come back 'n see 'im 'n he would give me a list."

"All right. I don't reckon your bein' gone is actual goin' to work no hardship on anyone."

"Thanks," Boone said.

"Stay out of trouble," Andy called as Boone turned his horse to leave.

Boone's answer was a wave thrown back over his shoulder.

"Ha. I coulda told you that Boone warn't goin' to be doin' no work today," Dub Wilkerson said as he and Andy watched Boone ride away.

"How did you know?" Andy asked. "Did he say somethin' to you?"

"Warn't no need for him to say nothin'. You could tell by lookin' at 'im. Din't you notice when he come up here that he was wearin' them fancy new boots of his?"

Andy chuckled. "Yeah, now that you mention it, he was wearin' 'em, wasn't he?"

* * *

At that very moment Big Jim was standing in the parlor drinking coffee and looking through the window.

"What are you looking at?" Julia asked.

"Heaven," Big Jim replied.

"What?"

Smiling, Big Jim turned toward her and held his arm out. "I am a very happy man, Julia. There is no way that heaven can be any sweeter than the life I am enjoying now."

Answering his unspoken summons, Julia smiled then walked over to him and let him put his arm around her. He pulled her to his side as she joined him in looking through the window.

"And to prove that this is heaven, I've got an angel by my side." Big Jim tightened his grip on her shoulder.

Julia chuckled. "My goodness, Jim, what did you sweeten your coffee with this morning? A bit o' the creature, perhaps?"

"You feel it, too, Julia. Don't tell me you don't. This year will be the biggest return we have ever received for our cattle. We're taking them in a thousand at a time, no two-month-long drives. We can go from here to the depot in two hours."

"That's true," Julia said.

"And look at our family. Becca is happily married, Dalton is, too, and even better, Dalton has decided to settle down and come back to help run the ranch. I know that Tamara isn't actually our child, but from the time she has come to live with us, she is in every way but actual blood."

Big Jim and Julia had taken Tamara in after her parents had been brutally murdered. Since that time she had become very much a part of the family.

"You're an old fool, Jim," Julia said, though the way she said it made it clear that it was more of an endearment than a criticism.

"Yes, but don't forget, I'm *your* old fool," he said, turning to kiss her.

"I don't know what has gotten into you this morning, Jim, but I like it," Julia said, smiling up at him.

Big Jim stepped away from her and set his empty coffee cup down.

"Well, I could stay here all morning, but I do have a ranch to run, so I think I'd better ride out and see how things are going."

"You don't need to, you know. Dalton has everything well in hand. If you start meddling it could—"

Big Jim interrupted her comment with a laugh. "I'm not going to meddle. I'm going to admire. Dalton has caught on to ranching quicker than I ever thought he would."

"I'm sure he would like to hear that," Julia replied.

"He doesn't need to hear it. He knows it." Big Jim leaned over and gave Julia a quick kiss. "I love you, Julia Marie. And I will love you forever.

As Julia watched him leave, her heart warmed to his words. "I love you, Julia Marie" had long been one of his expressions of endearment, but the, "and I will love you forever," was something he had never said before.

* * *

Big Jim went outside and saddled Shiloh, then rode out to check on things. At the moment most of the permanent hands, as well as those who were part-time cowboys were spread out over Live Oak Ranch, bringing in the cattle from the farthest reaches of the property. They would then break the herd into elements of one thousand head each. One such controlled herd had already been delivered. Four remained, each to be delivered on a schedule as established by Preston Miller.

On the bank of the West Fork of the Trinity River

Stacey Alford and Paul Butler were not regular hands, but they had worked for Big Jim in previous roundups. They liked working for him because he paid well and he treated his part-time help as well as he treated his permanent hands.

Most of the cattle would be shipped out and sold, but Alford and Butler knew that at least two thousand head would be held back in order to sustain the herd. It was Alford and Butler's job to look after the "keepers," as they were being called. So far fifteen hundred head had been gathered in the holding area, which was, by design, as far away from the rest of the cattle as they could be.

Because of water and ample grass, the cattle were content to stay where they were. That made Alford and Butler's job very easy, and though both men were mounted, their horses were standing quietly on the periphery of the herd.

"Say, Stacey, have you ever actual seen one o' them telyphones?" Butler asked.

"I've not only seen one, I've used one," Alford replied proudly.

"Uh-uh. No you ain't."

"I have, too. They's one in Dunagan's Gen'rul Store 'n oncet when I was cleanin' up for 'im, the phone rang, 'n bein' as I was the only one there I answered it. Turned out it was Mr. Dunagan his ownself. He was just checkin' to see if I was still there."

"What's it sound like? I mean, to hear a feller talkin' on one o' them thangs," Butler asked.

"Well sir, you can understand what it is they're a-sayin', but their voice is kind of high 'n scratchy."

"How far will one o' them telyphones reach?

"Well, sir, you can be in Fort Worth 'n talk to someone that's got a telyphone in Dallas now. And I reckon that iffen you had a line long enough, why you could even talk to someone in Chicago or New York or some such place," Alford said.

"I'm twenty-three years old now. What do you reckon things will be like when I'm sixty?" Butler asked.

"There ain't no tellin'."

At that moment some riders came across the West Fork Trinity.

"Hey, Stacey, lookie over there? Who are them fellers?" Butler asked.

Alford looked toward the approaching riders.

"I don't recognize none of 'em. Besides which, they're a-comin' from the wrong direction to be any o' the Colonel's hands," Alford replied. "Could be they're just cuttin' through."

"Well, they're comin' this way, so I reckon we're about to find out," Butler said.

"Who are you men 'n what can we do for you?" Alford challenged.

Neither Alford nor Butler was armed, so when they saw pistols appear in the hands of the approaching riders, they gasped in fear.

"What—" Butler was unable to finish his question as both he and Alford were shot down.

"All right, gentlemen, start the cows moving," Catron ordered.

As the rustlers got into position to move the cattle away, another man who hadn't crossed the river with them did so now.

"Good, good. These are the keepers, and there are about fifteen hundred of them gathered so far. This will make quite a nice bundle for us," the new man said as he started riding around the herd for a closer inspection.

"Professor, I've got a question about this new fella that we're workin' with," Dooley Evans said, nodding toward the new arrival.

"What is your inquiry, Mr. Evans?" Catron asked.

"What I want to know is, how much is he makin' out of this?"

"How is that any of your concern? Just concentrate on the job at hand," Catron said.

"Hey, Professor, you think maybe somebody mighta heard the shootin'?" Lattimore asked.

"No, we're a long way from the main part of the ranch, and the wind is against us. I think we will be able to move them off the ranch without any danger of being discovered."

"How far do we have to drive these critters?" Lattimore asked. "I mean fifteen hunnert head is damn near the same thing as a cattle drive."

"We don't have to take them any farther than we took the horses."

"Damn," Lattimore said with a wide smile. "If that's the case, then this here operation is slicker 'n goose poop."

CHAPTER TWENTY-ONE

Approximately two miles east, and a little south of where Catron and his men were working, Big Jim approached one of the gather areas. "How are things going?" he asked Dalton.

"Things are going just fine, Pop.'" Dalton said proudly. "Andy has a gather just to the north of us, 'n Gene is working to the east."

"You've been pushing our keepers to the west?"

"Yes, sir. We've got fifteen hundred there now. Stacey 'n Paul are lookin' after them. I plan on moving another two hundred and fifty out there later this afternoon and two hundred and fifty tomorrow. That'll finish the keepers. Then we can just work on getting the cattle together to take in to Mr. Miller."

"Good. Glad to see that everything is on schedule. I think I'll ride out that way just to have a look around and see how Alford and Butler are doing," Big Jim said.

"All right, thanks. I was goin' to do that myself after a while, but if you do it then I won't have to."

"Son?" Big Jim said.

"Yes, Pop?"

"You've been doing a great job since you came back home. I'm glad you came back, and I want you to know that I'm proud of you."

Dalton smiled self-consciously. "Thanks, Pop."

He watched his father ride away, feeling proud that he had won his praise. The relationship between father and son had not always been so good. Dalton had been somewhat rebellious when he was younger, but with maturity had come more responsibility, and he was glad that his father had not only stuck with him during those difficult times, but recognized that he had become more responsible.

"What did the Colonel want?" Roy Baker asked, his question interrupting Dalton's musing.

"Oh, nothing in particular. He's just out checking up on things. How many calves have to be branded?" Dalton asked, getting back to business.

"I think the count is forty, so far today, but we haven't counted them all."

"Good, good. It looks like we're going to have a pretty good increase this season."

"That'll make the Colonel happy, for sure," Roy said.

"Well, time to get back to work," Dalton said, turning his horse toward the gather.

About a fifteen minute ride after leaving Dalton, Big Jim saw several cows in front of him.

"Well, look here, Shiloh. All the cows we're keeping behind are waiting here in a bunch like a . . . who are those men with them? What the hell? I thought only Alford and Butler were here."

He was still too far away to be able to identify the riders, but he assumed they were part-time hands who had gotten a little confused. That was understandable; there were quite a few seasonal hands right now, and the ranch was so large that it was easy to lose one's direction.

Big Jim urged Shiloh into a rapid trot toward the gather, which he figured to be about five hundred cows. "Hold on there, men! These are our keepers! They stay here!" he shouted out to them.

"Here boys," he called out again. "You need to turn around and—" Big Jim stopped in midsentence, and the expression on his face turned from bemused observation to one of anger and understanding. These men weren't part of the gather. They were cattle rustlers.

At first, Big Jim thought all the rustlers were strangers, then with a gasp of shocked surprise, he recognized one of them.

"You? You're with them?"

"Kill him, Professor. If I'm identified it will ruin everything."

"Shoot him," Catron ordered his men.

Big Jim wasn't armed, and when he saw half a dozen guns pointed toward him, he jerked his horse around and tried to get away. Even as he heard the sound of gunshots, he felt a blow, as if someone had hit him in the back with a club, and though he tried to hang on, he was unable to stay in the saddle. He lay dying while his riderless horse, startled by the gunfire, galloped back toward the safety of the stable.

"Julia," he said with his dying breath.

"Somebody check him out. Is he dead?"

Dawkins rode over to where Big Jim was lying facedown on the ground. There were at least three bullet holes in his back.

"He's deader 'n a doornail," Dawkins replied.

"Hurry up. We need to get these cows out of here before anyone comes to check on him."

Back at the ranch headquarters, Clay Ramsey was looking over the horses in the corral when Dewey Gimlin came up beside him.

"You know, I been thinkin', Clay. Could be that maybe that the Colonel made a mistake when he done what he done," Dewey said.

Clay chuckled. "You, thinking? Now there's an interesting concept. What mistake did the Colonel make?"

"Well, here's the thing, Clay. Since half o' the new ones that the Colonel bought got themselves stoled, he maybe ought not to have sold them other ones. I say that, 'cause we're runnin' a little thin ain't we?"

"We're down some, but Smoke told the Colonel he'll be bringin' in another fifty to make up for the ones that were stolen. And we're far enough along with the gather that we're not really overworking the ones we have now."

"I wonder why it was that only fifty of 'em was stoled?" Dewey asked.

"I think what Smoke and the Colonel decided what happened is that they probably already had fifty horses sold, and they didn't want to have to deal with the rest of them."

"I reckon that could be so, but seems to me like there's somethin' just real strange about this."

"What do you mean?" Clay asked.

"Well, if they did already have fifty horses sold, how is it that they could do it so fast? I mean we didn't get them horses in until that day, 'n they only spent one night in the holding pen. How did they even know about 'em to sell in the first place?"

"That's a damn good question," Clay replied. "And I know for a fact that Smoke 'n the Colonel have already been thinkin' 'bout that very thing."

"I hate it when somethin' bad happens to the Colonel. He's a damn good man. Best man I've ever worked for," Dewey said.

Clay chuckled. "Best man I've ever worked for, too, but I've been with him since I was twelve years old, so that makes him the only man I've ever worked for."

Dewey saw a saddled but riderless horse coming in at a gallop.

"Hey, boss, ain't that the Colonel's horse, Shiloh, comin' in here?" Dewey asked, pointing toward the approaching horse.

"Yeah," Clay said, "Yeah, it damn sure is. Wonder what he's doin' back here? The Colonel left here no more than an hour ago. And why is the saddle empty?"

With an uneasy feeling, Clay started toward Shiloh. The horse, recognizing the ranch foreman, stopped his gallop, slowed to a trot, then to a walk as he approached. He lowered his head and let Clay take hold of his halter. He was breathing heavily.

"Here, boy, what has you so upset?" Clay asked as

he petted the horse on his forehead. "Where's the Colonel?"

"Clay?" Dewey said in a sense of awe. "Clay, lookie here."

Clay looked where Dewey had pointed and saw the reason for Dewey's anxious concern. There was blood on Shiloh's flanks, and not just a little blood.

"Dewey, I saw Dalton going into the Big House not more than ten minutes ago," Clay said in a voice filled with dread. "I'm thinking it might be a good idea for you to go get him."

"Clay, do you think maybe something has happened to the Colonel?"

Clay dipped his finger into some of the blood, which had not yet dried, then held his finger up for a closer examination. "It sure as hell doesn't look good. Don't say anything to anybody, not even Dalton. Just tell him I need to see him."

As Dewey went into the house to get Dalton, Clay removed the saddle from Shiloh. He had just taken it off when Dewey returned with Dalton, who had a worried look on his face.

"Clay, what is it? Dewey had a strange look on his face when he came to get me, and when I asked what it was about, he didn't answer. Hey, that's Pop's horse, isn't it? When did Pop come back?"

"He hasn't come back," Clay said.

"Why not? Clay, where is he?" Dalton asked with foreboding.

"I don't know," Clay answered. "But I think you had better see this."

Clay showed the blood to Dalton, and Dalton took a quick, audible breath.

"This . . . this can only mean that Pop is lying out there somewhere, badly hurt or—" Dalton couldn't bring himself to say the word. "We need to find him."

"He rode out onto the range to check everyone, and I know he was going to come see you. When's the last time you saw him?" Clay asked.

"No more than half an hour ago," Dalton said. "He stopped by where I was working, then he said he was going to check on the keeper cattle."

"I know where everyone is, but if this happened near any of them they would have sent someone back to tell us. Even near the keepers, Alford and Butler. One or the other would have come to get us. This can only mean that the Colonel is out there somewhere on his own, so we're going to have to look for him, and that's not going to be easy to do since we have two hundred square miles to search," Clay said.

"I've got an idea." Dalton patted Shiloh's face. "Shiloh, as soon as we get saddled, I want you to lead us to Pop. Will you do that for us?"

Shiloh nodded. Though it was in response to the patting, Dalton was sure, by the way Shiloh stared so directly at him, that the horse understood.

"Yes, that's a damn good idea," Clay said. "I think Shiloh understands."

It took but a few minutes for Clay, Dalton, and Dewey to get saddled. They went back to Shiloh, who was still standing where Dalton had left him.

"All right, Shiloh, take us to Pop," Dalton said.

For just a moment Shiloh looked at the others, his eyes reflecting his confusion.

"Go on! Get!" Dalton said, and he slapped Shiloh

on the rump. With a little whinny, Shiloh started west at a brisk trot, and the other three followed.

"Where the hell are the keepers?" Clay asked. "We should be seeing them by now."

Shiloh broke into a gallop then, and the other three followed. Then he stopped and looked down.

"Oh, my God, that's Pop," Dalton said, his voice filled with dread. He swung down from the saddle then knelt on one knee beside his father's body. "Pop? Pop?"

There was no answer, nor did Dalton actually expect one. Big Jim's back was covered with blood, though the blood was no longer flowing.

"Looks like he was shot 'n the back," Dewey said, pointing out the obvious.

"Who could have done something like this?" Dalton asked.

"Where are Alford and Butler?" Clay asked.

"Maybe they're the ones who done this 'n took the herd," Dewey suggested.

"No, it wasn't them," Clay said. He pointed to two dark forms lying on the ground. "They're both over here."

"Are they dead?" Dalton asked.

"Yeah, I'm sure they are," Clay replied.

"None of the cows are here, which means Pop must have happened on to a bunch of rustlers," Dalton suggested.

"It could be that they were frightened off by the gunshots," Dewey suggested.

"No, I don't think so. Look over here," Clay said. "Dalton is right. A lot of cows were headed out this way"—he pointed—"and you know damn well that isn't the way they're supposed to be going. They weren't just wandering around, either. The cows were in a tight bunch with at least four and maybe more horses moving with them. My guess is that the Colonel saw them and probably thought it was some of our men who weren't sure what they were doing. When he came up on him, they shot him."

"Clay, you don't think it was any of our men, do you? I mean, I know it wasn't any of our regulars, and a lot of the part-time people have worked for us before. But we do have some new—" Dalton started.

"It wasn't any of our people," Clay said, interrupting Dalton's question. "You know yourself, Dalton, everything was organized so the only part-time riders working anywhere on their own were Alford and Butler. They're laying over there dead, which means they didn't have anything to do with this. Every other part-timer is paired up so's that they're workin' with some of our regulars. No, sir, I don't who did this, but whoever it is, they aren't drawing a check from Live Oak."

"What do you want to do with the Colonel's body, Dalton?" Dewey asked. "Though I reckon I should start callin' you Mr. Conyers, now."

"Dewey," Clay said, answering before Dalton could, "go back to the barn and get a buckboard. Also, get some tarps so we can cover the bodies then take them into town to the undertaker. There's no need for Mrs. Conyers or any of the other ladies to see him like this. Let Mr. Ponder get the Colonel all cleaned up, before anyone else sees him.

"That is, if that's all right with you, Dalton," Clay added.

"Yes, of course it is, and thanks, Clay. That is the best thing to do. And Dewey? Tell Mr. Ponder I'll be responsible for whatever it costs to bury Stacey Alford and Paul Butler." Dalton wiped his eyes, then walked back to his horse. "I'd better go see Ma, now."

After Dalton and Dewey were gone, Clay was left alone with Big Jim's body. Clay had no idea who his own father was, so this man had filled that role in his life. As Dalton had done earlier, Clay fought hard to hold back the tears.

"Colonel, I want you to know, that because of you, I never missed having a father of my own. I loved you as much as any man could ever love a father. And I always looked to Dalton as if he was my brother. I promise you this, Colonel. I'll be as loyal to him as I was to you, and I'll look out for your family as if they're my own. 'Cause in my mind, by God, they are my family."

CHAPTER TWENTY-TWO

With a lump in his throat, and fighting to hold back tears, Dalton made the long, sorrowful ride back to the main compound. He was in the barn unsaddling his horse when Marjane came into the barn.

"Sweetheart, where did you disappear to so mysteriously a while ago? You've got everyone worried."

Dalton didn't turn to face her. He stood there for a long moment, his arms resting on the back of his horse, even though the saddle had been removed.

"Dalton?" Now there was some concern in Marjane's voice. "Dalton, honey?"

Dalton turned toward her, the red puffiness around his eyes clearly visible.

Marjane gasped. "Sweetheart, what is it? My God, Dalton, have you been crying? What's wrong?" she asked, her voice showing more fear than concern.

"I'm goin' to need your help, darlin'," he said in a quiet, thick voice. "I'm goin' to need you with me when I tell Ma."

"When you tell . . . oh, Dalton," she said, realizing

what must have happened. "Oh, sweetheart. Oh, no. It's your father?"

Dalton's response was a nod

"Oh, no. Oh, I'm so sorry." Marjane hurried over to him, and they stood in a tight embrace for a long moment.

"I have to tell Ma," Dalton said a moment later, pulling away from the embrace.

"Dalton, is your father still riding around somewhere?" Julia asked as he and Marjane stepped into the parlor of the Big House. "Filipa has a good dinner going and—" Julia stopped in midsentence when she saw the expressions on their faces. She gasped and raised her hand to her mouth. "Where is your father?" She asked the question as if already dreading the answer.

"I had Clay take him into town," Dalton replied.

"To the doctor?"

"No, Ma. To Mr. Ponder."

"Ponder?"

Dalton nodded, but didn't vocalize the answer. He didn't need to. Lou Ponder was the mortician.

"No," she said in a small voice that could barely be heard. "No," she repeated. "Please, God, no!"

"Ma," Dalton said, going to his mother and taking her into his arms as she began crying on his shoulder. He couldn't help but have a strange, irrelevant thought. Here he was, comforting his crying mother, and he knew there had been many times when he had been a crying child being comforted by this same woman.

"Why did you take him away before I could see him?"

"Ma, let Mr. Ponder . . . uh . . . get him ready for

you to see. You would not have wanted to see him the way he is now."

"What happened? Was he thrown from his horse? Shiloh would never do that. Why, he loves Jim as much as Jim loves him."

"He was shot, Ma. So were Mr. Alford and Mr. Butler. From the way it looks, a bunch of rustlers came up and shot Butler and Alford then started stealing the cows. Pop must have happened on to them while they doing that, and they shot him."

"What . . . what will I do now? Jim was my life, my whole life. I . . . I don't know how I can go on without him." Julia began sobbing almost uncontrollably and, like Dalton, Marjane shared in the embrace of the grieving woman.

Tamara and Filipa had been drawn to the room by the sound of Julia's weeping. Without having to be told, both women perceived what must have happened, and while Tamara joined in the group hug, Filipa stood in the door as tears slid down her brown cheeks. She made the sign of the cross.

Gradually, Julia managed to get hold of herself, and she began thinking of what must be done. "We'll need to take Jim's new suit in to Mr. Ponder so he can make him presentable, and I'll want to see him as soon as I can."

"Yes, Ma," Dalton agreed.

"Becca will need to be told. But, Dalton, send the telegram to Tom so he can break the news to her. I think it will be better coming from him than having her read it on a telegram."

"I agree. And Ma, I want to tell Smoke and Sally Jensen about it, too. They'll be returning soon with the replacement horses, and they need to know what they are going to find when they get here."

"Yes, of course, you must tell them, and also those nice young men who work for him, Pearlie and Cal. I do hope they can get here in time for the funeral."

"I'll take care of everything, Ma. In the meantime Marjane and Tamara will be here with you."

"And I will be here too, señora," Filipa said with a voice that broke as she spoke. "Anything you need done, you just tell me and I'll do it."

"Thank you, Filipa," Julia said, turning toward her and opening her arms in an invitation for an embrace.

"El Señor Jim está con Dios, Señora Conyers. Lo volverá a ver."

"Yes, Filipa, Jim is with God, and I will see him again," Julia agreed.

"I'll be goin' now, Ma, to do what has to be done," Dalton said.

Julia nodded, then took a handkerchief offered by Tamara and dabbed at her eyes.

Dalton went to the door then glanced back for one more look at the weeping women. With everything that was in him, he wanted to join them and cry with them. But he called upon all his reserve not to do so. Now, more than ever before, Dalton had to be strong.

Julia watched her son leave, then she thought of the last words Big Jim had said to her. *"I love you, Julia Marie, and I'll love you forever."*

Now, it truly would be forever.

* * *

The first thing Dalton did when he got to town was deliver the suit to Lou Ponder.

"Yes," Ponder said in a voice of practiced compassion. "This suit will look very good on him."

"How soon will you have him ready for Ma to see?"

"She can see him tomorrow morning," Ponder said. "Dalton, I am used to tragedy and sorrow in my business, and I have to be able to put it all aside. But Big Jim? He has always been bigger than life, so much a part of our community, so much a part of my own life, that, well, I must confess that I'm having a hard time with this."

"Thank you, Lou."

"Oh, and about the other two gentlemen?" Ponder asked. "Clay said they were from Dallas, so I've gotten in touch with Gene Welch, who is the undertaker I know there. He will come later today to pick them up."

"I know that Butler has a sister there, but I don't know if Alford has any family at all."

"Don't worry about it. Gene will take care of finding any relatives and notifying them."

Dalton put his hand on Lou Ponder's shoulder. "You're a good man to know, Lou."

"Although there is always the stress of dealing with sorrow in my profession, I take solace in the fact that I am able to provide closure and comfort the bereaved," Ponder said in a solemn, but dignified voice.

"Yes," Dalton said, nodding. "Yes, Lou, you do just that."

When Dalton left the mortuary he considered going to the saloon for a drink, but when he looked down the street he saw the Tarrant County Stock Broker building, and, steeling himself, walked down to give the news to one of his father's oldest friends.

Leonard McGee greeted Dalton when he stepped into the office.

"Mr. Conyers," Leonard said. "Are you here to make arrangements for the next one thousand head?"

"No," Dalton said. "Mr. McGee, I wonder if I could visit with Mr. Miller for a few minutes."

"Yes, of course. I'll tell him you are here."

Dalton started to sit down but within seconds of McGee going into Preston Miller's office, the broker came out into the reception area.

"Dalton, it's good to see you. There is no problem with bringing in the next one thousand head, is there? I'm making rail arrangements now."

"I think it might be best to delay that for a short while," Dalton replied. "Mr. Miller, I guess there's no good way of telling you this, so I'm just going to come right out and say it. My father is dead. He was shot and killed this morning, apparently by some cattle rustlers."

Preston gasped and raised his hand to his mouth. He stared at Dalton for a long wordless moment before he spoke. "You say *apparently*. So you don't know for sure?"

"If you mean were there any witnesses, there may have been, but, like Pop, they were killed as well. We found the tracks of a large number of cows and four or five riders. The cattle we were holding back as keepers are missing and the two hands who were tending them were killed. We found my father dead, shot in the back. His body was lying where the tracks of the horses and the cattle were, so it seems to me that it is a simple case of putting two and two together."

Preston nodded. "Yes, I've no doubt but you are right. How is your mother taking it?"

"As you would expect, she's taking it very hard. I came to town to make arrangements with Mr. Ponder and to send my sister a telegram telling her. Then I thought about you, and knowing how close you and Pop were, figured I should tell you next."

Preston reached out to put his hand on Dalton's shoulder. "Dalton, I am so sorry to hear this." He tried to chuckle, but it came out as an ironic chortle.

Preston was quiet for a long moment before he spoke again. "Here I am trying to comfort you, when I need comforting."

Dalton nodded. "I know you do, Mr. Miller. I know what you meant to my father and what my father meant to you. Like I said, I hated to bring the news to you, but I also knew that you would want to know."

"Yes, thank you. You did the right thing. Mr. McGee?" he called out.

"Yes, sir?" the bookish McGee replied.

"You heard what Dalton said?"

"Yes, sir, I heard." The clerk turned his attention to Dalton. "Mr. Conyers, I'm so sorry to hear about your father. You have my condolences."

"Thank you."

"Mr. McGee, this office is closed, and it will remain so until after the funeral. I intend to see that Jim Conyers gets all the respect he deserves. And Dalton, please tell Julia that I am here for her. If she needs anything done, I will take care of it for her."

"Thank you, Mister—"

"You're the head of the ranch now, Dalton," Preston said, interrupting him. "I think you should call me Preston. It is my hope that you become as good a friend to me, and I to you, as your father and I were."

Dalton smiled. "Thank you, Preston."

After leaving Preston's office, Dalton walked down to the Western Union office. He wasn't looking forward to letting his sister know what had happened, but it would be her husband, Tom, who would have to face her, not he.

"Mr. Conyers, I, uh, heard some very disturbing news," the telegrapher said when Dalton stepped into the telegraph office a few minutes later. "I hope your presence here isn't conformation of that news."

Dalton nodded. "I'm afraid it is. I'm going to have to send a couple of telegrams.

"Yes, sir, of course." The telegrapher got out a yellow tablet and a pencil. "You may dictate them."

When Dalton stepped into the Palace Saloon after sending the telegrams, the buzz of conversation stilled. The piano player was banging out a gay tune but Dalton saw one of the bar girls go over and whisper something to him, while pointing toward Dalton. The music stopped.

Without having to order, the bartender slid a shot of bourbon across the bar. "It's on the house, Mr. Conyers, with our condolences."

"You know?"

"The whole town knows. Someone saw his body when it was brought into town, and the news has reached everyone. It is an unbelievable tragedy. I can't imagine life in this town without the Colonel."

"Thank you, Michael," Dalton said. He lifted the whiskey in a salute to the bartender, then tossed it down. "I had better leave," he said. "I'm afraid that I have put a cloud over everyone here."

"Don't you worry about that, Mr. Conyers. You are welcome to stay as long as you wish."

Leaving the saloon, Dalton rode down Calhoun Street to the corner of Calhoun and Belknap. Sheriff Maddox looked up when Dalton stepped inside.

"I heard about your pa," Sheriff Maddox said. "I'm just real sorry."

"I thought you might want to ask me a few questions," Dalton said.

"I do, and I was going to ride out there after a while but I wanted to give you and Mrs. Conyers a little time first. I'm glad you came in. That will make it easier on your ma."

"Yes, I think so."

"Tell me how you found him."

"*Them,*" Dalton said. "Two of the part-time hands, Stacey Alford and Paul Butler, were also killed."

"Yes, I heard. I'm sorry to hear that, because they would have been my primary suspects. What about the rest of your hands? Are all of them accounted for?"

"Yes, the cattle that were taken were being held back, and Alford and Butler were the only ones with them. Every other hand, permanent and temporary, is accounted for."

"Well, one thing that might help us is that they took Angus. And since the Colonel was the only cattlemen growing Angus in Tarrant County, the rustlers are going to have a hard time getting rid of them. I'll check in Dallas, Parker, Johnson, and Denton counties to see if there are any Angus there."

"Tom Allen has Angus in Dallas County and Ken Smitten has Angus in Parker County," Dalton said.

"That's good to know. I'll contact the sheriffs in those counties and ask them to check with Allen and Smitten to see if anyone has tried to sell them any cattle."

"Sheriff, one thousand, five hundred head of Angus can't be hidden that easily. They moved them off our ranch and they had to go somewhere with them. You should check around to see if anyone saw a herd of Angus being moved."

"Yes," Maddox replied. "I'll do that."

CHAPTER TWENTY-THREE

Sugar Loaf Ranch

Buster Crabtree had gathered twenty horses and was taking them back to the paddock where they could be confined while he was breaking them. Smoke and Pearlie were sitting in their saddles watching as Buster brought in the horses in a column of twos, almost as if they were a military unit passing in review.

"I'll say this for the man," Pearlie said. "I've never seen anyone who could handle horses like he can. Why it's almost as if he can talk to the critters."

Smoke chuckled. "Everyone talks to their horses, Pearlie."

"Yeah, but in Buster's case the horses listen, and they talk back," Pearlie insisted.

Smoke's chuckle turned into an outright laugh. "Don't tell Cal that. He'll start repeating horse gossip."

"What are you laughing at?" Cal asked as he came riding up then.

"We're laughing at that story you said one of the horses told you," Pearlie said.

"I don't know what you're talkin' about, I never—" Cal started, but he interrupted his comment in mid-sentence. "One of the horses is trying to get out of line. I'd better go push him back." He galloped away toward the horses Buster was leading.

"It'll take him two days to figure out what I said to him," Pearlie said with a little laugh.

"No it won't. You're going to tell him you were just teasing, and you're going to apolo— Damn!"

Smoke urged Seven into a gallop before he could even explain the outburst. No explanation was needed, though. Pearlie also saw what had happened.

Just as Cal reached the errant horse the horse kicked out its back legs, catching Cal and knocking him from his saddle. As he fell, his horse and the errant horse ran off, leaving Cal on the ground.

Within seconds Smoke and Pearlie were at Cal's side.

"Cal!" Smoke called as he made a gentle exploration of Cal's head.

"Was he kicked in the head?" Pearlie asked, his voice showing his concern.

"I don't think so."

Cal opened his eyes and looked up at Smoke and Pearlie, both of whom were kneeling beside him.

"What are you two lookin' at me like that for?" Cal asked.

"Well, because you got knocked off your horse and you're lying on the ground," Pearlie answered.

"I am?" Cal looked around. "Damn, I am lying on

the ground. Help me up." He raised his arms, then let out a sharp exclamation of pain. "Oh, damn! My side!"

"He has three broken ribs," Dr. Parnell said. "I've got him pretty well bound up, but it's going to be a while before he'll able to walk."

"Ha, I'll think about you boys workin' out in the hot sun while I'm lying here in the guest bedroom drinking lemonade and eatin' all those bear claws Miz Sally will be making for me," Cal said, and though he tried to be jovial about it, his voice was laced with pain as he spoke.

"Who says I'm going to make you any bear claws?" Sally asked.

"Well, you're goin' to have to, aren't you? I mean, what with me being all stoved up and all. I mean, aren't you going to feel some sorry for me, Miz Sally?"

Sally laughed. "We'll see." The expression in the words as she answered indicated that she would do just that.

Cal smiled. "Maybe I should have broken my ribs a couple of years ago."

"Don't worry about missing any work while you're in here, napping and eating, Cal," Pearlie said.

"Oh, I'm not worried. I know you'll be taking care of it for me."

"You've got that right. I'll be saving it up for you so you can get to it when you're all healed up," Pearlie said with a laugh.

Boston General Hospital, Boston, Massachusetts

The incandescent bulbs over the operating table used the mirrored shrouds to greatly intensify the light on the patient, a twelve-year-old boy named David who had been diagnosed with appendicitis. Dr. Thomas Whitman, chief of surgery, was about to perform an appendectomy.

Prior to the surgery Tom had donned rubber gloves. This was a relatively late innovation, adopted in order to prevent sepsis. When he was certain that David was out, he used his scalpel to make an incision in the lower right side of the boy's abdomen. Reaching in through the incision, he found the little worm-shaped appendix and cut it out.

"All right," Tom said after the appendix was removed. "Let's take a look inside and see if there's any pus or anything that might have spilled into the abdominal cavity." Using a small, sterilized mirror on the end of a probe, Tom stuck it into the opening where a quick perusal told him that the cavity was clean. Satisfied by his examination, he closed the incision then stitched the wound shut.

"Let's get him out of here," Tom said. "I don't want him to wake up in the operating room. This whole thing has been frightening enough for him. There's no need to add this to it."

"Yes, Doctor," one of the nurses replied.

Tom removed the gloves, washed his hands, then took off his full-body apron and dropped it into a pile of laundry to be washed.

Tom returned to his office where he poured himself a cup of coffee. He had just sat down at his desk when his father stepped in. Like Tom, his father was a doctor. He was also the hospital administrator.

"Hi, Pop, what's up?" Tom asked cheerfully. When he saw the expression on his father's face, he asked the question again, this time with foreboding rather than cheer. "What's up?" he repeated.

"This telegram just arrived. It was sent to you, though it concerns Rebecca."

"Bad news?" Tom's concern was even greater.

Without answering, the senior Dr. Whitman handed the telegram to his son.

POP SHOT AND KILLED TODAY STOP
FUNERAL WILL BE ON THE 17TH
STOP HOPE YOU AND BECCA CAN COME
STOP

DALTON

After reading the message Tom looked up toward his father. "Dad, I need to—"

"I know you do," his father answered before Tom could finish his request. Take as much time as you need, son."

When Tom stepped out into the street a little later, the air was cool, and the low-hanging, dark clouds held the threat of rain. It exactly matched his mood, and he dreaded taking the message to Rebecca. He hailed a hansom cab and as he was pulled through the streets of Boston, contemplated the best way to tell Becca.

"There is no best way," he muttered.

"Beg pardon, sir?" the driver asked.

"Nothing," Tom said, waving him away. "I was just talking to myself."

The driver chuckled. "Yes, sir. Lots of folks do."

After a drive of about half an hour, Tom stepped out of the cab in front of the brownstone on Huntington Avenue. Adjusting his collar and squaring his shoulders, he climbed the steps.

"Tom!" Becca said with a happy smile. "What are you doing home at this time of—" She paused in midquestion when she saw the expression on Tom's face. "Tom?" she said in plaintive tone. "What is it? You are frightening me."

Tom stepped to her and, opening his arms pulled her to him. "It's your father, Becca."

He didn't need to say any more, all he needed to do was hold her as she wept.

"We must go. Mom will need me," Becca said into his shoulder.

"I'll start making arrangements," Tom replied, holding her close to him.

"I wonder what happened?" Becca asked. "Papa was such a strong man, and he was healthy. You said yourself, Tom, that he was a healthy man."

"He was"—Tom hesitated for a long moment before he gathered the strength to tell her everything—"he was murdered, Becca."

"Murdered? Oh, my God, that's even worse!" Rebecca said. "Do they know who . . ."

"The telegram doesn't say. It just says that he was murdered."

"Oh, poor Ma. How she must feel."

Big Rock

Smoke and Sally had come to town, Smoke to make arrangements for the cars that would be needed to transport the fifty replacement horses, and Sally for no reason other than she wanted to go to town.

"We can meet in Longmont's in an hour," Smoke said.

It took less than half an hour for Smoke to make shipping arrangements with the railroad, and when he stepped into Longmont's, he looked around for Sally, even though he didn't expect her to be there yet. A few women were present, but Sally was not among them.

There was no condemnation of the women who frequented Longmont's because it was more of a club than a saloon. Longmont's was, in fact, the preferred meeting place for some of the local women's groups— the garden club, the library club, and the firemen's auxiliary that frequently met there for lunch.

Phil Clinton, editor of the *Big Rock Journal,* and Sheriff Monte Carson were with Louis at his private table, so Smoke walked over to join them. Louis had just finished with some tall tale, and the others were laughing.

"Louis, I should start printing your stories in my newspaper," Clinton said. "I could probably double my circulation."

"Smoke, join us," Sheriff Carson said. "How is Cal getting along? I guess he's getting a little antsy, not being able to move around."

"Ha, are you kidding? Cal's living like a prince now,

having his meals brought to him, listening to music on the music box, reading penny-awfuls."

"I don't suppose he'll be going back down to Texas with you and Sally then, when you deliver the horses."

"No, he won't, and that is bothering him. He was looking forward to going back. But we're going to leave Pearlie here to take care of him."

Louis laughed. "I'm sure Pearlie is looking forward to playing nursemaid to Cal."

"Oh, you don't have to worry about that," Smoke said. "Pearlie will get his pound of flesh once Cal recovers."

"Tell me, Smoke, have you heard anything else about your stolen horses?" Sheriff Carson asked.

"Not a thing. I must confess that I feel like a fool letting them get away from me. That's why I'm replacing the horses."

"Surely Conyers doesn't blame you for the loss," Clinton said.

"No, Jim has been very resolute in saying I'm not to blame, and the truth is, I'm probably not to blame, but I feel honor bound to do this."

"Here comes *Madame* Sally," Louis said.

At Louis' announcement, Smoke turned to see her, pleased that she had come so quickly. His being pleased turned to concern though, when he saw the expression on her face. He stood and walked from the table to meet her. "Sally, what is it? What's wrong?"

"Oh, Smoke, it's awful. It's just awful," Sally said, the tone of her voice matching the dread of her words. "I just saw Mr. Deckert out front."

Hodge Deckert was the Western Union telegrapher.

"He was about to come in and deliver this, but

when he saw me, he asked me to do it." Sally held out a little yellow sheet of paper. "I've already read it," she added.

"Oh, don't tell me Jim has changed his mind and doesn't want the replacement horses now," Smoke said, reaching for the telegram

JIM HAS BEEN MURDERED STOP
THOUGHT YOU SHOULD KNOW STOP
HOPE YOU WILL ATTEND FUNERAL AND
STAY AS OUR GUESTS STOP

JULIA CONYERS

"We should answer so they know we got the message," Smoke said.

"We did respond. I sent our condolences and assured them we would be there for the funeral," Sally said.

"Good," Smoke said. "I guess we had better get back to the ranch and tell the others. Also, we should make arrangements to be gone longer than we had originally planned. I'll arrange for Herman to draw some operating funds from the bank if it becomes necessary.

"Herman? I thought Pearlie would be staying behind," Sally said.

"Not now. I want Pearlie with me."

"Even so, we aren't going to be gone for a whole month, are we?" Sally asked.

"A month at least, and maybe even a little longer."

"You're going to try and find out who killed him, aren't you?"

"No, Sally, I'm not going to try." Smoke was quiet for a moment before he added, "I damn well *will* find out."

Sally reached out to lay her hand on Smoke's and gave him a quiet smile. "I thought you might."

CHAPTER TWENTY-FOUR

Denton, Texas

Del Catron and his business partner were having a beer in the Four Aces Saloon.

"The final head count is one thousand, five hundred, and thirty-seven."

"So how much will that be worth?" Catron asked.

"I'm afraid there will be nothing for the additional thirty-seven."

"What do you mean nothing for them? At twenty-five dollars a head, our agreed-upon price, they should be worth another nine hundred and twenty-five dollars. That's too much money to just walk away from," Catron said.

"Yes, but unfortunately we have only booked one thousand five hundred head. If you are dissatisfied with that arrangement, you can take the extra thirty-seven back and try to sell them. But, as they are Angus, which is quite a rare breed here, trying to sell them on the open market would be a very foolish thing to do."

Catron frowned. "So, what happens to them?"

"We will just have to throw them in as an act of goodwill."

"I don't believe in goodwill."

"In this case, I don't see that we have any choice. We can't afford to be exposed. And remember, it isn't just a matter of rustling now. Big Jim Conyers was also killed. And while I know you have used your gun before, Jim Conyers has long been one of the most important men in Tarrant County, indeed, in this area of Texas."

"His demise was unplanned," Catron replied. "Unfortunately he arrived on the scene at an inappropriate time, and as you well know, we were left with no choice."

"Nor do we have a choice in this. We booked fifteen hundred head, and we will be paid for fifteen hundred head. That's thirty-seven thousand five hundred dollars for you and your men."

"What is your cut from that?" Catron asked.

"You need not worry about my cut. I'll get my cut from the buyer."

Del smiled. "Thirty-seven thousand five hundred dollars. I'm sure my men will be pleased."

"Mr. Catron, if you continue to do business with me, I'm quite certain that I will be able to provide you with many more opportunities to make a lot of money. But you must work within the system. Don't get greedy, and above all, don't let your men get greedy."

"Should any avarice be exhibited by my men I shall bring them under control. You need have no concern. And, if you have another job like this one, I will be glad to make myself available."

"Gentlemen, we got thirty thousand dollars for the cattle," Catron said when he returned to their hideout with the money. "That's four thousand, two hundred and eighty-five dollars for each of us."

Catron failed to tell them that he had already taken seventy-five hundred dollars off the top.

"Four thousand dollars apiece? That's a lot of money!" Lattimore said excitedly.

"I suppose it is. Still, it don't seem like all that much money for that many cows," Jory Gibbons said.

"Mr. Gibbons, I believe you told me that you and your brother once worked as drovers, taking a herd of cattle from Texas to Kansas. How long did that take you?"

"Three months."

"And I believe you said that you were paid thirty dollars a month which means for ninety days of work, you received the princely sum of ninety dollars. Is that correct?"

"Yeah," Gibbons replied.

"When we acquired the cattle in our last job, how many days were we involved in the cattle drive from acquisition to our disposal of the herd?"

"How many days?" Gibbons laughed. "Hell, it warn't no days a-tall. We done the whole thing in just a few hours."

"So let me see if I can completely comprehend your dissatisfaction. As I understand it, you are disappointed because in your previous experience in dealing with cattle you were paid one dollar per day, but in our most recent enterprise you received four thousand two hundred and eighty-five dollars for less than one day of work. Is that an accurate appraisal of your dissatisfaction?"

"What the hell, Jory?" Dooley said. "Have you gone crazy or somethin'? If you don't like the money go back to workin' for a dollar a day 'n I'll take your money."

The others laughed.

"Uh, no, you've got me all wrong," Gibbons said with a big smile. "I like the money. I like the money a lot, 'n I ain't complainin' 'bout nothin'."

"That's good to hear," Catron said. "A well-satisfied crew makes for efficient operations."

Nobody was more satisfied than the Professor, who had taken away eleven thousand, five hundred dollars from that one job. In his former profession, it would have taken him nearly four years to earn what he had earned in no more than eight hours.

St. Louis, Missouri

Rebecca Whitman stared through the window as the train rumbled across the Mississippi River on Eads Bridge. She saw a majestic stern-wheeler riverboat passing underneath, its gaudy red and white paint scheme belying her own melancholy. It just didn't seem possible that her father, who actually was bigger than life, could be dead. He had always been there, a looming presence even though she now lived in Boston.

Tom was sitting beside her and he reached over to take her hand. "Are you doing all right?"

Rebecca squeezed his hand. "I'm all right. It's just hard for me to comprehend that he's gone."

Like her father, Dr. Tom Whitman was a big and powerful man. Several years ago, when his first wife died on the operating table, in fact *his* operating table, Tom had turned his back on medicine. Becca had met him when he went west to get away from the sorrow of losing his wife.

Neither she nor anyone else knew that Tom was not only a doctor, but one of the most highly regarded surgeons in the nation. Tom was passing himself off as a hired hand. Running away from everything, he was so determined to start a new life that for a while he was an ordinary cowboy. As it turned out, he'd functioned quite well as a cowboy, keeping his medical background a secret from everyone until an emergency situation forced him to reveal himself.

He saved the life of a woman who, but for him, would have died giving birth . . . on Christmas Eve. After that, Tom had no recourse but to admit that he was a doctor.

It was during this hiatus from medicine that he'd met, fallen in love with, and married Rebecca Conyers, the daughter of his employer, Big Jim Conyers. Becca returned to Boston with him so he could resume his medical practice. It had been a happy marriage, her bliss marred only by the devastating news of the death of her father.

"We'll be changing trains here, in St. Louis," Tom said.

"How long will we have between trains?"

Tom checked his tickets. "It looks like three hours."

"Good. That will give us time to walk around and see some of the city."

Half an hour later, having detrained and checked their baggage through for the next train, Becca and Tom were walking down Clark Street. Passing a small pastry shop, they paused and looked in through the window.

"I remember this place from the last time I was in St. Louis," he said. "You wait here. I'm going to get us a butter cake. That's a St. Louis specialty, and it is so good it will melt in your mouth."

"All right," Becca said. She knew that Tom was trying to cheer her up, and she loved him for it. She watched him go inside.

A minute later Becca's contemplation was interrupted by someone who spoke in a low, and gravelly voice. "Lady, you look like the kind of woman that's prob'ly got a lot of money in that bag you're carryin'."

She turned to see a man with long, tangled hair, and an unkempt beard. "What did you say?"

"I'm a-tellin' you to take your money out of that bag 'n give it me."

"Now just why would I want to do such a thing?"

The man reached into his pocket and pulled out a pistol. "On account of 'cause if you don't, you're goin' to get yourself shot. Now do what I say."

"Hello. Becca, who is your new friend?" Tom asked, coming from the bakery holding two small pastries.

"I don't know who he is, he didn't give me his name."

"Oh? Well let's find out, shall we? What is your name, sir?" Tom asked with a friendly smile.

"Are you two crazy?" the hairy-faced man asked, his face showing his shock at the unexpected reaction of the two. "Now quit your jabberin' 'n give me all your money. Both of you." He took in Tom with a little wave of his pistol.

"Would you hang on to these for me for a minute, dear?" Tom said, holding out the two little cakes. "I need to deal with this unpleasant gentleman, and I wouldn't want the butter cakes to get soiled."

The robber smiled. "Now you're makin' sense. You're goin' to give me the money."

"Oh, no, my good man. You're going to give me your gun," Tom said and before the would-be robber could react, Tom reached down and grabbed the hand that held the gun.

Reacting quickly, the assailant tried to pull the trigger, but Tom's hand prevented the cylinder from rotating and that locked the hammer so the gun couldn't be fired.

"I'm Dr. Tom Whitman," Tom said, speaking as calmly as if this were a casual meeting. "This is my wife, Rebecca, but of course, you two have already met."

Tom squeezed harder, and the gunman began to feel the pain. "Say hello to our new friend, Becca."

"Hello," she said with a smile.

Tom squeezed harder, and the pain was evident in the gunman's face.

"If you would let go of the gun, this unpleasantness could end now," Tom said. "If you don't let go, I'm afraid I will have to crush your hand, and if I do, you'll never be able to use it again. Now which shall it be?"

"I'll let go. I'll let go!" the gunman said, pleading his case.

Tom loosened his grip just enough for the gunman to relinquish his gun. "Well now, I would say that you've made a wise decision."

The gunman was cradling his hurt hand and moaning in pain.

Tom held the gun out and looked at it. "Hmm, a Webly WG forty-five-caliber pistol. Now that is a nice pistol. How much will you take for it?"

"What?" the gunman asked, and though his voice was strained by pain it also reflected his confusion.

"I'll give you twenty dollars for it."

"You . . . you'll pay me for it?"

"Indeed I will. I think with twenty dollars you might be able to get yourself cleaned up and get a job somewhere. Apparently you're not all that good at this one. So, what do you say? Is twenty dollars fair?"

"Yes, uh, yes, sir. It's fair. It's more 'n fair. Uh, I mean, considerin'."

Tom gave the man a twenty-dollar bill, and he took it hesitantly, as if afraid Tom might be laying a trap for him.

"Well, I guess our business is concluded here," Tom said. "Oh, wait. Before you leave, you must try one of the butter cakes. Give him one, Becca."

She held out the cake and the would-be assailant took it gingerly, still not certain that he wasn't about to be the victim of some plot. He took a taste of the cake and the look of confusion was replaced by an expression of pure joy. He wolfed the cake down.

"Oh, our new friend must be hungry. Give him the other one, too, Becca. We can go into the store and get two more."

Becca held out the second one.

The man took it without caution and said, "Jib."

"I beg your pardon?" Tom asked, confused by the word.

"My name. It's Jib. Jib Roundtree."

"Well, Jib, take your twenty dollars and go in peace," Tom invited. "Do try and stay out of trouble."

"Yes, sir, yes, sir," Jib said. "I'm goin' to get myself cleaned up 'n get me some clean clothes, then go back to workin' down at the river docks loadin' 'n unloadin' boats, which is what I done before."

Becca and Tom watched him scurry away.

"We've just enough time for me to get another butter cake," Tom said. "You really do need to try one."

Becca laughed. "Thank you, sweetheart. I needed that."

CHAPTER TWENTY-FIVE

With Smoke, Sally, and Pearlie

Once again it was necessary for Smoke to assemble a special train to transport the horses. Like their previous private train had been, it was not part of any schedule of the railroad lines on which it passed, and it was frequently shuttled aside in order to allow the scheduled trains to pass. Three times during the journey he had sent telegrams to Dalton to apprise him of his progress.

Because of the frequent delays, the train arrived in Fort Worth only one day before the funeral was scheduled, and immediately upon arriving, was diverted to a sidetrack. However, since the trip was complete, the sidetrack was more of a convenience than an inconvenience and Smoke actually welcomed the space and time it would allow for off-loading the horses.

When he stepped down from the car, he was met by Clay Ramsey and six riders from Live Oak.

"The last time we left the horses here overnight, half of them were stolen," Clay reminded Smoke. "We aren't going to take a chance on losing them this time."

"Good idea," Smoke agreed.

"I'm glad you were able to make it in time for the funeral," Clay said. "Where's Cal?"

"He's back home with three broken ribs," Pearlie answered.

"What? How did that happen?"

"He got kicked by a horse. One of your new horses in fact," Pearlie said with a smile.

"Well, how bad is he? He's not going to wind up crippled, is he?"

"I hope not. The doc says if he did something crazy, like trying to walk around before he's well healed, he could wind up permanently crippled. But I'm not all that worried about it. I mean, yeah, sometimes Cal does some real crazy things, but even he has better sense than to try and start movin' around before he's good 'n healed."

"I sure hope he pays attention to the doc."

"Clay, do you have any idea who killed Jim?" Smoke asked.

"I don't have any proof or anything but if you ask me I would say that it was the people that call themselves the Sidewinder Gang."

Smoke nodded. "Yes, I heard of them when I was here before and looking for the stolen horses. The headman of the gang is supposed to be the one they call the Professor, isn't he?"

"Yeah, that's what they say."

"What do you know about the Professor? What is his real background? From what I've heard, he's supposed to be quite good with a pistol."

"They say he's the best there is," Clay replied. "Though I've told ever'one who's took on about him so, they ain't no way he's as good as you. At least in my mind."

Smoke chuckled. "Thanks for the vote of confidence. By the way, is the sheriff working on it?"

"He is—but to be honest, Smoke, it seems to me like he's not doin' nothin' but runnin' around here like a chicken with his head cut off. Beg your pardon, ma'am," he added as Sally approached.

"No need to apologize, Mr. Ramsey," Sally replied with a smile. "I would say that is an apt use of a metaphor."

"By the way, Tom and Becca have already arrived," Clay said.

Sally smiled. "Good. I'm glad they were able to come," Sally said.

"We can go on out to the ranch now, if you want to. Andy and the others will take care of the new remounts."

Half an hour's easy ride brought Smoke and the others to Live Oak. As they rode up, Julia and Becca were waiting with others on the front porch for them. Sally went straight to Julia and the two women embraced.

"Uncle Smoke," Becca said throwing her arms around him. In this case *uncle* wasn't merely a token of affection. Rebecca was not only Big Jim's daughter, she was also the daughter of Smoke's late sister, Janie. Becca had been raised by Julia from the time she was an infant, and didn't learn of her biological mother, and thus her relationship with Smoke, until she was an adult.

Dr. Tom Whitman was standing behind Julia and Rebecca, and alongside Marjane and Tamara. Tom was dressed in the attire of a businessman, but those who had questioned the ability of an "Eastern dude" to defend himself had done so at their own peril. He stepped forward to shake hands with Smoke and Pearlie. "Cal didn't come?"

Smoke gave the same explanation to Tom that Pearlie had given to Clay earlier.

"The doctor is right on restricting Cal's mobility," Tom said. "With an injury like that, there is always the danger of paraplegia, which could be brought on by movement-induced trauma to the central nervous system, or cause additional damage at the level of the thoracic or lumbar vertebrae of the spinal cord, or lower."

Smoke laughed. "That was the doctor talking, not Tom, but from what I understand, you just said that Cal ought not do much moving around."

Tom nodded. "That's exactly what I'm saying."

"Well, I don't think there's a whole lot of danger of him doing that. I don't think I've ever known anyone who enjoys lying around as much as Cal does."

"Did you hear that Jim was murdered?"

"Yes, it was in the telegram."

"I wonder who could do such a thing," Tom said.

"I intend to find out," Smoke insisted.

Big Jim had been brought home from Ponder's Mortuary, and his body was lying in an open coffin in the parlor. Several area ranchers and their families had dropped by to pay their respects, but the visitors weren't limited to the area ranchers; many from the town had come out as well. Preston Miller was standing at the coffin looking down at Jim when Smoke stepped up.

Jim was wearing his best suit, and he was positioned in the coffin with his hands clasped in front of him, giving him a more natural-looking appearance than the formal stiffness of most bodies.

"Mr. Jensen, it's good that you could come," Preston said.

"I was coming back anyway," Smoke said. "But I hadn't expected to come back to this."

"I was wondering about your connection to Jim, but then I was told that you are the reason Live Oak Ranch has such a wonderful herd of Angus cattle."

Smoke shook his head. "No, that would be Duff MacCallister. Duff introduced Jim to the Angus, but Duff is a good friend, and I helped him deliver the herd. That was when I learned I had a family connection.

"Yes, I heard that his daughter was your niece."

"Mr. Miller . . ."

"Preston, please."

"Preston, I understand that fifteen hundred cows were taken and that they, like the horses that were taken before, just disappeared almost overnight."

"Yes, apparently that is the case."

"You're a horse and cattle broker. Do you have any idea as to how that could possibly happen?"

"It's obvious that the rustlers already had the horses

and cows booked so they could sell them all at the same time, but how they could do so has me stumped."

"I intend to find out who it was," Smoke said. "They didn't just steal some horses and cattle, they killed Jim. I don't intend to let them get away with it."

"Nor should they," Preston said.

"What do you know about the Sidewinder Gang?" Smoke asked.

Preston nodded his head. "I know that many people are suggesting they are the ones who did this."

"Would a gang of outlaws like that be able to pull off something like this? I mean steal horses and cattle and have them sold and delivered within a matter of a few hours?"

"Well the gang is led by the man they call the Professor, and he actually is, or was, a professor. So he is certainly smart enough to do something like this."

"But he would have to have some accomplices, wouldn't he?" Smoke asked. "He would need someone who had knowledge of what Jim's plans were, and someone who would be able to handle the sale of the cattle and horses."

"You mean someone like me or Drew Burgess or Larry Cantor."

"Exactly. If you don't mind, from time to time I'll be checking in with you," Smoke said. "Being as you are a livestock broker, you might pick up some information that could be useful. That is, if you wouldn't mind helping me out."

"Of course I don't mind," Preston said. "As you know, Jim was a very dear friend of mine, perhaps, my best friend. I would very much like to see justice done."

Smoke extended his hand and Preston took it.

"We'll work together," Smoke said.

Sugarloaf Ranch

Buster brought Cal his dinner from the cookhouse, and helped Cal sit up to eat.

"I'm getting awfully tired of staying here in the bedroom all the time," Cal said.

"Yes, but you know what the doc told you. And I'd believe him if I were you. I know a cowboy that was ridin' on the rodeo circuit who got busted up pretty much the way you are, 'n he wound up not bein' able to walk anymore. You don't want that to happen."

"No, I sure don't want that," Cal said as he began eating.

Buster chuckled as he watched Cal eat.

"What is it? What are you laughin' at?"

"You might be busted up some, but it sure hasn't hurt your appetite."

"I reckon I'll still be hungry ten days after I'm dead," Cal replied with a laugh.

As the two men ate together, Buster talked about his wife. "Emma Jean Malcolm was the prettiest girl I ever knew. I fell in love with her first time I ever saw her. She was engaged to Hayes then." He was quiet for a moment. "I can understand how Marv come to hate me. I mean we were good friends 'n I took his woman away from 'im. But how is it that his hate was so much that he killed Emma?"

"Where is Hayes now?" Cal asked.

"I don't know where he is, but I've got a feeling I'll

run across him again, someday. And when I do, I'm going to kill him. Or he'll kill me."

Boulder, Colorado

"Buster Crabtree? Oh yeah, sure, I remember him. Best bronc rider I ever saw."

Marvin Hayes was playing cards in the Miner's Pick Saloon, and a moment earlier he had asked if anyone had ever heard of Buster Crabtree.

"I remember Crabtree," said one of the other card player. "I used to see 'im a lot, but I ain't seen 'im in quite a while."

"Yeah, it ain't likely that you woulda seen 'im," the first speaker said. "On account of he left here about three months ago."

"Well, I'd really like to see Buster again," Hayes said. "Me 'n him is old friends. We used to ride in the cowboy competitions together, but I kind of lost track of 'im."

"You 'n him rode together? Are you as good as he is?"

Hayes laughed. "Well, I'm pretty good, but I'll be the first to admit that I'm not as good as my friend Buster is. Truth to tell, he's about the best rider I ever seen."

"Takes an honest man to admit somethin' like that. I can see why you 'n him might be good friends," the first speaker said. "When he left here, he told me he was goin' over to Red Cliff. You might find 'im there."

"Thanks," Hayes said. "I reckon I will see if he's there."

"Boys, the bet is five dollars," one of the players

said, smiling broadly as he examined the cards he was holding.

"Too much for me," Hayes said as he folded. He didn't care that he hadn't done well in the game, but that wasn't the reason he had joined it. Learning where to find Buster Crabtree was worth the few dollars he had lost. He planned to surprise his erstwhile friend and kill him.

CHAPTER TWENTY-SIX

Episcopal Church of the Transfiguration, Fort Worth

Coaches, carriages, surreys, buggies, buckboards, and wagons lined both sides of Houston Street for several blocks to either side of the church. Directly in front of the church was a glistening black hearse, appointed in silver and with clear glass sides. Attached to the hearse, a team of black horses with black funereal accoutrements stood patiently awaiting the moment they would be needed.

The three coaches directly behind the hearse were for the family. Because of his relationship to Rebecca, Smoke and Sally were included. Pearlie would be riding with the ranch hands of Live Oak, a position he considered to be an honor.

All stood as the six pallbearers—Clay Ramsey, Andy Dunlap, Roy Baker, Gene Finley, and Burt Rowe, all of whom were longtime riders for the brand, and Preston Miller—brought the closed coffin as the choir sang the requiem music of *Pie Jesu* from Faure.

They set the coffin on the catafalque in the middle of the crossing transept in front of the nave.

When the pallbearers were all seated, Rebecca and Tom stepped up onto the sanctuary and with a nod from Rebecca, the organist began to play. In beautiful harmony, Tom and Rebecca began to sing the words of Saint Thomas Aquinas.

> *Panis angelicus*
> *Fit anis hominum*
> *Dat panis coelicus*
> *Figuris terminum*
> *O res mirabilis*
> *Manducat Dominum*
> *Paupier, Paupier*
> *Servus et humilis*
> *Paupier, Paupier*
> *Servus et humilis*

Their beautiful rendition of the anthem was all the more meaningful because it was Rebecca's father who was being buried.

"I know it will be difficult for you, darling," Julia had told her when she asked Rebecca to sing. "But you know how much your father loved that song, and how much he loved to hear you sing it. I know he will look down from heaven with particular pride as you are singing."

"I will sing it with you," Tom had promised, and it was the thought of her father and the presence beside her of the man she so dearly loved, that enabled her to get through it.

Though applause would have been inappropriate, the many tears shed by the parishioners were evidence of their approbation.

Father Bill Pyron read from the scriptures, including Big Jim's favorite passage. "A reading from Corinthians. 'When the perishable puts on the imperishable, and the mortal puts on immortality, then shall come to pass the saying that is written: Death is swallowed up in victory. O death, where is your victory? O death, where is your sting?'"

Clay Ramsey stepped behind the ambo and cleared his throat before he spoke. "I want to put you in mind of a frightened skinny, twelve-year-old orphan boy, a boy who had never even seen his real parents and had known nothing but that orphanage for as long as he could remember. Now, imagine what's going through that boy's mind when a six foot, seven inch–tall man looks down at him and says 'Boy, I've made all the arrangements. You are going to come work for me.'

"I was that boy, and I was terrified. Here was a giant, and he was taking me away from the only home I had ever known. What was he going to do to me?

"Well, I'll tell you what he did to me. He fed me, he bought me clothes, he saw to my education, not just in school, but in all things I would need in life. I had never known my father, but with the Colonel, that never became a missing part of my life. When he made me foreman of Live Oak, it was the happiest day of my life . . . just as this is the saddest day of my life."

Clay paused for a moment, and it was obvious to everyone that he was fighting to regain his composure.

He cleared his throat, then continued, with his

voice breaking on the first word. "Whe . . . when the history of this great state, of this West, and of this nation is remembered in the last recorded syllable of time, Colonel James, 'Big Jim' Conyers will occupy a position of honor. Colonel, I don't know as I ever told you while you were alive, because it's something that's hard for a man to say to another man. But I'll say it now in front of God and all these witnesses. I loved you Colonel. With all my heart, I loved you."

Clay returned to his seat, and Andy reached up to put his hand on his friend's shoulder.

When the church rites were concluded, every employee of the ranch and more than two hundred people from town formed a funeral cortege that made the seven-mile trip from the Church of Transfiguration to the ranch. Once there, they gathered on a small rise near the big house where the grave had already been dug.

As the walnut coffin was taken from the hearse and placed on the ground near the open grave, Julia Conyers, in widow's weeds, held a silken handkerchief to her nose. Becca stood on one side of her with Tamara standing beside Becca. Dalton was on the other side of Julia, and Dalton's wife, Marjane, was standing beside him.

Tom couldn't help but notice that, just as it was on the day he had received that terrible telegram, the sky was heavy with dark clouds. It was as if heaven itself was providing a funeral pall for the interment. Fortunately the threatened rain had not yet materialized.

After the six pallbearers lowered the casket into the

ground, Father Pyron made the sign of the cross at the graveside. "Grant that our brother James Conyers, known to many as Big Jim, may sleep here in peace until you awaken him to glory, for you are the resurrection and the life. Then he will see you face-to-face and in your light will see light and know the splendor of God, for you live and reign forever and ever. Amen."

"Amen," the mourners repeated.

At Maria Ramsey's urging, Manny stepped up to the closed coffin and lay upon it a single yellow rose. He genuflected before he left the side of the coffin, then came back and stopped beside Dalton, who reached down to put his arm around the boy and pull him close.

Afterward, a reception was held in the big house with all the ladies of the town offering what comfort they could to Julia, Becca, and Tamara, who were receiving in the parlor.

Maria and Filipa had worked together in the kitchen, and the results of their labor could be seen in the dining room. The table was filled with viands for the mourners.

Smoke was standing to one side of the room talking quietly with Dalton. "If you don't mind, tomorrow I would like for you to take me out to where you found him. I want to have a look around there."

"All right. I'll be glad to take you. I have to tell you, though, there's nothing left to see. It has rained twice since then, and one of them was a pretty hard rain, so there are no tracks left."

"If nothing else, visiting the place will give me a feel of the lay of the land."

"Smoke, with no witnesses and all the tracks washed out, do you really think you can find who did this?"

"I don't just think I can, Dalton. I damn well know I *will* find who did this, and the ones I don't kill will hang."

"But that might take some time, and you have your own ranch to look after."

"Don't worry about that. I have good men who will take care of Sugarloaf in my absence, and that means I can take as much time as I need."

"I-I thank you for that, Smoke," Dalton said, his voice choking at the words.

Preston Miller approached the two men. "Dalton, again, I want to offer you my condolences, and let you know that I will work with you just as I worked with your father. I will follow through on the cattle I was able to book for Jim."

"Thank you, Mr. Miller. And I thank you for your friendship and for your business help."

"Mr. Jensen, you said that you might call upon me from time to time to see what help I could offer in bringing to justice the men who killed Jim. I would like nothing better than to see those men pay for what they did, but you don't think they would be dumb enough to try and sell them to me."

"Oh, I would hardly think so. But, you might—"

"Be able to track them," Preston interrupted when he realized where Smoke was going with his line of reasoning. "Yes, I'm in constant touch with brokers all over this part of the state. And you're right. The rustlers had to go somewhere with those horses and cows, and it could be that I'll hear about it."

"Yes!" Dalton said, enthusiastically. "You know what? I think we may wind up catching them after all."

In the bunkhouse the cowboys were a rather morose lot, many of them still wearing their best jeans and shirts. They sat or lay on their bunks.

"I'll tell you one thing," Dewey Gimlin said. "I've rode for five or six outfits, 'n I ain't never rode for no better a man than the Colonel was. I don't know what it's goin' to be like 'round here now, what with Dalton in charge."

"Dalton is a good man," Andy said. "Him 'n Clay has known each other forever, 'n Clay will be pretty much in charge just like it's always been. I don't look for there to be no real change, 'ceptin' we'll all miss the Colonel. Like Dewey said, he was as good a man as they's ever been anywhere."

"Hey, Boone," Bert Rowe said, calling out to the young cowboy who was lying on his own bunk, somewhat separated from the others. "How come it is that you didn't wear them real fancy boots of your'n to the funeral?"

"Why should I?" Boone Caulder replied.

"Why should you? 'Cause it was a funeral is why, 'n most generally folks gets dressed up as best they can when they go to a funeral."

"Yeah, well, you just don't worry any about my boots."

"Oh, I ain't worried none about 'em. Just wonderin' why you didn't want to wear 'em to the funeral is all."

"Death happens to everyone," Boone Caulder said. "There's no need to be carrying on about this one, as if he was your pa. Clay could feel that way, seein' as he had been with him since he was a boy. But there isn't a one of us who didn't work somewhere else before we came here."

"Boone, are you tellin' us that you was not upset to see the Colonel kilt?" Donnie Webb asked.

"No, I'm not saying that I'm not saddened. It's just that I don't understand the depth of grief all of you seem to be showing."

"You're a young man, Boone," Andy said. "I don't reckon you've done much so as to have an idea of what we're talkin' about. But you're likely to wind up ridin' for quite a few brands before it's all over, 'n when you do, you'll be able to look back on this, 'n you'll see the Colonel for the fine man that he was."

"Well, that is yet to be seen, isn't it?" Boone asked.

"Boone, can I give you a suggestion?" Andy said. "Don't be sayin' nothin' like that around Clay. You know what the Colonel meant to Clay, 'n if hears you talkin' like that, he ain't goin' to like it."

"I doubt seriously that he will fire me just because I'm not crying enough for him."

"I wasn't talking about firing you. I was talking about him beating you to a pulp."

"I am not afraid of Clay Ramsey."

"If you ain't a-scairt of Clay, then you ain't got no sense a-tall," Andy said.

He and the others walked away from Boone then, and continued to share their own memories of the man who had been so important in their lives.

Boone lay on his back with his hands laced behind his head, staring up at the ceiling. Did he have enough money to leave here and take Maggie with him?

Not yet, he answered himself. But the time would come when he would have, he was certain of that.

From the *Fort Worth Gazette:*

Titan of Tarrant County
Laid to Rest

James R. Conyers, Colonel of the late war, was buried within the very shadow of the house he built on his ranch in the county he helped to build.

On the 12th, instant, the man known by all as Big Jim was murdered, shot in the back by cowards who by their dastardly act have taken from our midst a man who was a leader, a builder, and a friend to all who knew him.

I have been made aware of the intention of one Kirby Jensen to find the murderers of this good man and to bring them to justice. Kirby Jensen, better known as Smoke Jensen, is a man known to be expert in the employment of a pistol, and better known as one who employs his pistol only for good. If the perpetrators of this vile murder should read these words, be warned that you will be found and made to pay for your crime. As editor of this newspaper I, BB Paddock, give this promise. I will, to the best of my ability, follow and report upon the search for these contemptable, scurrilous, back-shooters, and when Mr. Jensen finds them, as I know he will, we will all rejoice in justice being served.

CHAPTER TWENTY-SEVEN

Fort Worth

"I didn't really like him all that much but ever'one else who worked for him thought he hung the moon," Boone said.

"Yes, and not just the people who worked for him. If you read the story in the newspaper you would think he was some kind of a saint," Maggie said.

"He was just at the wrong place at the wrong time," Boone said.

"So what happens now?"

"Well, I don't expect there to be any major changes. Clay Ramsey will still be the foreman, and I suppose he will just keep on as we have before. Of course Dalton is now the owner of the ranch, but there's not a dime's worth of difference between the two men."

"It is important that you keep your job there and don't arouse any suspicions," Maggie said.

"Suspicions about what?"

"Suspicions about anything. What I mean is, if you ever are going to get away from the ranch, and I to get away from Lattimore, we have to keep everyone off guard. Then, when we have enough money and no one is expecting anything, we'll leave together."

"Where will we go?"

"You ever see orange trees growing, Boone?"

"No, I can't say as I have."

"Have you ever seen the ocean?"

"No," Boone replied.

Maggie smiled. "Then you are going to love California."

Sidewinders' hideout

"Who the hell is this Jensen fella, anyway?" Jory Gibbons asked.

Merlin Dawkins had just read the newspaper article to the others, partly because a couple of them couldn't read, and partly just for the convenience of everyone hearing the article at the same time.

"Don't you 'member? He's the one that Delaport come out here to tell us about."

"Yeah, he come out here, but he din't go back," Morris said with a laugh

"Smoke Jensen is someone who is well-known for his proficiency with a pistol," the Professor said.

"He's what?" Parker asked.

"He is very good with a gun."

"Is he better 'n you, Professor?" Dawkins asked. "I mean, you're supposed to be good, too, aren't you?"

Catron glared at Dawkins. "I don't know. Why don't you try me and see how good I am?" the leader challenged.

"What? No. Now, hold on there. You just hold on,"

Dawkins said nervously, holding his hand out. "You took that all wrong. What I was actual sayin' was, there ain't no way this Jensen feller is as good as you. Which is why I ain't worried none about 'im comin' after us."

"Which he most likely can't do on account of they don't nobody know we're the ones that done it, anyhow," Lattimore said.

"Except for one person," Dawkins suggested. "What if this Jensen feller gets to him, 'n he talks?"

"Why would he talk?" Gibbons asked. "He's makin' as much money as any of us."

"He's makin' more, seein' as he's on the inside, givin' us all the information," Parker said.

"When are we goin' to get another job like that last one?" Lattimore smiled. "This here's the most money I've ever had in my life 'n I wouldn't mind doin' somethin' like that again."

"As soon as it is practicable to do so, we'll be going back to the same well," the Professor said.

"What?"

"Soon, we will have another job like the last one," the Professor said.

Red Cliff, Colorado

Marvin Hayes spent three days in Red Cliff before he found anyone who knew anything about Buster Crabtree.

"Yeah, he hung around here for a week or so," an employee of the Red Cliff Livery said. "He was tryin' to get someone to ride agin 'im in some sort of bucking contest. Seems he's pretty good at it, 'n he wanted to make some money from it. But he couldn't get nobody to put up any money, so he finally left."

Hayes chuckled and shook his head. "Well, that's just like my old pard, makin' money from ridin' like that. I'll tell you this. Them's that wouldn't enter into a ridin' contest with 'im was smart, 'cause they saved their money. Buster woulda beat 'em for sure. There ain't nobody, nowhere, that's no better 'n him. But I'm havin' the devil's own time tryin' to catch up with 'im."

"What is you are lookin' for 'im for?" the groom said.

"Well, his mama has took some sick, 'n the family don't know how to get a hold of 'im, so they've asked me to try 'n find 'im."

"Well, I'm always kind of careful when I tell someone how to get a holt of someone else 'cause you can't never tell why it is they're a-lookin' for 'im. But in this case, I don't see no reason why I shouldn't tell you. He was askin' me about a town not too far away called Big Rock. I don't know for sure that's where he went, but if I was to make a bet on it, that's where I'd bet he went."

"Big Rock," Hayes said. "I thank you, 'n his mama thanks you."

"I hope you find 'im in time," the groom said as Hayes left for Big Rock.

Live Oak Ranch

When Smoke and Dalton walked out to the barn the next morning, they were met by Clay and Pearlie.

Seven had already been saddled, as had Dalton's horse.

"How far is it to where you found him?" Smoke asked as he swung into the saddle.

"It's about two miles northwest of here," Dalton said.

"What was he doing out there by himself?" Smoke asked as they started riding.

"It's my fault," Dalton said quietly.

"How is it your fault?"

"Pop came by to see me while I was out with a gather. He said he was going to just ride out to have a look at the keepers. I should have stopped him."

Clay chuckled. "Now, tell me, Dalton, do you really think you could have stopped him, even if you had tried?"

Dalton couldn't help but chuckle as well. "No, I don't reckon I could have."

"Then quit beatin' yourself up over somethin' you couldn't control."

"I guess you're right."

The four men rode on without speaking, the silence broken only by the clopping sound of hoofbeats.

"We found him right over there," Dalton finally said, breaking the silence and pointing toward a clump of live oak trees.

"Where exactly?" Smoke asked.

"When I found him, he was right here," Clay said when he dismounted a moment later. He pointed straight down to a spot on the ground. "He was face-down, 'n he had been shot three times in the back."

"What about the other two men? Where were they?"

"Over there, about thirty or forty yards away from where we found the Colonel."

"Then it would appear they weren't shot at the same time," Smoke said. "In fact if they were that far away, it's likely that Jim never even saw them."

"It was not only murder, it was cold-blooded murder," Clay said. "Neither the Colonel nor either of the other two were armed."

"I've changed that," Dalton said. "Starting the very day Pop was killed, I told everyone to be armed, either with pistols or long guns in a saddle sheath."

"That's a very good idea." Smoke dismounted and knelt down over the spot that had been pointed out to him as the place where Big Jim was found.

"Which way was he facing?" Smoke asked.

"Well, his head was here, and his feet were here," Clay said, describing a line with his hand.

"And was shot in the back, which means that his killers were somewhere over there within pistol range," Smoke said, pointing back toward the trees then walking in the direction he had pointed.

"Before the rain washed them away there were tracks here," Dalton said, following Smoke. "Cattle, and shod horses."

"How many horses were there? Were you able to tell?"

"We found tracks for five at least, but there could have been a few more."

"I wonder where they were going," Pearlie said.

"One thing for sure, they weren't takin' the cows

to Fort Worth," Clay said. "There's no way to get to Fort Worth from here without crossin' over Live Oak."

"Yes, well, where could they go with them in Fort Worth anyway?" Dalton asked. "There are only three livestock brokers in Fort Worth, Preston Miller, Drew Burgess, and Larry Cantor of Trinity River Livestock Company. And since we're the only ones in Tarrant County raising Angus, any of the three of them would get suspicious right away if someone other than Live Oak came to them with Angus."

"Yeah, I guess you're right."

"Hey, what's this?" Pearlie called. He had been walking all over the area, searching the ground for anything he might find. He held up a little piece of silver. "Looks like one of those Indian things."

"You're right. It is an Indian totem," Smoke said after closer look at the little piece of silver. "It's a thunderbird."

"Good Lord, are you saying it might have been Indians?" Dalton asked. "We haven't had any Indian problems here within my lifetime, certainly none that I can remember."

"It could be Indians," Smoke said. "But if it is, I'm sure it would be nothing but a bunch of renegades, no actual Indian involvement. But Indians can go bad just like white men." He examined the little piece of silver more closely. "However, Indians would have an even more difficult time getting rid of the cattle. No, it's much more likely this came from some white man, from his saddle, boot, belt, or something."

"Boot?" Clay asked, reacting to Smoke's suggestion.

"Yes." Smoke chuckled. "You wouldn't find it on a work boot. It's more of a fancy boot thing."

"Dalton, Boone Caulder has a pair of boots with somethin' like that on 'em," Clay pointed out.

"He does? Hmm, I've never seen them."

"That's 'cause he only wears them when he gets fancied up to go into town or something."

"Where was Boone on the day Big Jim was killed?" Smoke asked.

"Oh, don't get me wrong, I'm not accusin' Boone of anything," Clay said. "Anyhow, he was with Andy Dunlap out in the eastern range the day the Colonel was killed."

"Let's go talk to Andy," Dalton suggested.

"Why are you asking me that, Clay?" Andy replied when Clay and the others came to question him. "You know where he was that day."

"Yes, he was with you, we just need . . ."

Andy shook his head. "No, he wasn't with me."

"What do you mean he wasn't? Where was he?" Dalton asked, surprised by the response.

"It's like I said, Clay knows where he was."

"Andy, why are you saying that I know? If he wasn't with you, how am I supposed to know where he was?"

"Clay, you sent him off somewhere to do an errand for you, don't you remember?" Andy asked.

"What?" Clay shook head. "I did no such thing. Why would you say that?"

"Because that's what Boone told me when he said

he needed to take some time off. He said you had an errand for him to run."

"Are you talking about the day the Colonel was killed?" Clay asked.

"Yes, that's exactly the day I'm talking about. He came out to where we were, wearin' those fancy boots of his, 'n he said he had to go to town to run an errand for you."

"Are you sure he was wearing his fancy boots?" Smoke asked.

Andy grinned. "Oh yeah, and I wasn't the only one who seen 'em. Dub Wilkerson seen 'em, too. He's the one that pointed 'em out to me."

"What time was that?" Smoke asked.

"He left really early that morning, just as the rest of us was startin' in to work. And now that I think about it, I didn't see him again until very late that day. Of course, he could've come back earlier, but bein' as the Colonel had just been kilt, things got a little confusin' for us for the rest of that day," Andy said. "So he could 'a come back some earlier 'n I wouldn'ta knowed nothin' 'bout it."

Dalton frowned. "I hate to say this, but we've been wondering how they knew just when and where to hit us. Like the horses, for example. Did the rustlers just happen on to them, or did they know when they would arrive and where they would be?"

"Same thing with the cattle," Clay said. "They knew what part of the range we were holding our keepers on. And if the Colonel hadn't happened to just ride out that way, they would have gotten away clean."

"As it turns out, they did get away with the cattle,

though you couldn't say they got away clean, because they killed Pop, and Alford, and Butler," Dalton said. "I wish they had gotten away clean, then Pop would still be with us."

"I ain't exactly makin' no accusations or nothin' like that, but, Clay, you're a-sayin' that you didn't give him no chore to do on the day he was supposed to be workin' with me?" Andy asked.

"That's what I'm saying," Clay said.

"I wonder why it is that he told me you did?"

"So, as it turns out there's a long period of time during the day when we don't know where Boone Caulder was," Smoke said. "And we know that he wears a pair of fancy boots that might have this little decoration." He held out the piece of silver Pearlie had found. "Andy, you said he was wearing his fancy boots the morning he came to tell you that Clay was sending him on an errand. Did you happen to notice if either one of his boots was missing this little thing?"

"Oh, no sir. They wasn't either one of 'em a-missin' that little thing 'cause I specially remember seein' 'em both there. Fact is, after he rode off me 'n Dub talked about them little things, wonderin' exactly what they was called."

"It's called a thunderbird," Smoke said.

"Here's somethin' else," Andy added. "Boone was gone on the night them horses was stoled, too. He didn't get back to the bunkhouse till early the next mornin'."

"Damn, it's not looking very good for Boone, is it?" Clay said.

"Dalton, Clay, tell me what you know about Boone Caulder," Smoke said.

Dalton sighed and shook his head. "I sort of hate to tell you, I mean, considering what we're talking about now, and considering the way everything is piling up on him, because it will look bad. I believe everyone ought to get a second chance. Pop believed that, too, and that's why he gave Boone a second chance."

"Why did he need a second chance?" Smoke asked.

Dalton hesitated for a moment before he responded. "Boone came here from Arizona, and while he was out there, he and another man were taking a hundred cows to market for the man they were working for. They never got there, claiming that that they had been held up and the cattle stolen from them. It turns out they sold the cows themselves, and Boone was charged with larceny after trust. He wound up serving two years in prison, and when he got out he found that he could no longer get a job in Arizona. That's when he came here."

"How did Jim know about that?" Smoke asked. "I mean, if he stole those cows and went to prison in Arizona, it wouldn't likely be common knowledge here, would it?"

"When Boone came to ask for the job, he said, right away, that he had just served time in Arizona, and he told Pop exactly why he had gone to jail."

"Yes, I remember the Colonel talking to me about it," Clay said. "He was impressed with Boone's honesty in tellin' the truth about himself. That was one of the reasons he hired him."

"So, the Colonel was impressed with Boone's honesty, was he? Well, Boone wasn't all that honest with me, was he?" Andy asked. "He lied when he said that you were sending him into town. And if he didn't go into town to get something for you, where was he on the day the Colonel was killed?"

"I don't know," Clay answered in a quiet, concerned voice.

"Gentlemen, I suggest that we find Mr. Caulder and get to the bottom of this," Smoke said.

CHAPTER TWENTY-EIGHT

When Smoke, Dalton, and Clay stepped into the bunkhouse half an hour later, a couple of men were playing blackjack on one of the bunks, a few others were in conversation, and one man was reading a book. Boone Caulder was stretched out on the bunk with his hands laced behind his head.

"That's Boone down there," Clay said.

The three men approached his bunk.

"Hello, Boone," Clay said.

Looking up, the expression on Boone's face changed from curiosity to concern. He swung his legs over the edge of the bunk and sat up. "What is it? What do you want?"

"We want to ask you a few questions," Dalton said.

"Questions about what?"

"For one thing, on the day Pop was killed, you were supposed to be working with Andy. But Andy says that you left."

"Andy said it would be all right."

"We spoke to Andy," Clay said. "He told us the

reason he let you go was because you told him I had said that I wanted you to go to town for me."

Boone didn't reply.

"Is that what you told him?"

After another beat of silence, Boone finally answered in a voice so subdued his response was barely audible. "Yeah, that's what I told 'im."

"You know damn well I didn't ask you to do anything for me. Why did you lie to Andy?"

"Because I needed to go somewhere. Look, I know it was wrong of me lyin' like that, 'n I'm willin' to work extra in order to make up for it."

"Where did you go?"

"I had some business that needed to be took care of."

"Where did you go, Boone?" Dalton asked.

"I'd rather not say."

"Caulder, I want you to think about this very hard. It is important that you tell us where you were, and it would help if you could give us a witness who would say you were where you say you were," Smoke said.

"What for? I admitted that I lied to get off, so what else do you need to know? And what difference does it make where I was?"

"Have you ever seen this before?" Smoke asked holding out the little silver thunderbird device Pearlie had found on the ground near where Big Jim had been killed.

Boone gasped in surprise.

"Have you seen this before?" Smoke repeated.

"I-I'm not sure."

"Where are your boots, Boone?" Clay asked.

"What boots?"

"What boots?" Clay responded. "Boone, you know damn well what boots. You've been showing them off to everyone, making sure everyone saw all the silver. I'm pretty sure one of those little silver doodads looked just like this, didn't it?"

"Where did you find that?"

"Before I answer that question, I would like to see the boots."

"Clay, what's this all about? Why do you want to see my boots, and why are you asking me all these questions?"

"We want to see your boots to see if you are missing a thunderbird."

"I, uh, don't have my boots right now," Boone replied.

"Why not? Where are they?"

"I'm not sure. I seem to have misplaced them."

"For crying out loud, Boone. I was told that you paid thirty-five dollars for those boots. That isn't the kind of thing that you just misplace," Clay said.

"Where were you?" Dalton asked again.

"Where was I when?"

"Don't play games with us, Caulder." Smoke said. "You said you had some personal business to take care of, but by your own admission you lied to get away."

"Yes, but what has that got to do with my—" Boone started to ask. "Wait a minute. This all happened on the day the Colonel was killed, didn't it?"

"Now do you see why are interested?" Smoke asked.

The expression on Boone's face had passed through the stages of agitation, curiosity, and concern. Suddenly, it was registering pure panic.

"We found this little piece of silver at the scene, just like the silver on your boots," Clay said, having taken over the interrogation.

"Y-you found that piece where the Colonel was killed?" Boone asked in quiet voice.

"Is it from one of your boots?"

"No."

"You could clear it up by showing us your boots or telling us where you were," Clay said. "Where did you go?"

"I-I can't tell you where I was."

"Why not?"

"I . . . I just can't. I promised I would never tell."

"Promised who?"

"I can't tell you that."

"Boone, whoever rustled the cattle also killed the Colonel. And whoever stole the cattle had to have some inside connection."

"What the hell? Clay, Mr. Conyers, Mr. Jensen, you all don't think I killed the Colonel, do you?"

"Did you or did you not serve time in prison for stealing cattle from the man you worked for?" Clay asked.

"Yeah, I did," Boone replied in a weak voice. "But Clay, I was up front with the Colonel about that when I come to work here. I was young then, 'n I made a mistake. I didn't kill the man I was workin' for then 'n I damn sure didn't kill the man I was workin' for now. Also, I'm tellin' you, I didn't have nothin' to do with stealin' the Colonel's cows."

"You could clear it all up by showing us your boots or telling us where you were," Smoke said.

"Open your trunk," Dalton ordered.

"You got no right to look into my trunk."

"I own this ranch, Caulder, and that means I own the horse you ride, I own this bunkhouse, I own this bunk, and I own this trunk. Now you open it, or I'll have someone open it with a hatchet," Dalton said.

Reluctantly, Boone opened the trunk. Clay started removing the contents of the trunk, but he found no boots.

"No boots here, Dalton."

"Where are they, Caulder?" Dalton asked.

"I told you, I seem to have misplaced them."

"Wait a minute." Dalton picked up a cloth bag from the bottom of the trunk, and when he opened it, he saw a large roll of money.

Sugarloaf Ranch

"Cal, I'm about to go into town," Herman said, "but Buster will still be out here to take care of you. Anything I can get you from town?"

"Yes, how about stopping by Nancy's Bakery and picking up some o' those peach scones she makes?"

"Well, now, here we all thought you were about to die, but you're a-wantin' some peach scones," Herman teased. "I guess we'll have to put up with you for a while longer."

"Oh, and can you help me out onto the chair on the front porch? I mean, wound up as tight as I am in the bandage I can barely move, much less walk. It gets stuffy staying cooped up in here all day."

"I s'pose I could, but no better 'n you're able to get around I'd better get Buster to help me."

A moment later, Herman got on one side of Cal and Buster the other side, then the two men started helping Cal. He felt several sharp pains in his side every time he moved, but finally, after much effort and many gasps of pain, he was ensconced in the rocking chair on the front porch.

"I hope you're satisfied there, for a while," Herman said. "I don't think I've got it in me to move you again, at least, not right away."

Cal chuckled. "To tell you the truth, boys, I know I don't have it in me to move again for a while. That took a lot more out of me than I thought it would."

"I'll be in the barn," Buster said as Herman rode off. If you need me, just give a call out."

"I'll be fine here, thanks," Cal replied.

Herman Nelson had gone into town to pick up some new bridles from Murchison's Leathergoods Store, but when he got there, Tim told him he had a few things to do with them before they were ready, so Herman stepped next door to Longmont's to have a beer while he was waiting.

"Herman, have you heard anything from Smoke?" Louis asked.

"Cal got a letter saying that the funeral was nice 'n all, but that they're goin' to stay down there a while longer to see if they can find out who did it."

"*Pitié pour l'homme qui a tué l'ami de Smoke,*" Louis said.

"What was that?"

"I said I feel sorry for the man who killed Smoke's friend," Louis said. "Oh, wait. I was talking about you just a moment or two ago."

"You were talking about me?" Herman asked.

"Well, not you, exactly, but about the ranch and Buster Crabtree."

"What about Buster?"

"There's someone here who is looking for him. Monsieur Johnson," Louis called out to one of the saloon patrons.

Louis had to call the name out twice because Marvin Hayes didn't answer to it the first time.

"Yeah?" Hayes answered.

"The man you're looking for is working out at Sugarloaf Ranch. This is Herman Nelson. He works there, as well."

"Is Buster out there now?" Hayes asked.

"Yes, why are you looking for him?"

"I have some news for him about his mother," Hayes said, using the same story that had worked so well before.

"What is it? I'll tell him."

"She asked me to tell him personally. She's a fine old lady, and I don't know how much longer she has left. I think I'd better do what she asked me to do."

"All right, sure. Go on out there."

"How do I get there?"

"Go on down Front Street till you get to the depot, then turn right across the railroad. That'll be Jensen Avenue. Follow it for a few miles and it ends at Sugarloaf. If you don't see Buster right away, ask Cal about him. When I left, Cal was sittin' on the front porch, 'n as stoved up as he is, he'll still be there. He can't even move without lots of help."

"Thanks," Hayes replied.

Sugarloaf Ranch

After Herman left for town and Buster went back to working in the barn, Cal was left alone on the front porch. He tried to rock, but a shooting pain through his side stopped him. "Damn, as long as I'm just going to be sitting here doing nothing, I should've had one of them bring me a cup of coffee before they left," Cal said aloud.

He thought about Smoke, Sally, and Pearlie. He heard Smoke say that he was going after whoever it was that killed Big Jim. Cal wished he wasn't hurt. He would give anything to be with them at Live Oak. It didn't matter that they didn't have any idea who killed Big Jim. Cal knew Smoke well enough to know that he would find out who did and it would just be a matter of time until the killer was brought to justice.

Cal had been sitting out on the porch for a little over an hour when he saw a rider coming up Jensen Avenue. At first he thought it was Herman, and he was glad, because he was in quite a bit of pain from sitting so long and he wanted to go back in and lie down for a while. It would take Herman and Buster both to move him.

As the rider got closer, though, Cal saw that it wasn't Herman. It wasn't anyone Cal had ever seen before. Whoever it was may not have intended to come to Sugarloaf but Jensen Avenue ended here so he had no choice.

The rider came through the gate and all the way up the long entry road, then stopped just in front of the porch and no more than a few feet from Cal.

"Tell me, is this here what they call Sugarloaf

Ranch?" There was something in the man's demeanor and in the tone of his voice that was off-putting.

Over the years Cal had spent with Smoke and Pearlie, he had learned from them to read people, and he didn't like what he was reading in this man.

"Yes, just like it says on that arch you passed under when you came riding up here," Cal replied.

"Good, that's good. I'm told there's a man working here by the name of Buster Crabtree. Is that right?"

"Who wants to know?" Cal said.

The man smiled, though the smile didn't reach his eyes. "Well now, is that any way for you to be treating a guest?"

"Mister, you're not a guest unless you are invited, and you weren't invited. Now I'm going to ask you again, why is it that you're looking for Buster?"

The man pulled a pistol from his holster. "You just let me worry about that. *Buster! Buster Crabtree, where are you, you wife-stealing thief?*"

"I'm right here, Hayes," Buster said, coming out of the barn.

Dismounting, Hayes started toward Buster.

"I never thought I would see you again, not after killin' my wife, like you done," Buster said.

"What makes you think I'm the one that done it?"

"Because she didn't die right away. She wrote your name," Buster said. "She left a note telling me who killed her."

"She called out your name, you know that?" Hayes asked. "All she had to do to save her life was come with me, but she wouldn't do it. When she seen that I was about to shoot her, she called out your name."

"I've been looking for you ever since," Buster said.

"Have you now? Well you've found me." Hayes laughed. "Actually I guess you could say that I found you. I can't have you out there, dogging me for the rest of my life, which is why I decided to come after you. And here you are."

"You do see that I'm not wearing a gun, don't you?" Buster said.

Hayes laughed, a high-pitched, insane-sounding laugh. "Yeah, well, you know what? Emma Jean wasn't wearing a gun, either."

"So you're planning on killing me, are you?" Buster asked.

"Oh, yes. I'm goin' to kill you, and then I'm goin' to kill that gimpy cowboy on the porch. And since neither one of you have a gun, it's goin' to be as easy as takin' candy from a baby."

Buster smiled. "Maybe not as easy as you think."

Hayes's easy, confident smile faded and he got a look of confusion on his face. "What are you talkin' about?"

"You tell him, Cal," Buster said.

Hayes shook his head. "Uh-uh. You ain't goin' to get me to fall for that old trick."

"What if it isn't an old trick?" Cal said from behind him. "What if it turns out that the gimpy cowboy on the porch has a gun?"

"What?" Hayes shouted, spinning around, pulling the trigger as he did so.

Cal let Hayes get all the way around and pull the hammer back to shoot a second time before he shot.

Cal's bullet plunged into Hayes's heart, killing him before he fell.

"I saw you comin' out here, and didn't know how long I could keep him talking," Buster said.

Cal looked at Buster with a pained expression on his face, then he collapsed.

"Oh, my God! Cal! Are you hit?"

CHAPTER TWENTY-NINE

Tarrant County Jail

"Two thousand, one hundred forty-two dollars and fifty cents," Sheriff Maddox said as he finished counting out the money that was in the cloth bag found in Boone's trunk. "Where did you get the money, Caulder?"

"I saved it."

"Boone, even if you had not spent one penny in all the time you were working out at Live Oak, you would not have saved as much money as there is in this bag." The sheriff picked up a ledger book Dalton had handed him a moment earlier.

"Big Jim Conyers kept very accurate records as to every cent that you have received since you started working at Live Oak, and according to those records, you have been paid a total of one thousand and forty dollars. You expect us to believe that you have saved over two thousand dollars?"

"I've made a little extra money, now and then."

"By giving the rustlers the information they need

in order to steal the horses and the cattle?" Sheriff Maddox asked.

"Who are you working with, Boone?" Smoke asked.

"I ain't workin' with nobody."

"I understand there is a man down here they call the Professor."

"Who?"

"The Professor. I heard about him when I was looking for the stolen horses. It is said that he has put together a gang he calls the Sidewinders. Have you ever heard of them?"

"I -I uh . . ." Boone stuttered.

"Caulder, you are in a lot of trouble," Sheriff Maddox said. "You had better tell us what we want to hear."

"I-I want to see a lawyer."

"Yes, I think you definitely need one," Sheriff Maddox said.

Sugarloaf Ranch

"He's lucky he didn't paralyze himself for life, walking out there like he did," Dr. Parnell said.

"I feel responsible for him, Doc," Buster said. "If it hadn't been for me, he would have never left the porch. He saved my life."

"And according to Cal, he saved his own life as well," Herman said. "Johnson was going to kill both of you."

"His name wasn't Johnson. It was Hayes," Buster corrected.

"Yeah, I forgot. In town, he told me his name was Johnson."

"How is Cal, Doc?" Buster asked.

"Well, you were both right to leave him alone until I got out here to stabilize him. If you had tried to pick him up right away, he would have been paralyzed."

"The way he fell, I thought he had been shot."

Dr. Parnell shook his head. "It is an absolute miracle that he was able to move at all, let alone stay on his feet for as long as he did."

"He stayed on his feet for just as long as he needed to," Herman said.

"Miz Sally," Cal mumbled.

"What?"

"Miz Sally," he said again.

"Miss Sally is down in Texas with Smoke," Herman said.

"Miz Sally," Cal repeated.

"Herman, if you know how to contact Mrs. Jensen, I would suggest that you do so. Cal needs every advantage if he is going to come through this, and having her here would be a great help."

"I'll send her a telegram today," Herman said.

The White Elephant Saloon, Fort Worth

The White Elephant reminded Smoke of Longmont's in that it was considerably upscale as far as saloons go. The bar was gleaming mahogany, the bar rail was brass, and polished every day. Three gilt-edged mirrors hung on the wall behind the bar, and every table was surrounded by four, red-cushioned chairs.

At the moment, Smoke, Dalton, Tom Whitman, and Preston Miller were sitting at one of the tables. Smoke and Dalton were drinking beer, Tom and

Preston were drinking brandy. Pearlie, Clay, and Andy were there, as well, but they were standing at the bar.

"I told Jim when he hired that man that he was making a mistake," Preston said. He sighed and took a swallow of his brandy before he spoke again. "I should have been more forceful with him. Perhaps if I had been, Jim would still be alive."

"Mr. Miller, it would appear to me as if you have convicted Boone Caulder before he has had his day in court," Tom said.

"Well, Doctor, you have only but to look at his past," Preston said. "He served two years in prison. And do you know why he served those two years? He served them for rustling cattle from the very man he was working for. Could it be, perhaps, that he has established a pattern?"

"Technically, it was larceny after trust." Tom waved his hand. "Though, admittedly, that is just a technicality. And, I must admit, the evidence we have against him does seem quite damning."

"I do wish we had something more substantial than an unaccounted-for wad of money," Dalton said.

"Wad is right," Preston said. "He had over two thousand dollars, which by your own books is almost twice as much as he has been paid in the whole time he has worked with you."

"Yes, the question is, where did he get all that money?" Dalton said.

"I understand he won't tell where he got the money," Tom said.

"No, he won't," Dalton said.

"Well, it's obvious where he got the money, isn't

it?" Preston asked. "It looks to me like this money is his cut from stealing the horses and the cows. They had to have an inside man, and that would be Boone Caulder."

"I might be able to believe that he was in on the stock rustling," Dalton said. "Like you said, he has a history of having done that before. But I just can't believe that he had anything to do with killing Pop."

"What you have to understand, Dalton, is that if he was part of the overall felony, that of stealing the horses and cattle, then he is also guilty of murder whether he pulled the trigger or not," Preston said.

"Is that right? I mean even if he didn't actually shoot Pop, he would still be guilty of killin' 'im just because he was part of the robbery?"

"If he was present on the scene when Jim was actually shot, then yes, he and everyone present at the time is technically guilty, no matter who did the shooting."

During their discussion Smoke noticed a smallish man, bald-headed and wearing glasses, standing at the bar. He seemed to be studying the table where Smoke and the others were sitting.

"Dalton, do you know that man at the bar?" Smoke asked. "He's the bald-headed one with glasses, and wearing a green shirt."

"No, I don't think I do," Dalton said. "Why do you ask?"

"He seems very interested—" Smoke didn't finish his answer. He didn't have to. The bald man at the bar, perhaps realizing that he was center of attention, started toward the table.

"Aren't you Mr. Conyers?" the man asked Dalton.

"Yes, I'm sure you are. I saw you at your father's funeral."

"Yes, I'm Dalton Conyers."

The man smiled. "Good, good. I was hoping it was you. The thing is, I'm not sure what I should do right now."

"I beg your pardon? Do about what?"

"I heard that Boone Caulder is in jail."

"Yes, he is, but how does that effect you?"

"My name is Lonnie Truax. I own the Boots and Saddle Shop. And the thing is, Mr. Caulder left some boots with me 'n they're ready for 'im to pick up, but with him bein' in jail, I don't know what to do with them."

"Work boots?" Smoke asked.

Truax chuckled and shook his head. "Oh, no sir. I don't reckon anyone would ever wear these boots to work in. They're much too pretty for that."

"Is there a bill due?" Dalton asked.

"Well, yes sir, there is. It comes to seven dollars and fifty cents."

"Whoa, that's a lot of money, isn't it? You can buy a whole pair of boots for five dollars."

"Not like these, you can't. Anyhow the work is only a dollar. It was the silver that cost so much."

The four men at the table—Smoke, Dalton, Tom, and Preston—looked at each other.

"I'll tell you what, Mr. Truax, as Boone Caulder is my employee and, as you said, he is currently in jail, I'll take the responsibility for paying the bill and picking them up. Can I do so now?"

"Sure. I'd better go back to the shop with you,

though. Mr. Puddle is there now, and he might not want to give the boots to you."

Smoke and Dalton followed Truax down to his Boots and Saddle shop, the little bell on the door tingling as it was opened.

"Be right with you," someone called from the back of the shop.

"It's all right, Mr. Puddle, it's me," Truax replied. "Go ahead with what you're doing." Truax took the boots from the shelf and put them on the counter.

They were trimmed with a white filigree and within the swirls at the top of the boot shank were little silver decorative pieces on each side of each boot.

Smoke removed the silver thunderbird from his pocket and held it up against the decorative silver piece in the boot. It was a perfect match.

"Oh, my," Truax said. "I didn't know he had the thunderbird accoutrement. It would have been much cheaper for him if he had brought it with him when he brought the boots in."

"By the way, when did he bring the boots in?" Smoke asked.

"That would be Friday, the seventh. I've marked it on the bill," Truax said.

"Pop was killed on the twelfth, five days later." Dalton paid the bill, then he and Smoke carried the boots down to the sheriff's office.

"What have you there?" Sheriff Maddox asked.

"These boots belong to Caulder," Dalton said, showing them. "Take a look at the silver decoration. Smoke, show him."

He pulled the little silver thunderbird from his pocket and showed it to the sheriff.

"We found this where Pop was killed. We just picked up these boots from the Boots and Saddle Shop. Mr. Truax says Boone Caulder brought them to him to have this very piece replaced, and he brought them in two days after Pop was killed."

"Dalton, I would say that you just put the noose around Caulder's neck," the sheriff said.

"Wait," Smoke said.

"What? What is it?" the sheriff asked now.

"If Boone Caulder was there, we know he wasn't alone. Perhaps if you offer him a deal, he will tell us who the others were. The thought of a hangman's noose is a pretty good way of loosening the tongue."

"Yes," Sheriff Maddox said. "I've seen that work before."

"Let's go talk to him."

Boone was lying on his bunk, and he looked up when Sheriff Maddox, Dalton, and Smoke Jensen went back to his cell.

"Have you seen these before?" Dalton asked, showing Boone the boots.

"They're my boots. Thanks for picking them up for me. I'll pay you back when I get out of here and my money is returned."

"What makes you think you're going to get out of here?" Sheriff Maddox asked. "I would say you are soon to have a hangman's noose put around your neck."

"I didn't do it!" Boone said.

"Caulder, there is a way you could avoid being hanged," Smoke said.

"How?"

"By telling us who the others are that were involved," Sheriff Maddox said.

"Lord, I wish I could, but I don't know who was involved because I wasn't there," Boone said. "I'm telling you, I didn't kill the Colonel!"

"We'll give you some time to think about it between now and your trial," Maddox said.

CHAPTER THIRTY

Live Oak Ranch

"I'm not as convinced that Boone Caulder is guilty as the rest of you seem to be," Tom Whitman said as he, Dalton, and Smoke sat in the parlor that afternoon, discussing their visit to the jail.

"Why not?" Dalton asked. "I mean, we found that silver thunderbird where Pop was killed. And Boone had all that money on him. Where did he get the money?"

"I admit that it looks very bad for him," Tom said. "But it just doesn't feel right to me."

"What do you think, Smoke?" Dalton asked.

"I don't know."

"You don't know? Smoke, I thought you were more convinced than anyone," Dalton said.

"Why didn't he talk?" Smoke asked. "Why didn't he tell us who the others were?"

"Because he was probably afraid," Dalton said. "Most people think it might have been Del Catron, and Boone is afraid that if he talks, Catron will kill him."

Smoke chuckled.

"What is it? What's funny?"

"If he doesn't talk, it is a lead-pipe cinch that he's going to hang. Seems to me like that would be the greater danger for him."

"Yeah," Dalton said. "Yeah, I hadn't looked at it like that. All right. I don't know why he won't talk, but I'm totally convinced he's guilty.

Sally came into the parlor. "Smoke?" Something in the way she spoke his name alerted him.

When he looked toward her the expression on her face caused him even more concern. "Sally, what is it?" Smoke set his coffee cup down and stood up to go toward her.

"Oh, Smoke, it's Cal," Sally said in a trembling voice. She showed him the telegram.

CAL IN CRITICAL CONDITION ASKING
FOR MRS. JENSEN STOP PLEASE COME
QUICK STOP

HERMAN NELSON

"I wonder what happened?" Smoke asked after reading the telegram.

"Oh, Smoke, I must go. I have to," Sally said.

Smoke pulled her to him and held her in a warm embrace. "Yes, of course you must."

Texas and Pacific depot, Fort Worth

Andy had attached a team to a buckboard, which Smoke used to bring Sally into town. She got there in time to catch the eight o'clock train that evening. Because it was a scheduled train and would not be subject to all the delays they had experienced in the special train that had brought the horses down, she would be back in Big Rock within a day and a half.

"I'll send you a telegram with a report on his condition," she promised as they waited for the train.

"Sally, if anyone can get him through this, you can." He knew she'd felt a very special attachment to the young man ever since Cal, when not much more than a mere boy, had tried to rob her of enough money to buy something to eat. Instead of giving him money, she'd taken him home with her, fed him, and convinced Smoke to give him a job. Over the intervening years Cal had not only become one of Smoke's most loyal workers, he, like Pearlie, had become family.

Two days after putting Sally on the train, Smoke got a telegram from her.

AM WITH CAL STOP PARALYSIS HANGS IN THE BALANCE STOP DOCTOR SAYS PRAYERS AND LOVE WILL HELP STOP

LOVE SALLY

On the same day an article about the upcoming trial of Boone Caulder appeared in the *Fort Worth Messenger*.

Murder Trial to Begin

It has been less than a month since one of the most honored and respected residents of Tarrant County was murdered, but already a suspect is in custody and about to face trial.

Boone Caulder, an employee of Big Jim Conyers, has been arrested and will soon be tried for first-degree murder. This will not be Caulder's first encounter with the law. Five years previous he was arrested tried, and convicted for stealing cattle from Steve Emerson, for whom, at the time, he was employed.

In addition to his felonious past, there is a growing mountain of evidence against Caulder, who has been offered exemption from the hangman's noose if he will cooperate with prosecution and name the others concerned. This, he has refused to do.

It may be of interest that Preston Miller has hired Jim Robinson, the Doyen of Dallas Lawyers, to act as lead prosecutor in the trial. Although such a thing is legal, it is very rarely done.

"As everyone knows, Jim Conyers was my closest friend," Preston Miller told this newspaper. "And I intend to do all in my power to see to it that justice is served against the man who killed him."

The Tarrant County Prosecuting Attorney, Bob Dempster, must, by law, be the lead prosecutor, but the case for the prosecution will be presented by Mr. Robinson.

Jeremiah Madison will be Boone Caulder's court-appointed lawyer for the defense.

Live Oak Ranch

"Dalton, do you know this man, Jeremiah Madison?" Tom asked.

"Yes, though to be honest, it is more that I know *of* him, than that I know him."

"What kind of a lawyer is he?"

"From what I understand he was a good lawyer at one time."

"At one time?"

"He drinks a lot."

"How much is a lot?"

"He's an alcoholic," Dalton said.

"Then I'm going to hire another lawyer for him."

"Tom," Becca said with a pained expression in her voice. "This is my father you're talking about."

"I know."

"And you're wanting to hire a lawyer to defend the man who killed him? How could you do such a thing?"

"Becca, you know what I thought of your father. What if, just what if Caulder is innocent, as he says he is? If he is innocent and he is convicted, that means the real guilty party would go free."

"With everything that we have found about Caulder, how can you not believe he is guilty?" Becca asked.

"I don't know, Becca. God help me, I don't know why I have this nagging feeling everything isn't quite what it appears to be, but I can't shake it."

"I have to confess," Smoke said a little later when he was told of Tom's reservations, "that I agree with

Tom. Something about this whole thing just doesn't ring true for some reason."

"Would you go into town with me?" Tom asked. "I want to talk to the lawyer they appointed, and also to Caulder."

"All right. I'll go."

"Dalton, are you all right with this?" Tom asked.

"If you and Smoke both feel this way, I'll do nothing to hold you back. But do let me know what you find out."

Jeremiah Madison's office in Fort Worth wasn't in a stand-alone building. Rather his office was upstairs over the City Gas Works on Calhoun Street. One would have to already know, or as Smoke and Tom did, inquire as to the location of his office, because there was no sign out front of the City Gas Works to indicate his occupancy. The only notice was his name painted on the window of the door to his office, accessed by a rickety set of stairs on the back side of the City Gas Works building.

When Smoke and Tom reached the top of the stairs, they hesitated for a second. They didn't know if they should knock or just push open the door. Since most offices open for business required no announcement before entering, they assumed this was the case, and stepped inside.

The office furniture consisted of his desk and chair, and a faded, cloth-covered sofa. The only thing that stood out was a well-stocked bookshelf.

The man behind the desk had a defeated look about him. His hair was white and disheveled, his collar was frayed, and his jacket was well worn. A half-full glass and an empty bottle of whiskey sat on the desk before him. He held a piece of paper in his hand and looked up as Smoke and Tom entered.

"What can I do for you gentlemen?"

"Are you Jeremiah Madison?" Tom asked.

"At one time, sir, I would have responded by saying I have that pleasure." Madison held out his hand to take in his office. "But circumstances force me to say that I have that displeasure."

"You are the court-appointed counsel for Boone Caulder."

"I am, sir."

"No other lawyer in Fort Worth or Dallas will take the case," Tom said.

"As it turns out, Mr. Caulder seems to be indigent and doesn't have the means to hire any other lawyer. But as our constitution affords everyone the right to have an attorney, the court has appointed me, and I will be representing him."

"I want you to refuse the court appointment," Tom said.

"What?"

"The Colonel was my father-in-law, and I thought the world of him. I want you to refuse the court appointment."

"No, sir, I most definitely will not do that!" Madison said vehemently. "I will not help you deny the defendant his constitutional right to be represented. I may have lost my respect, sir, but I have not lost my honor."

"Good, that makes you just the man I want," Tom said.

"I don't understand."

"I want to pay you to represent him to the best of your ability," Tom said. "Something about this case just doesn't ring true to me."

"You mean, such as all the evidence against Mr. Caulder being just a little 'too' perfect?"

"Yes! Yes, you do understand, don't you?"

"I can add one more thing," Madison said. "I don't believe it was by chance I was chosen to defend Caulder." The lawyer lifted the empty whiskey bottle. "I was chosen because of this. Preston Miller has hired Jim Robinson to prosecute. Robinson's latest court case was for the Texas and Pacific Railroad against the United States Government. Robinson won his case.

"My last case was Peters verses the North Texas Stagecoach Company. I represented Mr. Peters, who was suing the stagecoach company for one hundred dollars. North Texas Stagecoach Company won."

"Yes," Tom said. "I did a little research on you before I came to see you."

"And yet, here you are."

"I also read about the Sam Jenkins trial in New Orleans. He was arrested for murdering his wife and two children. With every newspaper in the state clamoring for his conviction, and with the power of the entire state judicial system against you, you successfully argued his case and got the jury to find for a not guilty verdict. The newspapers, even those who were the most strident against you, said that your defense of Jenkins was the most brilliant case they had ever seen."

Madison picked up his half-full glass of whiskey and finished it off before he responded.

"There is an aspect to that case that nobody knows," Madison said his voice low and contrite.

"Oh?"

"After Jenkins was found not guilty, he left New Orleans. Two weeks later I got a letter from him, thanking me for getting him off, then confessing to the murder, pointing out that because of double jeopardy he couldn't be tried again."

"Is that what—" Tom didn't finish the question. He just pointed to the bottle.

"Yes."

"Mr. Madison, I have confidence in you. If you are willing to do it, I want you to withdraw from your position as court-appointed attorney, and let me hire you."

"Are you saying that you want to hire me to defend Caulder?"

"That is exactly what I'm saying."

"All right. I don't see how I can turn down such a proposition as that. You have just hired an attorney, sir." Madison stood and extended his hand to Tom.

"However, my hiring you is contingent upon two conditions. One, that you let me buy you a new suit and perhaps even get you a haircut so that you will be more presentable in court."

Madison smiled. "That condition I can gladly accede to. I have a feeling that your second requirement will be a little more difficult for me."

"I want you to stop drinking. At least until after the trial."

"As I said, that will be very difficult. But I will try."

"Don't try. Do it," Tom said.

* * *

"You didn't say a word the whole time we were in there," Tom said to Smoke as the two of them left Madison's office.

"You seemed to have everything under control."

"Smoke, am I doing the right thing?"

"I would say yes."

"The last thing I want to do is have the Colonel's family and friends turn against me for this, especially Becca," Tom said. "Having you agree that I'm doing the right thing may help me with them. I know that every one of them holds you in very high esteem."

"The problem is, Caulder isn't doing much to help his own case," Smoke said. "He says he doesn't know who was involved in stealing the horses and the cattle, but he has over two thousand dollars he is unwilling to account for. I think we should go talk to him again."

"With or without Madison?" Tom asked.

"Has Madison met his new client yet?"

"No."

"All right. Let's get him cleaned up and take him to meet Caulder."

Smoke, Tom, and a cleaned-up Jeremiah Madison went to the jail to have a talk with Boone Caulder.

"I'll let you three back in the cell to talk to him." Sheriff Maddox pointed to Smoke. "But, Smoke, you'll have to leave your gun with me."

"All right," Smoke agreed, unbuckling his gun belt and holding it out toward the sheriff.

Maddox took the three into the back of the jail. "You've got company, Caulder," he said as he unlocked the cell door to let the three in.

"I've already told you, I didn't do it, and I don't know who did," Caulder said before any of his visitors said a word.

"Boone, this is Jeremiah Madison. He is going to be your lawyer," Smoke said.

"The court appointed you, did they?" Caulder asked.

"Initially I was a court appointment, yes," Madison replied. "But I have subsequently been hired by Dr. Tom Whitman."

"You?" Caulder asked, surprised by the announcement. "I don't understand. Why would you want to defend me? You're married to the Colonel's daughter, aren't you?"

"Yes."

"Then why would you believe I'm innocent?"

"I don't know that you *are* innocent," Tom said. "But I want you to have the best possible trial so that, if you didn't do it, we can get you out of the way and move on to the actual guilty party. I just want to be sure."

"I didn't do it," Caulder said.

"How did that silver piece from your boot get out there where Jim was killed?" Smoke asked.

Caulder shook his head. "I don't have any idea how it got there."

"And yet, there it was," Smoke said. "What about the money? How did you come by the two thousand dollars that was found on you? And don't tell us you don't know where that money came from."

"Oh, I know where it came from, all right, but I

can't tell you." Caulder looked at Madison. "Ain't there some kind of law that says I don't have to answer questions if I don't want to?"

"Yes, the fifth amendment," Madison replied. "But that is to keep you from self-incrimination when you're being interrogated by the law, or being examined while in the witness chair. Right now you are among friends. I am your defense counsel so you can tell us anything. It would make my job of defending you considerably easier if you would confide in us. Where did you get the money?"

"I can't tell you."

Madison sighed and shook his head. "Dr. Whitman, I'm afraid you have invested your money in a lost cause. I will defend this man, but unless he is more forthcoming with us there is only one way this case can turn out. Mr. Caulder, you will be going to the gallows."

CHAPTER THIRTY-ONE

Dalton had not moved into the Big House at the ranch yet, and he was telling Marjane what Smoke and Tom had reported on their meeting with the lawyer.

"Dalton, do you think Boone Caulder did it?" Marjane asked.

"There is no doubt in my mind," he said.

"Then why in heaven's name did you agree to let Tom pay for the lawyer?"

"Because he and Smoke do have some doubt. And when they lead Caulder up those thirteen steps, I want Tom and Smoke to be as satisfied that he is guilty as I am."

"What does Becca think about this?"

"I've spoken with her. I think she and I feel about the same. We believe Caulder is guilty, but like me, she wants Tom and Smoke to be as convinced as we are. A fair trial with a defense attorney who is actually doing his best and not just satisfying some court-appointed obligation will guarantee a fair trial that should certainly satisfy Tom and Smoke."

There was a knock on his front door, and Clay called out.

"Dalton, Preston Miller is coming up the road."

When Dalton and Clay stepped outside, he saw that Smoke and Tom were watching the surrey as it approached.

"What do you suppose he wants?" Dalton asked.

"It would be my guess that he has heard we are paying Madison to defend Boone Caulder," Tom replied.

Miller approached with his team at a rapid trot so that when he stopped, the rooster tail of dust the spinning wheels had kicked up rolled back over him.

"Hello, Preston, what brings you here?"

"Are you aware, Dalton, that you have a viper in your midst? And not just one viper, but a nest of vipers." He pointed to Smoke and Tom.

"Sheriff Maddox told me that these two came to the jail with Jeremiah Madison to discuss defense tactics with the man who murdered your father and my best friend."

"I know," Dalton said.

"And do you also know that they have had him set aside the court appointment so they could pay his fee themselves?"

"Yes, I know that, too. And I know they paid to get him cleaned up."

"And you are all right with that?"

"Mr. Miller," Tom said, "I acted on my own. Dalton was not a part of this."

"And yet he says he is aware of it," Preston replied. He shook his head, slowly. "Would you mind telling me what in the hell gave you the idea to do such a thing? Why would you defend the man who murdered your own father-in-law?"

"Because I'm not entirely convinced that Boone Caulder is guilty," Tom said.

"What? How can you possibly doubt it? Good Lord, man, the evidence against him is overwhelming!"

"It's just a feeling I have. Anyway, if he is guilty he obviously didn't act alone. By defending him and gaining his confidence, we might learn who else was involved."

"Has he told you anything yet?" Preston asked.

"No."

"Nor will he."

"If he is found guilty, and he begins to feel the gravity of his situation, he may talk to keep from hanging," Smoke said.

"To keep from hanging? Whether he talks or not, I want him to hang. Don't you understand? This man murdered my friend. I want him to hang!"

"Preston, even if he was there, there's no proof that he's the one who pulled the trigger," Dalton said. "I want the murderer as much as you do, perhaps even more because the victim was my father. But I want to make certain we get the right killer. I would hate to think Boone is hanged while the real killer gets away."

"There is no doubt in my mind but that Boone Caulder is the real killer, and I intend to do all I can do to make certain he pays for it. Whatever expense the court is out in prosecuting this case, I will pay. I want the full power of the law to come down on this man."

Preston clucked at his team then jerked them around and left as rapidly as he had arrived.

"Dalton, regardless of how this turns out, I have a

feeling your relationship with Miller will never be like it was between him and the Colonel," Smoke said.

"I have that same feeling," Dalton said. "Oh, and Clay? Let's hold off on sending any more cattle through Mr. Miller until after the trial."

"All right. You're the boss."

"Hello, Burgess. What can I do for you?" Preston asked when he saw his competitor come into his office.

"Is it true that Tom Whitman is paying the lawyer to defend the man that murdered his own father-in-law?"

"Yes, it's true. I didn't want to believe it, but I had a visit with him today and he told me himself."

"Why would he do such a thing?"

"I don't know. I just know that I'm very disappointed in him."

Burgess smiled. "So disappointed that you don't want to represent Dalton anymore?"

"Why would I do that? We don't have to be friends for me to continue to broker his cattle. Business is business, after all."

"So you say now, but haven't you always made a big thing about business and friendship? Isn't that why you are charging Live Oak Ranch a brokerage fee of only three dollars per head?"

"I have a feeling circumstances may bring about a few changes," Preston said.

Burgess smiled. "Yeah, I got that same feeling."

* * *

The Tarrant County Courthouse was the most impressive building in Fort Worth. It was a two-story building, with its four wings forming a cross. Topping the junction of the cross was a magnificent dome that overlooked the Trinity River. It was still an hour before the trial was scheduled to begin, but already every seat in the courtroom was filled. In addition to the filled courtroom, a rather substantial crowd of people were gathered on Belknap Street in front of the courthouse.

As lawyer for the defense, Madison was able to reserve one entire row of seats. It was occupied by Smoke, Julia, Tamara, Tom, Rebecca, Dalton, and Marjane. Pearlie, Clay, and Andy had their own seats by virtue of having been subpoenaed as witnesses. Dalton would be a witness as well, but he preferred sitting with his family.

Scores of conversations were going in the gallery, and though they were subdued, the mere number of them created a din.

Lattimore and Maggie were in the gallery. So were Jory Gibbon and Dooley Evans.

"All rise!" the bailiff called from the front of the room and the gallery grew quiet except for the rustling sounds of all the people standing.

"This court in and for the county of Tarrant and the state of Texas is now in session, the Honorable Fielding Potlatch presiding."

Judge Potlatch was a man of medium size with blue eyes enlarged by the glasses he wore, a flushed face, and a rather prominent nose. He was wearing a black robe and a powdered, white wig. The judge swept his robe back, took his seat behind the bench, stared out for a moment at the standing gallery, then struck the bench one time with his gavel. "You may be seated."

The rustling sound was repeated as all sat.

"Bailiff, would you call the case, please?"

"Your Honor, there comes now before this court Boone Caulder who has been charged with first-degree murder," the bailiff said.

"Is counselor for the defense present?" Judge Potlatch asked.

Wearing the new suit Tom had bought for him, Madison stood. "Jeremiah Madison for the defense, Your Honor."

"I thought you had withdrawn from the court appointment," Potlatch said.

"I did, Your Honor. I am being compensated by the defendant."

"And how does your client plead?"

"My client pleads not guilty, Your Honor."

"Very well. Let the plea of not guilty be entered. Is the prosecutor present?"

Two men were sitting at the prosecutor's table and one stood up. He was short, with a protruding stomach and a bald head.

"Your Honor, I am Bob Dempster, Prosecuting Attorney for Tarrant County and as such, I will be the lead lawyer on the case. However, Jim Robinson has been hired to assist, and because of that he will handle the case."

At Dempster's invitation Jim Robinson stood. He was tall with dark hair and a well-trimmed moustache.

"You are recognized, counselor," Judge Potlach said.

Robinson retook his seat.

"Very well. With counselors present for prosecution

and defense, the trial may begin. Prosecutor, you may give your opening remarks."

Standing again, Robinson walked over to the jury box and was quiet for a long moment as he made eye contact with every juror present. "I am not from Fort Worth. I am not even from Tarrant County. I live and practice my profession in Dallas, and, upon occasion, in Austin. But even in Dallas I knew of Jim Conyers, the man that friends and family referred to with affection, as Big Jim, or the Colonel.

"Big Jim Conyers was a Texas giant, and I don't mean just his size. When he built Live Oak he was building more than just a ranch. He was rebuilding Texas from the ashes it had become as a result of the terrible War Between the States. His name will stand with other Texas icons, Sam Houston, Stephen Austin, James Bowie, William Travis, and yes, even Davy Crockett."

Robinson looked over at Boone Caulder, glared at him for a moment, then pointing at him, turned to face the jury again. "And that hero of Texas was murdered by this man!"

Even as the words *murdered by this man* still resonated with the gallery, Jeremiah Madison stood to present his opening statement. Unlike Robinson, he didn't approach the jurors, and in contrast to Robinson's loud, bombastic charge, Madison's voice, while audible, was well modulated. "Like the esteemed assistant to the prosecutor, I too am well-known. But there, the similarity between us ends. While Mr. Robinson is known as an outstanding attorney, one who has won many cases, I am known primarily as a drunk and a failure.

"Why is Mr. Robinson, a lawyer from Dallas, city

and county, pleading a case for the prosecution here in Tarrant County? It is because he is being paid to do so by someone with a vested interest in this case." Madison held up his index finger. "Now, don't get me wrong. It is perfectly all right for that to be done, and I'm casting no doubt as to the legality.

"And now we come to me. Of all the lawyers in Tarrant County, why was I chosen? As you know, I'm a drunk and it has been three years since I actually tried a case before the bench. Could it be that I was chosen because I am the yin, to Mr. Robinson's yang? How better to load a case than to arrange for one of the most successful lawyers in Texas, Jim Robinson, to argue the case with a proven, alcoholic failure like me? If the case for the prosecution was well enough supported by the evidence, why weigh the outcome on such an uneven scale?"

CHAPTER THIRTY-TWO

Robinson's case was well constructed, and he built it upon blocks of irrefutable evidence. First, he informed the jury of Caulder's felonious background, providing documented evidence of him having served a prison term for stealing cattle from his employer. Then, he called his first witness.

Andy Dunlap testified that not only had Caulder left his work area on the same day, and at least an hour before Big Jim was killed, but that he and others had noticed that Caulder was wearing his silver-decorated boots at the time.

Robinson pointed out the fact that Caulder was wearing those particular boots would be significant at a later point in the presentation of his case.

Clay Ramsey testified that though Caulder had claimed he was being sent to town to run an errand, that it wasn't true. He could not account for his absence from about an hour before the murder took place until late in the afternoon of that same day.

Pearlie identified the silver thunderbird as the one he had found at the site where Big Jim was killed.

Lonnie Truax testified that he had repaired Caulder's boots by replacing the missing silver thunderbird.

"This thunderbird?" Robinson asked, showing it to Truax.

"Yes, that's the one."

Although Madison had not questioned any of the other witnesses, he did cross-examine Truax. "Are you sure this is the same silver thunderbird that was missing from the boot?"

"Oh yes, I'm positive. Caulder brought the boot in to me with a missing piece, this same piece, and I replaced it with another."

"You replaced it with another thunderbird?"

"Yes sir. The right boot."

"Where did you get the other thunderbird?"

"Oh, I've got a few," Truax answered.

"So, there are more thunderbirds than just the two that were on Mr. Caulder's boots?"

"Yes, of course. It's a very popular design."

"Bearing in mind, Mr. Truax, that it is a popular design and there are many of them, I'm going to ask you again. Are you absolutely positive that the thunderbird Mr. Fontane found, this thunderbird"—Madison extended the little piece of prosecutor's evidence for Trotter to see—"is the very same one that was missing from Mr. Caulder's boot? Would you swear that on penalty of death?"

"Would I swear that on penalty of death? Well no, of course not. I couldn't do that."

"But you just *did* swear it on penalty of death, Mr.

Truax. Not your death, of course, but it could well be the death of my client. So your swearing as to the exact identity is subject to change depending on whether it's your death or my client's death. Would that be an accurate statement?"

"No, I, uh, well, since there are so many of them, I suppose it could have come from somewhere other than Caulder's boot."

"Thank you. No further questions, Your Honor."

Robinson's last witness was Dalton Conyers, who testified that he had found two thousand, one hundred forty-two dollars and fifty cents in the storage trunk used by Caulder.

"I understand there is a ledger in which your father recorded every dollar paid to all of his employees for the last five years," Robinson said.

"Yes, there is."

"And what is the total amount that has been paid to Caulder?"

"One thousand and forty dollars since the time he arrived."

"One thousand and forty dollars. Now, let us make a most unlikely supposition that Caulder left prison with roughly two thousand, one hundred and forty-two dollars, said sum being the difference between what he has drawn since coming to work at Live Oak, and the amount of cash that was found on him.

"During the time he has been here, he has also bought an expensive pair of boots, a stereopticon, drinks, clothes, and yet, somehow he managed to hang on to every dollar he was paid, plus the . . . mysterious one thousand and change he would have brought with him from the prison. Does that seem plausible to you?"

"No, sir, it does not," Dalton said.

"Your witness, counselor."

Unlike Robinson, who had paced back and forth between the witness and the jury, and whose examination had been bombastic, Madison stood, but didn't leave the defense table.

"The case against Boone Caulder seems quite strong, doesn't it, Mr. Conyers? He served time in prison for stealing cattle, his absence during the time of the murder is unaccounted for, the thunderbird missing from his boot was found at the scene of the crime, and an excessive amount of money with an unknown origin was found in his trunk. Mr. Conyers, were you aware of all that before the trial started?" Madison asked.

"Yes, I was."

"And yet, when you learned that your brother-in-law was paying me to represent Mr. Caulder, you made no protest. Why not? I mean it was your own father that was killed."

"If Boone Caulder killed my father, then yes, of course, I will want him to pay the penalty for it. But Boone says he didn't do it. My brother-in-law is not convinced that he did it, nor is Smoke Jensen entirely convinced that he did it. I have enough respect for the opinion of those two men that I am open to the possibility that Boone might be innocent."

"Despite the mountain of evidence against him?"

"Yes."

"Why don't you believe the evidence?"

"It isn't that I don't believe it. It's just that, somehow, it all seems too pat."

"No further questions, Your Honor."

The next witness for the prosecution was Preston Miller.

"Mr. Miller, it was alleged by Mr. Madison in his opening comments that you are paying me a fee to prosecute this case. Is that true? Are you paying me to prosecute?"

"Yes, I am."

"Why are you doing that? You are aware, are you not, a prosecuting attorney works for Tarrant County, and that he is compensated by the county?"

"Yes, but Big Jim Conyers was my best friend, and I wanted to make certain that the man who murdered him pays the penalty." Preston stared angrily at Boone.

"Your witness, counselor," Robinson said.

"No questions."

"I have no more witnesses, Your Honor."

"Defense may call their first witness," Judge Potlach said.

"Your Honor, despite my admonitions against it, my client wishes to take the stand in his own defense, and he will be my only witness."

"Very well. You may proceed."

After Boone was given the oath, he took his seat on the witness chair. Looking out over the gallery he saw nothing but a sea of angry, condemning faces. Then his eyes fell upon Maggie and her husband, Lattimore. At first he almost didn't recognize Maggie because she wasn't wearing even the makeup he was used to seeing. Also she was so modestly dressed that she could have been any woman you might pass on the street. When Maggie saw that he was looking right at her, she looked down, unable to meet his gaze.

"Mr. Caulder, the evidence against you is quite strong," Madison said. "If you don't mind I would like to go through it with you, one piece at a time. First, let us begin with your prior record. Is it true that you served two years in prison for stealing cattle from your employer?"

"Yes, sir, that is true."

"And you served your entire term, is that correct? What I mean is, you are not wanted in Arizona for escaping jail?"

"No sir, I am not."

Madison glanced toward the judge. "Your Honor, I would like to submit into evidence a telegram that I received from the warden of the Arizona Territorial Prison in Yuma, testifying that my client served his entire time and was discharged."

"You may do so."

Madison turned back to Boone. "The next link in the chain of evidence is your absence during the time of the murder. You told Andy Dunlap that your foreman, Clay Ramsey, was sending you on an errand. Did he assign you an errand?"

"No, sir, I made that up."

"Where were you?"

"I was with a woman."

"Who were you with?"

"I'd rather not say."

"Why not? Don't you understand, Mr. Caulder that if she could testify that you were with her, that you would be found innocent?"

"I don't think it would be fair to get her into this."

"Very well. The next piece of evidence is the little silver thunderbird that was missing from your boot. Is the thunderbird that was found at the scene of the crime the one that was missing from your boot?"

"I don't see how it could be. I mean, I might have been out there a few times, but I never wore them boots while I was there. Them was my goin'-into-town-only boots."

"I have no further questions, Your Honor."

The judge looked at Robinson. "Prosecutor?"

"Caulder, where did you get that two thousand, one hundred forty-two dollars and fifty cents that was found in a bag in your trunk?"

"It ain't money I got paid from stealin' the Colonel's cattle on account of I didn't do that."

"Where did you get it, Caulder?"

Boone looked at Maggie again, and he saw a pleading in her eyes. "I ain't a-goin' to say."

"No more questions for this . . . witness, Your Honor," Robinson said, putting as much vitriol into his dismissal as he could.

"Defense, you may make your closing argument," Judge Potlatch said.

This time Madison did approach the jury. "Gentlemen, there is something about our legal system unlike the legal system of any other civilized nation in the world. In our legal system that man"—he pointed to Boone—"came into this courtroom an innocent man. For the entire time of this trial, Boone Caulder has been an innocent man. As he sits there now, he is an innocent man. This principle is called the presumption of innocence, and that presumption of innocence is absolute! It cannot be violated unless you, the jury, declare him guilty. And if there is any doubt in your mind as to his guilt, then he will continue to be innocent.

"You have heard the evidence against him. He does not deny that he served a previous term in prison, but he served his complete term and he is not a wanted man in Arizona or anywhere else. He admits that he lied to Mr. Dunlap to get off on the day in question, doing so to visit a woman. What woman? Well here, gentlemen of the jury, we get a good look at the honor and integrity of this man because he would rather put his own life at risk than sully the innocence of a woman.

"He admits that the little silver thunderbird found at the scene of the crime *might* be his, but he also says that he was never at that part of the ranch in those boots. And a few questions to the other cowboys riding for the Live Oak brand will verify that he never wore these boots to work. So how did that silver thunderbird get there? I remind you that you cannot guess. You must *know* how it got there if you are going to use this as evidence for conviction.

"I want you to remember this. When I retake my seat at the defense table, unless it is declared otherwise, I will be sitting by an innocent man.

"Your Honor, the defense rests."

"Prosecutor, closing statement?" Judge Potlach invited.

Robinson stood. He was the one who remained at

the counselor's table. "Mr. Madison is quite right in his discussion of the presumption of innocence. The defendant, any defendant in any trial, has the constitutional right of presumption of innocence"—he paused for a moment—"just as you, the gentlemen of the jury, have the right to remove that presumption and replace it with an absolute declaration of guilty.

"This case has been laid out for you with geometric logic and axiomatic fact. I will not revisit the details as I am certain they are well lodged by now and you cannot, in good conscience, return any verdict but guilty. I charge you now, as twelve good men and true of this county where the crime was committed, as residents of this state, and as citizens of this great nation, to do your duty and find Boone Caulder guilty of the crime of murder in the first degree."

The jury was out for no more than thirty minutes when Smoke and the others were called back into court. The twelve jurors filed back into the box then took their seat.

"Has the jury reached a verdict?" Judge Potlatch asked.

One of the jurors stood. "We have, Your Honor. I'm Dean Pollard, and I have been selected foreman of the jury."

"Mr. Pollard, would you publish your verdict, please?"

"Your Honor, we find the defendant, Boone Caulder, guilty as charged, of first-degree murder."

"So say you one, so say you all?"

"So say we all, Your Honor."

"Thank you. Counselor for the defense, would you please bring your client before the bench?"

Standing, Madison urged Caulder to stand as well and the two of them walked up to the bench to face the judge.

"Mr. Boone Caulder, you have been tried by a jury of your peers, and you have been found guilty of the heinous crime of murder in the first degree. And though this trial was for the murder of Jim Conyers, two more men were murdered on that same day, and had you not been found guilty of this particular crime, we could have tried you two more times for the murders of Stacey Alford and Paul Butler. I mention their names now, so that it will be known that they, too, will receive justice.

"It is the sentence of this court that you be re-turned to jail and on this very day, two weeks hence, you will be taken to a gallows that shall be specifically constructed for the purpose and there, suspended by the neck until all life has left your body." Judge Pot-latch brought the gavel down sharply. "This court is adjourned."

Caulder hung his head then waited as two sheriff's deputies came up to him and put him in handcuffs. As they led him away, he made one plaintive glance toward the bench where sat Smoke, Tom, Rebecca, Dalton, Marjane, Julia, and Tamara.

Preston Miller came over to stand in front of the bench where all were seated.

"Julia, I know that this justice, once it is carried out, will not bring my friend and your husband back to us. But I hope that you, as I, will take some satisfaction in knowing the man who killed Jim will be paying for his crime with his life."

"I . . . I find that I can't take satisfaction in anyone's death," Julia replied.

"And you, Dr. Whitman," Preston said. "I hope you have learned a lesson that true justice cannot be thwarted."

"If it is justice," Tom said.

Preston was silent for a moment, then he shook his head. "I don't know what got into all of you, but I'm sure that, within a short while, you will understand that what I did in bringing in Jim Robinson to try this case was the right thing to do. And after we recover from the sorrow of losing someone who was so close to all of us, we will renew our friendship so that it is stronger than before."

CHAPTER THIRTY-THREE

As Maggie and Lattimore left the trial, she couldn't get Boone out of her mind. He could have betrayed her, but he didn't. Now he was going to hang for it. He was going to hang for her.

Until then Boone Caulder had been little more than one of many men she had been with. Well, if she were truthful with herself, she would admit Boone was more than that. Yes, she was using him. She had even given him money she had stolen from Lattimore's stash. He could have used that in his defense, but he didn't.

Maggie felt an intense sadness. Could it be that she actually loved him?

"Looks to me like you're 'bout to lose one of your customers," Lattimore said with a laugh, his comment interrupting her musings. "Boone Caulder's 'bout to get his neck stretched. He's one of your customers, ain't he? One of your regulars?"

"I see him from time to time," Maggie said, keeping her voice as calm as she could.

"I'm the reason he's goin' to hang," Lattimore said.

"What do you mean?"

"You seen that they was talkin' about that little silver doodad durin' the trial? The one that was found out there where the cows was all took?"

"Yes, of course I remember. It was one of the main reasons why he was convicted."

"I put it there," Lattimore said with a self-satisfied, smug grin. "When me 'n the other boys was out there takin' the cows, I dropped it thinkin' that if it was found, the law might get the idea that it was Boone Caulder what done it."

"I don't understand. I mean how did you come by that thing in the first place?"

"It was one o' them times when he come here to see you here, 'stead at Lena Watkins's house. I happened to come in, but you two was too *busy* to notice." Lattimore chuckled at his use of the word *busy*. "Anyhow, I seen them fancy boots he was a-wearin', 'n what I done is, I took my knife 'n pried off one o' them little silver doodads that was on it. The reason I done it is 'cause I figured on keepin' it for my ownself. But when we took them cows 'n shot Conyers 'n the other two fellers, that's when I got the idea to just drop that little silver doodad there."

He laughed. "That was pretty smart of me, don't you think? I didn't know that worked till the trial today when they was talkin' about it. I think I'll ride out 'n tell the Professor about it. I figure he'll be pretty pleased by that."

"Where are you goin'?"

"Like I told you, I'm goin' to see the Professor 'n the other boys."

"No, I mean where is it that you go? You ain't never told me."

"Oh, they got 'em a real jim-dandy of a hideout. It's a cabin on the West Fork Trinity River 'bout four miles south of Azle. There ain't nobody around it so it's real private."

"Take me with you."

"Hell no, I ain't goin' to take you with me. The Professor wouldn't like that 'n if there's one thing I've learned since joinin' up with this band, it's that you don't want to do nothin' that's likely to get the Professor pissed off at you."

"When will you be back?"

"Well I ain't likely to go there 'n then come right back. I'll prob'ly be there two or three days, 'n maybe longer if the Professor has another job for us to do."

"All right."

"Hey, what about the money I left here? It's still all here, ain't it?" Lattimore asked.

"Of course it's all here. Where else would it be? You want to see it?"

"Nah, I was just thinkin' I might get a hunnert dollars from it."

Maggie managed a smile. "You just stay right there, honey, I'll get it for you."

"I'll come with you. Then you won't have to come back in here. When I've got it, I can go on."

Maggie hurried on ahead of him and in the bedroom reached to the back of the top shelf of the chifforobe. From there she took down a box, opened it, and pulled out five twenty-dollar bills. "Here you are," she said with a sweet smile, handing him the money then closing the box and putting it back on the shelf.

Lattimore took the bills and stuffed them down into his pocket. "Don't be takin' no more money from that box. I intend to keep enough money to maybe buy a saloon someday. Then, maybe we can hire us some more whores 'n you can be in charge of 'em."

Maggie walked to the door with him and not until she saw him ride off did she breathe a sigh of relief. If he had looked into the box, he might have seen that half the money was gone, the money she had given to Boone to keep for her.

Although Dalton and the other Live Oak hands had returned to the ranch, Smoke, Pearlie, and Tom remained in town. At the moment they were in the jail talking to the sheriff about the trial, and about the upcoming execution.

"I'll get Billy Baker to build the gallows," Sheriff Maddox said. "He's about the best carpenter I've ever seen. He works quick, good, 'n he don't charge much."

"I hate to think of that boy hanging," Tom said.

"Doc, after sitting through that trial, even you have to be convinced now that Caulder killed the Colonel, aren't you?" the sheriff asked.

"The evidence that he was there is pretty convincing, I agree," Tom replied. "But that doesn't mean he pulled the trigger."

"In a crime like this, you know it doesn't matter whether he pulled the trigger or not," the sheriff replied. "If he was there, then he is guilty."

"He says that he wasn't there," Pearlie said. "He says he was with a woman."

"If he really was with a woman, why won't he tell us who it was?" the sheriff asked.

"Because he was with me, and he didn't want to get me involved," a woman said from the doorway.

Surprised by the announcement, the four men looked toward the front door as she stepped inside.

"You're Maggie, aren't you? You are one of Miz Watkins's girls?" Sheriff Maddox asked.

"Yes."

"Well, Maggie, don't take this wrong, but you being a, uh, soiled dove, why would he worry one way or another about getting you involved?"

"Because we wasn't at Lena's place. We was at my house. I'm married to Eb Lattimore."

"Lattimore, the hostler down at the stagecoach depot?"

"Yes, but he is also a member of the Sidewinder Gang. And the money that Boone wouldn't talk about? That was to protect me. That money came from Eb's share of the money the Sidewinders got from stealing the horses and the cattle from Mr. Conyers."

"Mrs. Lattimore, if Boone wasn't there, how do you explain that the thunderbird was there?" Smoke asked.

"Thunderbird? Oh, you mean that little silver doodad that came off his boot?"

"Yes."

"Eb put it there. He told me himself that he took it off Boone's boot when Boone wasn't lookin' 'n he dropped it there when he 'n the Professor 'n the others was stealin' the cows 'n killin' the two that was watchin' 'em. From what Eb told me, the only reason they kilt Mr. Conyers is 'cause he come up 'n seen what they was doin'.'"

"Why are you telling us this, Mrs. Lattimore?" the sheriff asked. "You do understand that you are implicating your own husband, don't you?"

"I'm tellin' you this 'cause I don't want to see Boone get hung for somethin' he didn't do. Especially when I know he didn't do it, on account of he was with me when it happened."

"Sheriff, may I suggest that we take this conversation next door and continue it in front of Judge Potlatch?" Tom said.

"Will you be willing to say everything you just said in front of the judge and under oath?" the sheriff asked.

"Yes."

"Mrs. Lattimore, if you say this under oath and it proves to be false, you can go to prison for perjury. Are you sure you want to testify under oath?"

"Yes, but please call me Maggie. I don't want to be Mrs. Lattimore anymore. When I married him, he worked for the stagecoach company. I didn't know he was a thief and a murderer."

Because the courthouse was next door to the county jail, it was very easy for the sheriff, Maggie, Smoke, Pearlie, and Tom to move the conversation to the judge's office. There she told the judge everything she had told the sheriff, including the story of how the silver thunderbird wound up at the scene of the crime, how Boone came by so much money, and how she and Boone had been together on the day of the murder.

"Is there any way you can prove that you and Caulder were together that day?" Judge Potlatch asked.

"Yes, just ask him."

The judge shook his head. "I'm afraid that won't do. His testimony would be self-serving."

"Your Honor, I have a suggestion as to how we might prove it," Tom said.

"What is your suggestion?"

"Maggie, is there anything special that you did that day . . . something that Boone might remember?"

"Well, we had lunch."

"No, that isn't what I mean. Is there something that is different about that day from any other day, something that Boone might also remember?"

"He, uh, he had a poke," Maggie said, and because she was modestly dressed she blushed a little at the revelation.

"How unusual is that?" the judge asked. "I mean given your 'profession,' one might think it has happened before."

"Yeah, it has."

"Think, Maggie. Boone's very life may depend upon it," Tom said.

"Oh, wait. I do remember something. Mr. Poindexter was drivin' by in front of the house, and a wheel fell off his wagon. His dog was ridin' with 'im 'n got scared and run over 'n jumped through the window into the house. Me 'n Boone caught it 'n took it back out to Mr. Poindexter."

"Wait a minute," Smoke said quickly. "Are you saying that you and Boone took the dog back to Poindexter?"

"Yes, 'n he was real glad to get 'im back, too. He

thought that—" Maggie stopped in midsentence when she saw the men were smiling broadly.

"I think we need to go see Mr. Poindexter," Smoke said.

The Texas Wagon Yard of Fort Worth occupied one entire block between Rusk and Main, and Sixth and Seventh Streets.

"Yeah, he's here. He's puttin' 'is wagon away. He just got back from Birdville. Sheriff, he ain't in no kind of trouble, is he? He's one o' my best drivers."

"Mr. Weaver, do you know if Mr. Poindexter attended the trial this morning?" Sheriff Maddox asked.

"Oh, heck no. He left for Birdville first thing this morning, and like I say, he just got back."

"Thank you."

They found Hugh Poindexter in the middle of the wagon yard. He was a muscular man, the result of loading and unloading wagonloads, and at the moment he was standing beside the wagon drinking a cup of water he had drawn from the attached keg. A cocker spaniel dog was sitting on the wagon seat watching as Smoke and the others approached.

When the dog saw Maggie she stood up on the seat and began wagging her tail.

"Hello, Dixie," Maggie greeted as she approached.

The dog lowered her head, inviting a rub behind her ears.

"She remembers you," Poindexter said.

"Mr. Poindexter, do you remember losing a wheel on your wagon?" Smoke asked.

"I'll say I do." He nodded toward Maggie and the dog. "That's where they met."

"Was there a man with her then?"

"Yes, a young cowboy. Blue, Booth, somethin' like that."

"It was . . ." Maggie started, but the judge held out his hand to stop her from saying any more.

"Would you recognize him if you saw him?" Smoke asked.

"Oh, yeah. He and this lady brought Dixie back to me."

"What day was that, do you remember?" Pointdexter said.

"I'll say I remember. You don't lose a wagon wheel every day. It was a little over two weeks ago. It was on the twelfth."

"Thank you, Judge, thank you, Sheriff, thank you, Smoke, thank you, Pearlie, thank you, Tom, thank you, Mr. Poindexter," Boone looked toward Maggie with a huge smile on his face. "And, especially, thank you, Maggie."

"Sheriff?" Maggie opened her reticule and took out a wad of money, then held it out toward him.

"No, no," Sheriff Maddox said. "Don't you go spoiling this by offering a bribe."

Maggie laughed. "This isn't a bribe, Sheriff. This is the rest of the money Eb got for stealin' those cows."

The sheriff laughed as well. "You're a good woman, Mrs. Lat— uh, Maggie."

"Boone, I expect we had better go back to the ranch with you," Smoke said. "Everyone needs to know that the judge reversed the verdict and you are a free man."

Boone put his hand to his neck. "Yeah. A free man. That sure sounds good.

CHAPTER THIRTY-FOUR

"That must be the cabin," Pearlie said.

Smoke and Pearlie were now Tarrant County deputy sheriffs, thanks to Sheriff Maddox. Following the West Fork Trinity River, they had located the isolated cabin just where Maggie had said they would.

"Yeah, it has to be," Smoke agreed.

"So, what do we do now?"

"I don't know. I thought maybe if we found it, you would have an idea as to what we do next," Smoke said.

"What?"

Smoke laughed. "I guess what we do now is up to them."

"Maggie said there were seven of them. I wish we had Cal with us. It would even up the odds a bit."

"No, the odds would still be uneven," Smoke said. "Three into seven means two of us would have to deal with two apiece, and one of us would have three. Now there are two of us, which mean one of us is going to have three and one of us is going to have four. So you see, the odds are still uneven."

"I swear, Smoke, sometimes you do say the damndest things."

Smoke dismounted and pulled his rifle from the saddle sheath. Pearlie did the same.

"How far do you think that house is set back from the river?" Smoke asked.

"Oh, I'd say no more than thirty yards."

"Ninety feet," Smoke said. "All right. I can throw that far." Smoke reached down into his saddlebag. "I'll throw two of them, and you can throw two of them."

"Uh-uh. I'll light 'em. You throw 'em," Pearlie said as Smoke pulled out four sticks of dynamite.

"Stay here, Seven," Smoke said, holding out his hand toward his horse.

Seven was well enough trained that he would remain without being tethered and Pearlie's horse would stay with Seven.

The two men walked along the bank of the river shielded from view by a head-high line of vegetation. They came even with the cabin, which put them, as Pearlie had guessed, about thirty yards away.

Smoke looked at his foreman. "What do you say we invite them to the dance?"

Pearlie jacked a round into the chamber of his rifle. "I'm ready."

"Catron!" Smoke shouted. "Catron! You and your men come out with your hands up!"

Inside the cabin, five of the men were playing poker, and because they had a lot of money from the cattle deal, they were playing for very high stakes—

betting a hundred dollars on a card as easily as they once bet a dollar. Only Lattimore and Catron were not playing.

"*Catron! You and your men come out with your hands up!*"

What the hell!" Lattimore said, looking around when he heard the call. "Professor, did you hear that?"

"*Catron!*"

"Who is it, Professor? Who's out there?" Parker asked.

"Damn! We're surrounded!" Dawkins said.

"We ain't surrounded," Lattimore replied. "Hell, where would they be? They's open fields on three sides of us. Whoever is there has to be down to the river."

"*Catron! This is your last warning! You and all of your men come out with your hands up!*"

"Lattimore is right. Whoever it is has to be down on the river." The Professor looked at the two windows and the single door on the front of the cabin, which faced the river.

"Gibbons, you and Evans take the door. Parker, Lattimore, you take the window on the right, Morris, you and Dawkins take the window to the left. Keep a very close observation of the river. When they start shooting you will, no doubt, be able to see the gun smoke, and perhaps even the muzzle flash. As soon as you have located your target, return fire. We have the advantage. These walls are so thick even if a bullet gets through it will have lost enough of its velocity as to be rendered harmless."

The men moved into the defensive locations that had been assigned to them by the Professor.

"Remember," he said from his command position, which for the moment was standing against the back wall so that he could observe all six of his men. "Keep your eyes open so you can see where they are from the moment they begin shooting."

The engagement opened with an explosion just in front of the window being manned by Morris and Dawkins. With wounds to their faces and arms from the flying glass, both of them spun away from the window.

"What the hell was that?" Gibbons shouted.

"Shoot at them! Shoot at them!" the Professor ordered.

"Shoot at what? I ain't seen nobody yet!" Evans said.

"Damn! There he is!" Lattimore said. "He's throwin' dynamite!"

Instead of shooting at him, the four men who had not been hurt by the previous blast backed away from the front wall. The next explosion took out the door.

"Keep your eyes open!" the Professor called. "He'll have to show himself to throw another stick at us. The next time he does that, don't back away! Shoot him down before he is able to throw it."

"Yeah," Lattimore said. "Come on. Throw another one at us." He got into position again, as did all the others.

"Shoot," the Professor ordered.

"Shoot at what? We ain't seen nothin' yet," Dawkins said. He and Morris, realizing that their wounds were superficial, had returned to their post, though the window was gone. They were actually standing on either side of an open hole.

"Just shoot. All of you shoot toward the river."

"So much for the heavy artillery," Smoke said as the defenders in the house began shooting. "I won't be able to stand up anymore. You take the two that are shooting at us from the right window, I'll take the left."

Pearlie fired, and someone pitched forward through the hole the dynamite blast had left of the window. He looked at Smoke. "What are you waiting on?" he asked as he worked the lever of his Winchester.

Smoke fired and was rewarded by the sight of a sudden spray of blood against the window. With that much blood from a head wound he was certain that he had put that shooter out of business.

When targets at the two windows no longer presented themselves, Smoke and Pearlie turned their attention to the empty door frame in the middle of the front wall of the house. Quite by coincidence their next shots were simultaneous, and two men tumbled out through the hole where the front door had been.

"Pearlie, if there were seven of them, looks to me now like there are only three of them left."

In the besieged cabin, Lattimore took a look around. Parker was dead on the floor beside him. The two half brothers, Gibbons and Evans, were lying facedown on the ground in front of what had been the door. Morris was also dead. Dawkins was still shooting through the window, but even as Lattimore was looking toward him, he saw Dawkins drop his gun and go to the floor with a head wound.

"Damn! Professor, me 'n you 's the only ones left!" Lattimore shouted in fear. He turned toward The Professor but saw that he was gone. "Catron! You thievin' traitor! Where are you?"

With a yell of rage, Lattimore ran out the front door. His pistol was in his hand, but he wasn't shooting it.

Pearlie and Smoke raised their rifles.

"Wait, Pearlie. Don't shoot," Smoke said. Laying the rifle down, he stood up, and with pistol in hand, walked out to face the man who was charging toward him. "Drop your gun," he ordered.

Lattimore stopped and stared at Smoke with a shocked look on his face. "Where are the rest of you?"

Pearlie stood. "I'm the rest."

"Two of you? Two of you did this?"

"Which one are you?" Smoke asked.

"I'm Lattimore."

"Where is Catron?"

"He's gone. The thievin' traitor ran out on us!"

"Drop your gun, Lattimore," Smoke said again.

"No, I ain't goin' to do it."

"Drop your gun, Lattimore. You know you don't have a chance."

"Yeah, I know."

With a smile that could only be described as insane, Lattimore raised the pistol to the side of his head and pulled the trigger.

CHAPTER THIRTY-FIVE

Fort Worth

When Leonard McGee looked into Preston Miller's office, he saw his boss putting stacks of banded greenbacks into a safe. "My goodness!" he said in surprise. "How much money is that?"

"One hundred and twenty thousand dollars," Preston said easily. "It is the money from the sale of the Live Oak cattle. I'm taking it out to the ranch."

"In cash? You made the sale in cash? But don't you normally arrange for the money to be deposited in the bank?"

"It's different now that Jim Conyers is gone," Preston said as he continued to put the money in the safe.

McGee had to leave the office for a few minutes and when he returned, he heard voices coming from Preston Miller's office.

"Professor Catron," Preston said.

Upon hearing the name *Professor Catron*, McGee froze in place. He had heard of the man people called the Professor. The thought that he was in the building and in the office was frightening.

McGee thought of the money Mr. Miller had put in the safe and wondered if that was what had drawn the Professor. It was obvious he had come to rob Mr. Miller, but how would he have known about the money?

"Where are the others?" Preston asked.

McGee was surprised to hear there was no anxiety in the question.

"They are dead," Catron answered.

"Dead? All of them?"

"As it developed, our secluded hideout wasn't secluded enough. Smoke Jensen found us."

"Are you telling me that one man killed all of you?" Preston asked.

"Not all of us. As you can see, I'm still alive."

"Yes, you are still alive. I'm sorry for the loss of your friends."

"They weren't my friends," the Professor replied. "They were merely people I worked with, just as you were someone I worked with when you made all the arrangements for us to steal the cattle and kill the three men. You aren't my friend, either."

Preston Miller was involved? McGee thought, smothering a gasp of surprise.

"Killing Conyers has made things very difficult," the Professor said. "Nobody would have paid any attention to the killing of two cowhands, but Conyers's stature was such that it caused an unrelenting search, which resulted in our being discovered."

"We had no choice. Jim Conyers recognized me. If we hadn't killed him, I would have been ruined."

"I have found it necessary to relocate," the Professor said. "I'll take the money now."

"What money? I don't understand. I've already given you your share of the money."

"I'm not talking about my share. I'm talking about all of it."

McGee was able to follow what was going on, not only by listening to the conversation, but by moving into position to see through the crack of the barely open door.

"I . . . I am going to have to leave as well," Preston said. "May I propose a bargain? I will split the money evenly with you, if you will act as my bodyguard until we are clear of this place."

"Where is the money now?"

"It's in the safe."

"All right. I'll accept that deal. Open the safe, take out the money, and we'll leave by train."

McGee watched as his boss opened the safe, and in doing so exposed the money he had so recently stacked on the shelf. Then, shockingly, the Professor shot him.

"What . . .?" Preston asked, his voice and face contorted with pain.

"I have decided to renege on our bargain," the Professor said calmly.

"You'll never get the money," Preston said, slamming the safe shut with his dying act.

McGee had watched it all, then realizing that he, too, might be in danger, he slipped out of the building and ran to the first place he thought of, the Fort Worth Livestock Exchange. "Mr. Burgess! Mr. Burgess!" he shouted as he ran into the office.

"Here, McGee, what's gotten into you?" asked Howard Pringle, Burgess's clerk.

"He killed him! He killed him!" McGee said. "Mr. Burgess! Mr. Burgess!"

Drawn by commotion in the outer office, Drew Burgess came out to see what was going on. "Leonard, for crying out loud, why are you taking on so?"

"He killed him, Mr. Burgess. Mr. Miller was working with the Professor and the Sidewinder Gang when they killed the Colonel 'n stole his cattle. The Professor just shot and killed Mr. Miller."

"Wait a minute! Are you telling me that it was Preston Miller who killed Conyers and stole his cattle? Are you a part of this, McGee?"

"No, no! I didn't know anything about it until just now when the Professor came into the office and killed Mr. Miller."

"Did Catron see you?"

"No, I don't think so. The door to Mr. Miller's office was just open a crack and I was looking through it. The Professor never looked in my direction, so I know he didn't see me."

"Is he still there?"

"I don't know. I just know that he was still there when I left."

"We'd better go see the sheriff."

* * *

Smoke and Pearlie went straight to the sheriff's office after the shoot-out at the little cabin on the West Fork Trinity River. Smoke poured the contents out of the cloth bag he was carrying onto the sheriff's desk.

"My word, what is this?" Sheriff Maddox asked in surprise.

"It's money," Smoke said as the last of it came from the bag.

"I can see that. How much is there? Do you know? And where did it come from?"

"It's a little over eighteen thousand dollars, and we found it in the cabin the Sidewinders were using as their hideout," Smoke said. "It has to be money that came from the horse and cattle rustling."

"That means it belongs to the Colonel," Sheriff Maddox said. "Or actually, to his son, now."

"Yes. I'll take it out to them, but I thought you should see it first."

"How did you come by it? I mean, did you just happen on to the empty cabin?"

"It wasn't empty," Pearlie said. "The whole gang was there. They're still out there, except for Catron. According to Lattimore, Catron got away."

"Still there?"

"They're dead," Smoke said.

"I'll send a couple of deputies out there with a wagon to bring the bodies in. I wonder where—"

"Sheriff, the Professor just killed Preston Miller!" McGee said as he and Burgess came barging into the sheriff's office.

"Where did this happen?" the sheriff asked.

"Down at our office."

"Where did Catron go?" Smoke asked.

"He's most likely still down there. Mr. Miller slammed the safe door shut so's not to give Catron any of the money Mr. Miller stole from the Colonel."

"Wait a minute! Did you say money that *Miller* stole from the Colonel?" Sheriff Maddox asked.

"Yes, sir. A hundred and twenty thousand dollars it was. That's why I think Catron is more 'n likely still down there, tryin' to open the safe so he can get the money."

Every drawer of Miller's desk was pulled out and every piece of paper removed. Catron had hoped to find the combination to the safe recorded somewhere and he had spent several minutes looking for it without success. Standing over Preston Miller's body, he stared at the safe in frustration. *Should have shot him in the head. Then Miller wouldn't have had time to slam the safe door shut.*

What to do? It wasn't a particularly large safe. Maybe he could carry it out of the office, hide it somewhere, then come back with a surrey or something and take it where he would have the time to open it. If he did that, he could even blast the door open. But how was he going to do that? He couldn't be seen walking through the streets of Fort Worth carrying a safe.

The more he thought about his situation, the greater his frustration. He had fled the hideout so quickly that he'd left his money there. He was flat broke, but just on the other side of that iron door was all the money he would need for the rest of his life.

He could go anywhere with it, San Francisco, New York. Why, he could even go to London or Paris.

He knew that some people could open a safe just by holding their ear to the door and listening to the tumblers as the dial was turned.

As the dial was turned. Miller didn't twist the dial when he slammed the door shut! He didn't have time!

If that's the case, the door could be opened either by pulling on it or by just barely turning the dial one way or the other because it would still be on the last number of the combination.

Putting that idea to the test Catron tried first to pull the door open. When that didn't work he turned the dial a very small way to the left, still without success. Turning the dial to the right in a very small turn, he heard a little click and smiled in triumph. Even before he pulled on the door, he knew he had succeeded.

Smoke was approaching the Fort Worth Livestock Exchange building when he saw someone coming outside. Although he had never met the one they called the Professor, this man certainly fit the description. He was also carrying a small valise.

"Mr. Catron," Smoke said. "I see that you have the money ready to be delivered to the Live Oak Ranch. I think it would be better if you gave it to me."

"And you would be the one they call Smoke Jensen?" Catron's reply had no more inflection than it would have had he been ordering a cup of coffee.

"Kirby, actually, though most people do call me

Smoke. Just as most people call you the Professor, I understand."

"It's an earned sobriquet," Catron replied. "Tell me, Mr. Jensen, why should I give the money to you?"

"Oh, because you are either going to be in jail or dead," Smoke said.

"That's rather an absolute, isn't it?" Catron said. "You must know that, according to Friedrich Nietzsche, 'There are no eternal facts, as there are no absolute truths.'"

"Well, I never met your friend Neechy, but the man I learned the most from, a man everyone called Preacher, told me once that the best way for me to get by in life is to always know what is true. And here is what is true, Mr. Catron. In the next few seconds I'm going to have that satchel of money in my hand and you're going to be walking down to the jail with me as my prisoner . . . or you're going to be lying here in the street dead. It's up to you."

Catron dropped the bag and dipped his hand toward his pistol. He was fast, about as fast as anyone Smoke had ever faced, but Smoke was a heartbeat faster. Even as Catron was pulling the trigger, a bullet energized by the pistol in Smoke's hand was already plunging into Catron's chest.

The impact of Smoke's bullet caused the Professor to pull his shot slightly, and Smoke heard the pop as the bullet came within an inch of his head.

Smoke held the pistol for a moment longer, but saw quickly that a second shot wouldn't be necessary. With his pistol ready, he looked down at Catron, who was drawing intermittent, wheezing breaths.

"I must say I thought your current age would bring about a loss of quickness in your ability to extract your pistol," Catron said in a strained voice. He chuckled, the laugh as strained as his voice. "Apparently, I failed to take into my calculations the fact that any diminution brought on by increased years, would be offset by your considerable experience."

"I have to say, Catron that you are about the strangest man I've ever shot."

Catron coughed before he spoke again. "I will take that as a compliment, sir."

Those were his last words.

Kansas and Pacific Railroad depot, Big Rock

"There's Cal!" Pearlie said when the train pulled into the depot. "Damn, I'm glad to see that he's up and around."

"He'll be glad to hear that you were worrying about him," Smoke said with a chuckle. Looking through the window, he saw that Sally and Cal were both there to meet them. Sally was standing on the depot platform and Cal was sitting in the seat of the surrey.

Smoke stepped down to a welcoming kiss and hug from Sally. Pearlie also got a hug from her.

"How 'bout you, Cal? No hug from you?" Pearlie teased.

"I wouldn't hug you, you ugly old fart, even if I wasn't stoved in like this."

"It's good to see him moving around," Smoke said.

"He is doing much better, but he really shouldn't have come here today," Sally said. "That business of him getting up when Buster was threatened nearly did him in. I tried to make him stay home this morning , but I couldn't keep him away. He was determined to come meet the train."

"What about Buster? Is he still here?"

"No, he left a few days ago, but he wanted me to tell you how thankful he was to you for believing in him when he really needed it," Sally said.

"Well, he was a good man," Smoke said. "I hope things go well for him."

"He'll be fine," Cal said. "With the man dead who killed his wife, Buster has found peace."

Keep reading for a special excerpt of the new
Western adventure!

National Bestselling Authors
WILLIAM W. JOHNSTONE
and J. A. JOHNSTONE

SHOTGUN WEDDING
A Have Brides, Will Travel Western

**The all-time masters of the classic Western cordially
invite you to another trip down the aisle with America's
mail-order brides—and the foolhardy men who
thought they could tame them.**

Bo Creel and Scratch Morton are mighty proud.
They managed to deliver five mail-order brides to
the New Mexico mining town of Silverhill in one
piece. The town is so grateful, they want to make
Bo their marshal and Scratch his deputy.
They are happy to accept the job—and even happier
to attend the weddings of the fine young women
they brought here. . . .

Cecelia has two young suitors—a well-off rancher
and a low-born miner—but one of them is not what he
seems. Tomboyish Rose has gotten herself roped into a
cow-rustling scheme—with the wild young buck who's
stolen her heart. Luella has a not-so-secret admirer of
her own, a former journalist who's making headlines—
with a gang of Mexican bandits. And the refined Jean
Parker thinks she's finally found a suitable match in
this raucous boomtown. But it turns out her educated
doctor has a dishonorary degree—in killing.

With marriage prospects like these, Bo and Scratch will
have to fight tooth and nail to keep the ladies safe and
sound—and a real shotgun wedding is about to begin.

Look for THE SHOTGUN WEDDING on sale now.

CHAPTER ONE

"You take the one on the right," Bo Creel said as he walked forward slowly, holding the Winchester at a slant across his chest. "I can handle the other two."

"Wait a minute," Scratch Morton said. "You mean their right or our right?"

"Our right. Your man's the one with the rattlesnake band around his hat."

"You mean the ugly one?"

"They're *all* ugly."

"Bein' dead ain't gonna make 'em any prettier," Scratch said, "but I reckon that's where they're headin' mighty quick-like."

Bo said, "We'll give them a chance to surrender. That's the only proper thing to do, seeing as we're duly appointed lawmen and all."

Scratch muttered under his breath about that, something that included the words "dad-blasted tin stars" and some other, more colorful comments, then said, "All right, Deputy Creel, let's get this done."

"Sure thing, Marshal Morton."

They continued up the dusty street toward the

three hard cases standing in front of the Silver King Palace, the largest and fanciest drinking establishment in the settlement of Silverhill, New Mexico Territory. The gun-wolves wore arrogant sneers on their beard-stubbled faces. They were killers and didn't care who knew it. In fact, they were proud of their infamous deeds.

And clearly, they weren't the least bit worried about the two older men approaching them.

They should have been. They didn't know what ornery sidewinders Bo Creel and Scratch Morton could be.

At first glance, the two Texans didn't look that formidable, although they stood straight and moved with an easy, athletic grace not that common in men of their years. Both had weathered, sun-bronzed faces, which testified to decades spent out in the elements. Bo's dark brown hair under his flat-crowned black hat was shot through heavily with white. Scratch's creamcolored Stetson topped a full head of pure silver hair.

Bo looked a little like a preacher, with his long black coat, black trousers, and white shirt, and with a string tie around his neck. Scratch was more of a dandy, wearing a fringed buckskin jacket over a butternut shirt and brown whipcord trousers tucked into hightopped boots.

Both men were well armed at the moment. Bo had the Winchester in his hands and a Colt .45 revolver riding in a black holster on his right hip. Scratch carried a pair of long-barreled, silvered, ivory-handled Remington .44s in a hand-tooled buscadero gun rig.

All the weapons were very well cared for but also showed signs of long and frequent use.

Bo and Scratch had been best friends since they met more than forty years earlier, during the Runaway Scrape, when the citizens of Texas fled across the countryside before Santa Anna's vengeful army. Though only boys at the time, they had fought side by side in the Battle of San Jacinto, when those Texans finally turned around and, against overwhelming odds, gave the Mexican dictator's forces a good whipping. Texas had won its freedom that fine spring day in 1836, and a lifelong friendship had been formed between Bo and Scratch.

In the decades since, they had roamed from one end of the West to the other, enduring much tragedy and trouble but also living a life of adventure that perfectly suited their fiddle-footed nature. Every attempt they had made to settle down had ended badly, until finally they had given up trying and accepted their wanderlust. Along the way they had worked at almost every sort of job to make ends meet.

Every now and then they had even found themselves on the wrong side of the law.

But right now they wore badges, which was mighty uncommon in their checkered careers. Despite being handier than most with guns and fists, they had hardly ever been peace officers.

More likely they'd be *disturbing* the peace . . .

The "peace" of Silverhill was about to be disturbed, all right. Like most mining boomtowns, this could be a raucous, wide-open place, but there weren't many gunfights on Main Street in the middle of the day.

Bo hoped there wouldn't be this time, either, but he wasn't convinced of that. Not by a long shot.

Bo and Scratch came to a stop about twenty feet away from the trio of hard cases. The one in the middle, who had long, greasy red hair under a black hat with a Montana pinch, clenched a thin black cigarillo between his large, horselike teeth and growled, "We heard the law was on the way. What in blazes do you old pelicans want?"

Scratch said, "We want you boys to unbuckle your gun belts and let 'em drop, then hoist those dewclaws and march on down to the jailhouse. You're under arrest."

"Under arrest?" the redhead repeated mockingly. "What for?" The second man, short and stocky, with a walrus mustache, said, "It's probably got somethin' to do with that piano player you plugged, Bugle."

"Shut up, Tater," the bucktoothed redhead snapped.

The third man, who had the gaunt, hollow-eyed look of a lunger, said, "Now you've gone and told these lawdogs your names."

"We already knew who you are, Scanlon," Bo said. "There are wanted posters for all three of you in the files in the marshal's office."

"So we wouldn't have been inclined to just let you ride out of town, anyway," Scratch added. "But killing a man . . . well, that sort of leveled it off and nailed it down. You're goin' to jail, all right, and then, in the due course of things, to the gallows, I expect."

Tater looked up at Bugle and said, "See, I done told you we oughta start shootin' as soon as we seen 'em headed this way. Now it's gonna be an even break."

"An even break?" Bugle said. He seemed to like to

repeat things. "How in blazes do you figure that? These two old fools ought to be sittin' in rockin' chairs somewhere, instead of bein' about to die in the middle of a dusty street!"

"Oh," Bo said, "I don't reckon we're quite *that* old."

Bugle's sneer twisted into a hate-filled grimace as his hands darted toward the guns on his hips.

Bo snapped the Winchester to his shoulder. He had already jacked a round into the chamber before he and Scratch started down here, so all he had to do was squeeze the trigger. The rifle cracked.

Bugle's head jerked back and the cigarillo flew out of his mouth as Bo neatly drilled a slug an inch above his right eye. The bullet made a nice round hole going in but blew a fist-sized chunk out of the back of Bugle's skull when it erupted in a pink spray of blood and brain matter. He went over backward, with his guns still in their holsters.

Beside Bo, Scratch slapped leather. The Remingtons came out of their holsters so fast, they were a silver blur. The cadaverous-looking gent called Scanlon was a noted shootist, but Scratch shaded him on the draw by a fraction of a second.

That was enough. Flame shot from the muzzles of both Remingtons. The .44 caliber slugs hammered into Scanlon's chest and knocked him back a step just as his fingers tightened on the triggers of his own guns. One bullet plowed into the dirt a few feet ahead of Scanlon. The other went high and wild. He caught his balance and tried to swing the guns in line for another shot, but Scratch, with time to aim now, calmly shot the gun-wolf in the head.

Meanwhile, Bo was realizing that he might have

made a mistake in shooting Bugle first. The short, dumpy Tater didn't look like he'd be much of a threat when it came to gunplay, and Bugle was the one who'd shot and killed the piano player in the Silver King, after all.

But while Bo was busy blowing Bugle's brains out, Tater drew an old Griswold & Gunnison .36 with blinding speed and thumbed off a shot. Bo felt the heat of the round against his cheek as it barely missed spreading *his* brains on the street.

Brass sparkled in the hot, dry air as Bo worked the Winchester's lever and sent the empty he had just fired spinning high in the air. He slammed the lever up and fired again, but not in time to prevent Tater from getting off a second shot. This bullet tugged at Bo's coat, but this attempt was a narrow miss, too.

"A miss is as good as a mile," the old saying went. But Bo hadn't missed. His bullet shattered Tater's right shoulder and knocked him halfway around.

Tater was stubborn. Not only did he stay on his feet, but he also didn't even drop the gun. Grimacing in pain, he reached over with his left hand and plucked the weapon out of his now useless right hand.

Bo cranked the Winchester and fired his third shot. This one ripped through Tater's throat and severed his jugular vein, judging by the arcing spray of blood from the wound. He dropped to the dirt like a discarded toy. The other two hard cases hadn't moved at all once they hit the ground, but Tater flopped and thrashed a little and made a gurgling sound as he drowned in his own blood.

Then he was still, too.

The battle had lasted five seconds. Maybe a hair

under. Echoes of the shots hung over Silverhill for a moment and then faded away.

"You hit?" Bo asked his old friend.

"Mine didn't even come close," the silver-haired Texan replied. "How about yours?"

"Close," Bo admitted. "No cigar, though. But that's because I misjudged old Tater. I thought Bugle was the more dangerous of the two."

Scratch shook his head. "Hard to be sure about such a thing, just from lookin' at a fella. I got to say, though, if I'd been in your place, I think I'd've made the same mistake. Comes down to it, those varmints are dead and we're still kickin', and that's all that matters, ain't it?"

"Yeah." Bo took cartridges from his coat pocket and thumbed them through the Winchester's loading gate to replace the rounds he'd fired. Quietly, he added, "Looks like folks are coming out of their holes."

The street and the boardwalks had cleared out in a hurry when it became obvious gun trouble was imminent. Nobody wanted to get in the way of a stray bullet, and you couldn't blame them for that. Now, up and down the street, people were stepping out of the businesses into which they had retreated and were peering toward the three bodies sprawled in front of the Silver King. A few even took tentative steps in that direction to get a better look. Before too much longer, a crowd would gather around the corpses, Bo knew, as the curiosity on the part of Silverhill's citizens overpowered their revulsion.

"Reckon we ought the fetch the undertaker?" Scratch asked.

"I'm sure Clarence Appleyard is already hitching up

his wagon," Bo replied. "It never takes him long to get to the scene of a shooting."

"No, he's Johnny-on-the-spot. You got to give him that." They turned and walked back toward the squat stone building that housed the marshal's office.

"Hell of a first day on the job, ain't it?" Scratch asked.

"Well," Bo said, "we knew the job might be dangerous when we took it."

They were passing the Territorial House, the biggest and best hotel in Silverhill, and before either man could say anything else, the front doors flew open and several figures rushed out.

Almost before Bo and Scratch knew what was going on, they were surrounded by a handful of femininity as anxious, questioning voices filled the air around them.

CHAPTER TWO

The five young women who surrounded Bo and Scratch were a study in contrasts. Two were blondes, one had hair black as midnight, another was a brunette, and the fifth and final female had a mane of thick chestnut hair falling around her shoulders. One blonde was small, dainty, and curly haired; the other was taller, with her wheat-colored tresses pulled back and tied behind her head. The young woman with dark brown hair had an elegant but cool and reserved look about her, while the one with raven's-wing hair was sultry and exotic looking. Unlike the others, the tomboyish gal with chestnut hair wore boots, trousers, and a man's shirt, and looked like she was ready to go out and ride the range.

The one thing they all had in common was that they were beautiful. The sort of beauty that made men take a second and even a third look as their jaws dropped. In a boomtown such as Silverhill, they were definitely diamonds in the rough.

With a tone of command in her voice, the cool-looking brunette, Cecilia Spaulding, said, "Everyone just be quiet! Mr. Creel and Mr. Morton can't answer our questions if everybody is talking at once."

"That's easy for you to say," chestnut-haired Rose Winston shot back at her. "You heard all that shooting, same as we did. We just want to know if they're all right."

"I don't see any blood on them," the taller, more athletic-looking blonde, Beth Macy, said.

Bo figured it was time he got a word in edgewise. He said, "No, neither of us was hit."

"You killed the men you were after, though, didn't you?" Rose asked with a bloodthirsty note in her voice. "Those hombres who shot the piano player at the Silver King?"

"Seemed like the thing to do at the time," Scratch replied with a grin. "How'd you know what happened to that ivory pounder?"

"People were talking about it in the hotel lobby," Cecilia explained. "It was quite the topic of conversation . . . as violence usually is."

Jean Parker, the dainty, curly-haired blonde, sniffed and said, "It seems like a day can't go by in this town without a killing of some sort."

"You're exaggerating, Jean," exotic-looking Luella Tolman said. "Why, until today it's been almost two weeks since there was a real gun battle here!"

"Two weeks ago," Jean said. "You mean when that horde of Mexican bandits and that other gang of outlaws and those horrible gunslingers and those wild cowboys all converged on the town and we were nearly killed? Is *that* what you're talking about, Luella?"

"Now, ladies," Bo said, "there's nothing to worry about."

"Oh?" Cecilia raised a finely arched eyebrow. "Can you guarantee that nothing like that will happen again, Mr. Creel?"

Rose said, "You should call him Deputy Creel now. He's a lawman."

"And Mr. Morton is the marshal," Beth said. She tilted her head a little to the side. "Although, for some reason, I would have thought it would be the other way around. No offense, Mr. Morton. But, anyway, with the two of them in charge of enforcing the law now, I'm certain what happened today was just an isolated incident. Silverhill will settle right down and actually become peaceful."

Bo wished he was as convinced of that as Beth seemed to be. He pinched the brim of his hat, nodded, and said, "We'll do our best to make sure that happens, ladies."

Scratch tipped his hat to the five lovelies but stopped short of bowing. Then he and Bo moved on toward the sheriff's office.

"Beth's right," Scratch said quietly. "You really ought to be wearin' this marshal's badge, Bo. I ain't sure why you insisted I'd be the marshal and you'd be the deputy."

Bo snorted. "It's bad enough we agreed to be star packers. I didn't want to be in charge."

"We could've told those fellas no when they came to see us yesterday."

Bo nodded slowly and said, "I've got a hunch that

we may wind up wishing we had slammed the door in that poor young fella's face."

The Territorial House,
the previous afternoon . . .

Bo and Scratch were in their room in the hotel when a knock sounded on the door. Scratch was dealing a hand of solitaire on the table that also contained a basin and a pitcher of water, while Bo had his Colt taken apart and spread out on a towel he'd put on the bed so he could clean the revolver.

Scratch turned on his chair to look over his shoulder at his old friend and ask, "You expectin' company?"

"Not me," Bo replied. "It might be one of the girls looking for us for some reason."

Several weeks earlier, Bo and Scratch had set out from Fort Worth in the company of five beautiful young women: Cecilia Spaulding, Jean Parker, Luella Tolman, Beth Macy, and Rose Winston. The five of them were from the town of Four Corners, Iowa, and had known each other all their lives. They were mail-order brides, and Bo and Scratch had been hired by Cyrus Keegan, whose matrimonial agency had arranged the matches, to accompany them to their destination, the mining boomtown of Silverhill, in New Mexico Territory, and act as bodyguards during the trip.

That journey had been filled with excitement and danger, and things hadn't really calmed down once the group reached Silverhill. Actually, even more hell had started popping. Once Bo and Scratch, with some help from new friends, had straightened out that mess, they had decided to remain in Silverhill for a while. Cyrus Keegan had informed them by a letter delivered on the twice-weekly stagecoach run from El Paso that he didn't have any more work for them at the moment, and the two foot- loose drifters had taken an avuncular interest in the five young women, who had wound up not getting married, after all.

But as lovely as they were, none of them lacked for suitors.

Scratch stood up and went to the door, drawing his righthand Remington as he did so. Caution was a habit of long standing with the two Texans. Scratch called through the panel, "Who's there?" and then stepped quickly to the side, just in case whoever was in the hall had a shotgun and decided to answer the question with a double load of buckshot.

Instead, a boy's reedy voice replied, "It is only Pablo, señores." Bo and Scratch had gotten acquainted with the youngster since they'd been staying at the Territorial House. He ran errands and did odd jobs around the hotel. Bo didn't hear any strain in Pablo's voice, like there would have been if somebody had a gun on him and was forcing him to try to get them to open the door, so he nodded to Scratch, who turned the knob—but didn't holster the Remington just yet.

Pablo was alone in the hall, they saw as Scratch swung the door back. He gazed with big eyes at the gun in Scratch's hand, clearly impressed by it, but then quickly remembered why he was here.

"Some gentlemen downstairs wish to see you, Señor Creel, Señor Morton."

"Which gentlemen would they be, Pablo?" Bo asked from the bed.

"Señor Hopkins, Señor Carling, Señor Esperanza, and Señor Dubonnet."

Scratch looked at Bo and raised an eyebrow. Both drifters recognized those names. Albert Hopkins and W. J. M. Carling owned two of the largest silver mines in the area. Hector Esperanza ran Silverhill's largest and most successful livery stable. Francis Dubonnet's general mercantile store took up almost an entire block. All four men were wealthy and influential. Silver- hill had no mayor and no official town council, but for all practical purposes, these men occupied those positions.

The former owner of the Silver King Saloon, Forbes Dyson, had been part of that circle, as well, but Dyson was six feet under now.

"What do a bunch of high rollers like that want with the likes of us?" Scratch asked.

Pablo shrugged. "They did not tell me, señor. They said only that they wished to speak with both of you. They wait in the lobby." The boy shook his head. "Hombres such as those four do not like to wait, señores."

"Well, they'll have to for a few minutes, anyway," Bo said. "I'm putting my gun back together."

"Tell 'em we'll be down in a spell and they shouldn't get their fur in an uproar," Scratch said.

Pablo's eyes widened again. He said, "I will tell them, Señor Morton. Perhaps not in those *exact* words . . ."

Scratch grinned and took a coin from his pocket, and flipped it to the youngster, who snatched it out of the air and then hurried toward the landing. Scratch closed the door and turned to Bo, who was deliberately reassembling the Colt.

"Usually when the leadin' citizens of a place want to see us, it's to tell us to rattle our hocks and shake the dust o' their fine community off our no-good heels."

"And they say that in no uncertain terms," Bo agreed without looking up from his task.

"You reckon that's what these fellas want with us?"

"I don't know. There's been a lot of trouble since we got here, but none of it was really any of our doing and, anyway, it's been quiet for a while."

"Could be they've decided that trouble just sort of follows us around, whether it's our fault or not."

"Well, considering our history," Bo said, "you couldn't blame them for feeling that way." He stood up, slid the cleaned and reassembled Colt back in its holster, and reached for his coat. "Let's go ask them."

When they went down the stairs and reached the lobby, they found the four men looking impatient as they stood beside some potted plants. As mining tycoons, Hopkins and Carling dressed the part, with frock coats, bowler hats, fancy vests, and cravats. Hopkins wore a close-cropped beard, while Carling sported bushy gray muttonchop whiskers and a jaw like a slab of stone. Both men smoked fat cigars.

Despite owning the general store and being worth a small fortune, Francis Dubonnet usually wore a canvas apron and worked behind the counter, alongside his clerks. He had discarded the apron today in favor of a brown tweed suit. His wavy black hair was plastered down with pomade, and wax curled the tips of his impressive mustache.

Hector Esperanza also had a mustache, but it was a thin gray line on his upper lip. He was short, lean, leathery, and wiry and had a reputation as one of the best men with horses in the entire territory. He wore a brown tweed suit, as well, with a collarless shirt and no tie, and didn't look anything at all like the rich man he was. He had a pipe clamped between his teeth.

"There you are," Hopkins greeted Bo and Scratch.

"Sorry to keep you waiting," Bo said, even though he really wasn't. Texans were courteous when they could be, though. "What can we do for you?"

Carling said, "I'm not in the habit of talking business while standing in a hotel lobby."

Bo and Scratch exchanged a glance. Neither of them had any idea what sort of business they might have with men such as these.

Esperanza took the pipe out of his mouth and suggested, "Why don't we go in the dining room and have some coffee?"

Carling and Hopkins scowled, but Dubonnet said, "That's an excellent idea."

The dining room was empty at this time of day. The six men sat down at a large round table. The lone waitress who was working hurried over to them, and Hopkins ordered coffee all around.

Then he leaned forward slightly, clasped his hands together on the fine Irish linen tablecloth, and said, "We'll get right down to business. Creel, Morton, we want you men to work for us."

Again, Bo and Scratch looked at each other. Bo

said, "We don't really know much about mining, but we've guarded ore shipments before—"

Hopkins made a curt gesture. "Not at the mines."

"Well," Scratch said, "it's true we've clerked in stores and mucked out stables, but we ain't really lookin' for jobs like that right now—"

"We don't want to hire you to work at any of our own businesses," Esperanza said. "We want to hire you to work for the town of Silverhill."

"As lawmen," Dubonnet added.

"Specifically," Carling said, "we're offering you the job of town marshal, Mr. Creel, and we'd like you to serve as deputy, Mr. Morton."

Connect with  Us

Visit us online at
KensingtonBooks.com
to read more from your favorite authors, see books
by series, view reading group guides, and more.

Join us on social media

for sneak peeks, chances to win books and prize packs,
and to share your thoughts with other readers.

facebook.com/kensingtonpublishing
twitter.com/kensingtonbooks

Tell us what you think!

To share your thoughts, submit a review,
or sign up for our eNewsletters, please visit:
KensingtonBooks.com/TellUs.